'Yes, I will m

It was not until th
how much he had
agree to his propo
smiled, Nicola caught her breath at the change it
wrought in his appearance. She was hardly to
know that it was a smile which only a few close
friends and family members were ever privileged
enough to see.

'There is...something I should like to ask you.'

'You may ask of me anything you wish, my
dear.'

The endearment caused the strangest flutter in
the pit of Nicola's stomach, but she forced
herself to concentrate on what she had to say.
'My lord, I was wondering...how do you feel
about...animals?'

Originally hailing from Pembrokeshire, **Gail Whitiker** now lives on beautiful Vancouver Island on the west coast of Canada. When she isn't indulging her love of writing, you'll find her enjoying brisk walks along the Island's many fine beaches, or trying to catch up on her second love, reading. She wrote her first novel when she was in her teens, and still blesses her English teacher for not telling her how bad it really was.

Recent titles by the same author:

LETTERS TO A LADY

BLACKWOOD'S LADY

Gail Whitiker

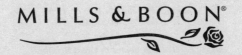

To Mum and Dad, the best parents in the world

And to Ron, for encouraging me to strive, and for
never forgetting the little things that are so important

*MILLS & BOON and MILLS & BOON with the Rose Device
are registered trademarks of the publisher.*

*First published in Great Britain 1999
Harlequin Mills & Boon Limited,
Eton House, 18-24 Paradise Road, Richmond, Surrey TW9 1SR*

© Gail Whitiker 1999

ISBN 0 263 81658 3

Set in Times Roman 10½ on 12 pt.
04-9905-80530 C1

*Printed and bound in Great Britain
by Caledonian International Book Manufacturing Ltd, Glasgow*

Chapter One

'So, my boy, are the rumours true?' a beaming Sir Giles Chapman enquired of the younger gentleman sitting across from him. 'Have you really decided to do it or is the story nothing more than hearsay spread on the lips of fools?'

A brief flicker of amusement lit the silvery blue eyes of David Penscott, fifth Marquis of Blackwood, as he settled back into the comfort of the deeply padded armchair and reached for the glass of brandy his uncle's manservant had just refilled. 'I'm afraid you're going to have to be more specific than that if I am to give you an intelligent answer, Uncle Giles, since I've no idea which rumours you're referring to.'

'No idea! My dear boy, I am referring to the ones that have you marrying the Earl of Wyndham's daughter. Everyone knows how loath you are to enter the wedded state, and given that the lady is something of a mystery to Society circles the subject is generating considerable interest. So, I am asking you straight out. Are the rumours true?'

David raised the cut-crystal glass to his lips and smiled at his uncle over the rim. 'That depends. Does your interest stem from the fact that you've money riding on my answer or from a genuine interest in my welfare?'

'Money riding on my— Egods, sir, you wound me!' Sir Giles cried, clasping his hand over his heart as though he had been grievously injured. 'You know I don't wager on my family.'

'I know that you have been warned *not* to,' David replied, his smile broadening, 'but I wasn't sure how seriously you were taking the threat.'

'I am taking it very seriously indeed, considering that it was levied by your aunt Hortensia. That meddlesome woman has threatened to sell off my entire collection of snuff boxes if I so much as look at another betting book. And she'd do it too,' Sir Giles muttered, the tips of his silvery moustache bristling with indignation as he thought about his eldest sister and her much publicized campaign to reform his character. 'Hence, I fear I must consider myself cured of the dreaded vice. But, as regards these rumours, I do admit to being curious. I never thought to see you brought to heel by a woman, David, and certainly not by a dark horse like the Lady Nicola Wyndham.'

'I hardly call making the decision to marry at four-and-thirty being brought to heel, Uncle,' David replied, choosing for a moment to ignore the latter part of his uncle's comment. 'It simply suits my purposes, that is all.'

'I see. Then is it indeed the Lady Nicola upon whom you have set your heart?'

'It is, though I fail to see why you would doubt one part of the rumour if you believed the other.'

'Because I would doubt anything that was being hailed as the truth by the likes of Humphrey O'Donnell and his cronies.'

'O'Donnell!' David's smile faded as an image of the handsome but far too cocky young dandy appeared in his mind. 'I am surprised that young scapegrace would trouble himself over my affairs. He has been overheard to say that no intelligent woman would be foolish enough to take me on.'

'Yes, and so he would once he'd learned that the lady in question was the Earl of Wyndham's daughter. Are you not aware that O'Donnell has been casting after Lady Nicola himself these past few weeks?'

David frowned. 'As a matter of fact I was not.'

'No, I thought not. I hate to sound like an interfering old busybody, David, but you really should pay more mind to what goes on in the drawing rooms of London if you are at all serious about this marriage business,' Sir Giles advised. 'The hunting fields can wait.'

'I am very serious about this marriage business, as you call it, Uncle Giles, but no man could possibly be expected to keep up with *all* the rumours drifting through London's drawing rooms,' David objected. 'As for the hunting fields, I take leave to tell you that this proposed alliance with Lady Nicola may well have been forged through the very sport you now decry.'

'Really? I was not aware Lady Nicola rode to hounds.'

'She doesn't, but her father does, and I thought perchance the number of times he and I have hunted together might have made him look more favourably upon my suit.'

'More favourably? My dear boy, an offer of marriage from the Marquis of Blackwood would be viewed as exceptional even for the daughter of an earl. Especially one who, at five-and-twenty, is—' Sir Giles broke off in midsentence and stared at his nephew. 'Tell me that you *are* at least aware of the lady's age?'

A glimmer of mirth danced in David's eyes. 'I am well

aware of the lady's age, Uncle, and I considered it a point
in her favour, rather than against it.'

'You did?'

'Most assuredly. At five-and-twenty, Lady Nicola is far
more likely to possess the qualities I seek than any of the
simpering young ladies making their bows at court. And,
while I know that it is well past time I settled down,
having had it pointed out to me time without number, and
by people whose opinions I value, that does not mean I
intend to plunge into the situation with my eyes closed.
Marriage is far too important a decision to make based
solely upon the feelings of the heart.'

Sir Giles couldn't help smiling. 'Some gentlemen consider it the *only* way to make this particular decision, David.'

'Possibly, but *I* am not one of them. I can think of
nothing worse than leg-shackling myself to a vapid young
woman whose head is filled with silly romantic nonsense
and little else.'

'I see. Then what kind of wife do you seek?'

'I seek a competent hostess and a loyal companion,'
David replied, without hesitation. 'A woman who will be
a good mother to my children, and who will discharge her
role as Marchioness of Blackwood with dignity and style,
as my mother did. And I believe Lady Nicola to be precisely that type of female.'

'She also happens to be a remarkably beautiful young
woman,' Sir Giles remarked idly. 'Or had you taken time
to notice that during your rather clinical assessment of her
many other fine attributes?'

'I have most certainly taken note of the fact that Lady
Nicola is an exceedingly lovely young woman, but more
important to me than her beauty is the fact that she has
been raised in a nobleman's house—an upbringing which

will have equipped her with the knowledge and refinement necessary to take her place in mine.'

'Knowledge and refinement. Dear me.' Sir Giles regarded the only child of his much loved younger sister, Jane—who, sadly, had succumbed to a virulent lung infection eight years ago—with an expression akin to pity. 'Is that all you can say about the woman you intend to marry?'

'Is that not enough?'

'Have you spoken to the young lady?'

'Of course. I accompanied her on the pianoforte at Lady Rutherford's musicale last month, and we danced twice at Lady Dunbarton's ball just a few weeks ago.'

'And you feel that to be a sufficient foundation upon which to make a decision that will affect the rest of your life?'

David's brows drew together in a dark line. 'I take it you do not.'

Sir Giles shrugged eloquently. 'Doesn't matter what I think, David; I'm not marrying the girl. I simply thought you might have…well, taken time to get to know her before offering for her hand.' Then, seeing the look which appeared on his nephew's face, Sir Giles chuckled. 'Forgive me. I thought love and marriage went hand in hand.'

'Only in penny romances,' David retorted dryly. 'I am not looking to fall head over heels like some moonstruck young cub, Uncle, or to cast away duty and obligation in the name of undying love, as my father did.'

'Your father did nothing of the sort,' Sir Giles replied mildly, having had this conversation with his nephew before. 'Richard was as respectful of the title as you are, and he was well aware of the obligation he owed to the family. But when he met Stephanie de Charbier nothing else mattered to him except that they be together.'

David stiffened as he always did at the mention of his father's second wife. 'I do not care to discuss her.'

'I know, but I will not have you accusing my brother-in-law of shunning his responsibilities. Your father was a lonely man, David. Jane had been dead for over four years, and not once in all that time did Richard so much as look at another woman. Until he met Stephanie—'

'I said, I don't want to hear—'

'But you will hear it, sir,' Sir Giles said, with more firmness than he usually employed when in conversation with his favourite nephew. 'Stephanie brought happiness and joy back into your father's life. The family didn't approve of her and neither did you, but she stood by him regardless. Even you can't deny how much her love changed him.'

'No, I can't deny it,' David agreed, the bitterness evident in his voice. 'Because it was that same love that turned his life upside down and eventually killed him.'

Sir Giles shook his head sadly. 'Love didn't kill your father, David. Grief did. Surely you understand that now? He never recovered from the shock of losing her.'

'What I understand is that he locked himself away in a room refusing to eat or drink, until there was nothing left of him,' David said woodenly. 'And all in the name of love. Well, if that is what passion does to a man, you can keep it. I have neither the time nor the inclination for such foolishness.'

'Then why bother to marry at all?' Sir Giles asked quietly. 'You say you are content as a bachelor. And as your cousin Arabella is happy enough to act the part of your hostess when you do trouble yourself to entertain, why spoil such an amicable arrangement by bringing in a wife?'

'Because there is the matter of progeny,' David said,

his brief spurt of anger deserting him as the melancholy he had never quite been able to overcome moved in to take its place. 'It is my duty to marry and produce the requisite heir, and I can't very well do *that* with Arabella, even if I were of a mind to.'

'No, I dare say there would be those who would take exception. First cousin?'

'Second, but it is of no consequence. Belle's always been like a sister to me.'

Pity she's never thought of you as a brother, Sir Giles was tempted to say, but then thought better of it. If David wasn't aware of his beautiful cousin's affection, perhaps it was just as well.

'Well, then, all things considered, I suppose there is nothing for it *but* to marry,' Sir Giles said at length. 'So, when does the courtship begin?'

'There isn't going to be a formal courtship,' David informed him. 'I am expected at Wyndham Hall tomorrow afternoon, at which time I shall set forth my offer of marriage. I have already secured the Earl's blessing.'

'Yes, and why would you not?' Sir Giles said fondly. 'You are considered a splendid catch, my boy, and I wager there will be many a broken-hearted young lady moping about Town when news of your betrothal appears in *The Times.*'

'Perhaps, but, as there are an equal number of gallant young gentlemen to console them, I doubt anyone is in fear of losing sleep over it. Besides,' David said, lifting his impeccably clad shoulders in an eloquent shrug, 'it may be the Lady Nicola for whom you should be reserving your sympathies. I am not as dashing as some of the young bucks parading around Town, and I have never been known for my gay outlook on life.'

'No, but what you lack in spontaneity is more than made up for by your cutting wit and rapier-sharp mind.'

One corner of David's mouth lifted in a smile that could almost have been called wistful. 'I hardly think wit and intelligence will endear me to a lady unless she happens to be something of a scholar herself. And I don't know that I am predisposed to spending the rest of my life with a bluestocking.'

'Rest assured, Lady Nicola has a fine mind and a lively sense of humour, but she is no bluestocking,' Sir Giles assured his nephew. 'In fact, I believe the only reason she is still unwed is as a result of her having been in mourning for so long.'

'Yes, what a tragic set of circumstances,' David observed soberly. 'First her maternal aunt and uncle killed in that freak carriage accident, and, then less than a year later, her mother in a riding mishap. And then her paternal uncle, most unexpectedly.'

'Tragic indeed,' Sir Giles agreed. 'Especially considering how close Lady Nicola was to her mother. But she has come through it all, and now Lord Wyndham is anxious that she marry and start a family of her own. And, given her devotion to him, I dare say she would marry you just to please him.'

'Not the most flattering of reasons for accepting a man's offer of marriage—'

'But acceptable enough under the circumstances,' Sir Giles pointed out sagely. 'After all, *you* were the one who said that love was not a consideration in the asking, David, so why should the lack of it be a consideration in the acceptance?'

'Why indeed?' David agreed ruefully, admiring the finesse with which his uncle had just swung the argument in his favour. 'And, with that in mind, I shall propose to

Lady Nicola tomorrow afternoon in the hopes of achieving two goals. One, that she will accept my suit and agree to become my wife. And, two, that we may put an end to this matrimonial fussing once and for all!'

'Alistair, you really are becoming quite impossible!' Nicola scolded gently. 'How do you expect to win Father over if you keep on misbehaving like this?'

The eyes gazing up at Lady Nicola Wyndham—while unquestionably bright and endearing—were patently devoid of contrition, and, recognizing that, Nicola shook her head in resignation. 'Very well. I can see that I am not making any headway with you, so I'll not waste my breath further. It would break my heart if we were to be separated, but we both know that Father will turn you out in a trice if your behaviour does not improve. Now, be a good boy and do not try to escape again.'

Fine words, Nicola thought ironically. A lot of good they were going to do a fox!

Picking up the wooden bucket, Nicola tipped fresh water into Alistair's drinking bowl, shut the cage door and locked it, and then stood back to watch him. It was hard to believe that this glossy, bright-eyed creature was the same pathetic, shivering animal she had found close to death in the woods last year, his front leg having been cruelly broken in a trap. Now, after Nicola's faithful ministering, the leg was all but healed. Even the fur had grown back, though for some strange reason it had come back white, serving as a permanent reminder of his injury.

Unfortunately, Alistair—as Nicola had affectionately named the cub—was showing no signs at all of wishing to return to his life in the wild. Rather, the little imp had become quite adept at getting out of his cage and turning up in the gardens near the back of the house—a situation which could only bode ill for both of them. After all, it was perfectly understandable that, as an avid hunter, Lord Wyndham believed the only place for a healthy fox was in the field. And, while he had long since resigned himself to the endless stream of small birds and injured animals she was forever bringing home, he had tried to draw the line at a fox cub—until Nicola had reminded him that her mother had never turned away any animal in need.

At that point, the argument had been as good as lost. Lord Wyndham had adored his beautiful wife, and had denied her nothing. Nor, it seemed, could he deny his only daughter, who was showing definite signs of having inherited both her mother's affinity for, and skill with, animals.

'Now, be a good boy, Alistair, and perhaps I shall come and see you again before I go riding this afternoon,' Nicola told the young fox as she collected her supplies and made ready to return to the house. 'No doubt I shall be in need of a diversion after my visit from the Marquis of Blackwood.'

Giving the fox's silky ears an affectionate tweak, Nicola started back towards the house, her mind drifting ahead to the upcoming meeting with Lord Blackwood. She knew why he was coming, of course. Her father had already hinted at the marquis's intentions, and, all things considered, she was not opposed to the match. She had always longed for a home and children of her own, and at her age she had almost given up hope of such things coming to pass.

But to think that the Marquis of Blackwood might actually be the man to make them happen…well, it was all but unthinkable. As a nonpareil and pink of the *ton*, Blackwood could have had his pick of any number of younger and—to Nicola's way of thinking—eminently more suitable girls than herself. Why, then, would he choose to wed the countrified daughter of a widowed earl, who spent far more time in the country than she did in Town?

And what would the exceedingly correct marquis say, Nicola wondered, if he were to discover that his future wife was tending a menagerie of wounded animals, which at the moment included two silky black puppies she had found half drowned by the edge of the river, an assortment of injured birds—including a falcon with a broken wing—and a wily fox named Alistair? Somehow, she could not imagine him being pleased.

Wives of the nobility simply do not indulge in such pastimes, Nicola could almost hear her stodgy old governess saying.

Well, maybe they didn't, but, if an alliance between the two of them was what he wished for, Nicola would certainly listen to his proposal. Her father seemed favourably disposed towards the match, and Nicola knew that he would never approve of a suitor who was not acceptable in every way. Clearly, Lord Blackwood had earned her father's approval.

Now, all he had to do was earn hers!

David set out upon his mission of matrimony in a spirit of amiable resignation. Resignation because, to him, marriage was a necessity of life—an obligation one undertook for the good of the family. And to David Penscott, Marquis of Blackwood, Earl of Winsmore and Viscount Huntley, obligation was a duty that went before all.

His feelings of amiability stemmed from the fact that he believed his selection of Lady Nicola Wyndham to be a judicious one. Her past was unblemished, and if she had spent somewhat more time in the country than most young ladies of her class it did not seem to have affected her adversely. Certainly her manners were all that he could have wished. She neither laughed too much, nor too loud, she was lovely enough to suit his rather exacting standards, and, by all accounts, she was not prone to vapours. If these were qualities to be gained by sacrificing the first blush of youth, it was a sacrifice David was more than willing to make.

Reaching Wyndham Hall just before three o'clock, David was greeted at the door by the steadfast Trethewy—an elderly retainer who had been with the Wyndham family for over forty-five years—and relieved of his hat, gloves and whip. From there, he was shown into the spacious green salon where, as expected, Nicola's father was waiting to greet him.

'Ah, Blackwood, good to see you again,' Lord Wyndham said in a rich voice that carried easily to every corner of the room. 'Ready to do the deed?'

'I am, my lord, though I admit to being somewhat anxious as to your daughter's reply.'

'Anxious? Good Lord, man, there's no need for apprehension. Nicola didn't seem at all unhappy when I informed her of your intentions. Once she had recovered from her surprise, that is.'

Surprise? David wondered ruefully. Or shock?

'Now, before Nicola joins us, might I interest you in a glass of wine? I have just received a shipment from France and I would welcome your opinion on this particular Bordeaux.'

Already familiar with the size and quality of the earl's cellar, David nodded in anticipation of a rare treat. 'I should be pleased to, thank you.'

'Splendid. I've not a bad nose for wine, but it doesn't hold a candle to a connoisseur's like yours,' Wyndham said as he poured out two glasses. 'Right, then, your good health, Blackwood.'

'And yours, my lord.'

The wine proved to be of excellent vintage, and David was persuaded to enjoy another glass before Lord Wyndham resumed the conversation.

'No, my Nicki's not at all like those other flibbertigibbets at court. She's a sensible lass, always has been. Takes after her mother in that regard. There were always rumours about her, of course, but I never paid them any mind.'

'Rumours?' David repeated cautiously.

'Aye. Superstitious fools. Thought she was a witch.'

'Lady Nicola?'

'Nicola?' Lord Wyndham frowned. 'Good Lord, no. Nicola's not been bothered by any rumours in that regard. At least, not yet.'

David cast a surreptitious glance at the older man. *Yet?*

'No, I was referring to Elizabeth. Personally, I could never understand what all the fuss was about,' the earl continued blithely. 'Just because the parson's wife saw Elizabeth feeding a wild buck at the edge of the common was hardly reason to think her odd.'

David's hand stopped the glass halfway to his lips. 'A buck?'

'Aye. Magnificent beast. Twelve pointer, as I recall.'

'And you say that Lady Wyndham was feeding it…by hand?'

'As though she were holding out crusts of bread to a lamb. Amazing woman,' Lord Wyndham said in a tone of mild bewilderment. 'But a witch? Rubbish! And so I told them, for all the good it did me. Thick-headed bunch,' he muttered as he crossed to the bell pull and gave it a tug. 'Still, no point in standing here reminiscing;

you've important business to get on with. Ah, Trethewy, there you are. Would you tell Lady Nicola that Lord Blackwood is here and ask her to join us?'

'Very good, m'lord.'

When the butler had gone, Wyndham gruffly cleared his throat. 'Sorry about that, Blackwood, didn't mean to ramble on about my wife. It's just that Elizabeth was very special to me. We were blessed, the two of us, and not a day goes by that I don't miss her. But then, I'm sure you can understand what I'm talking about, given your father's second marriage to Madame de Charbier. Now there was a love match if ever.'

The proffered statement—well intentioned as David felt sure it was meant to be—caused the words of condolence he had been about to offer Lord Wyndham to die on his lips, and he turned towards the window, fighting down his resentment. Stephanie de Charbier had been a beautiful young Frenchwoman who had come to England shortly after Napoleon's banishment to Elba. The widow of an influential Parisian diplomat, she had been left a wealthy young woman, and had purchased a charming house on Green Street, where, along with a small staff brought with her from Paris, she had set about re-establishing her life.

Stephanie had been twenty years younger than his father, but her age had made no difference to either of them. They had met quite by chance at the Royal Art Gallery and had fallen in love almost immediately. They had been married a mere three weeks later.

To be fair, David had no doubt that Stephanie de Charbier had loved his father. She had not been deceitful by nature, and, given her great beauty and genteel background, he knew that she could have had her choice of any number of titled English gentlemen. Certainly enough of them had danced attendance upon her.

But it was Richard Penscott whom she had chosen. And that he'd loved her in return, David did not doubt either. One had only needed to listen to the sound of his father's voice to know that he'd adored his beautiful French émigré. But what David had never been able to come to terms with was the fact that his father—whom he had loved and respected more than anyone else in the world—had perished *because* of that love. That on the day Stephanie de Charbier had died from a raging fever Richard Penscott had died too. By simply refusing to go on. By giving up on life.

That David could never forgive the young French-woman for. Not even in death.

Moments later, blissfully unaware of her visitor's agitation, Nicola walked into the room and hurried to her father's side. 'Good afternoon, Papa. I am so sorry to have kept you waiting, but I stayed rather longer at the stables than I meant to.'

'You did not keep us waiting, my dear,' Lord Wyndham assured her. 'Lord Blackwood and I were just discussing your dear mother.'

'Ah, then I dare say it is a good thing I came when I did, for it is a subject upon which you could converse for hours,' Nicola said, a silvery ripple of laughter accompanying her words. 'Good afternoon, Lord Blackwood, how very nice to see—'

The rest of the greeting came to an abrupt halt as Lord Blackwood turned and Nicola was given a glimpse of eyes that were so black, so...distant that they froze the laughter in her throat and caused her to take an involuntary step backwards. Good Lord, whatever could have happened to make him so angry? The tension was etched into his handsome face like lines carved into granite, and even under the impeccably fitted jacket Nicola could sense the rigidity of his broad shoulders.

A swift glance in her father's direction provided no clue as to Lord Blackwood's state. If anything, her father seemed blissfully unaware that anything was wrong. What, then, was the cause of it? Was the marquis unhappy about the deed he had come to enact today? Or was he— as a stickler for propriety and punctuality—displeased by her own tardy arrival?

'Lord Blackwood, pray…forgive my delay in arriving,' Nicola apologized uncertainly. 'I fear I…lost track of the time.'

Her apprehension was palpable and, recognizing that he was the cause of it, David swore softly under his breath. How stupid of him to have allowed his emotions to get the upper hand, especially in front of her.

He quickly forced a smile to his lips and bowed over her hand. 'On the contrary, it is I who should be offering you an apology, Lady Nicola. I did not give you a great deal of notice as regards my intention to call this after-noon.'

His words were all that were polite, but Nicola was not convinced that he had recovered from his anger. Whatever had caused his anger in the first place must yet be linger-ing in his mind. Still, he was obviously making an effort to be civil, which meant that the least *she* could do was to accommodate him. Her mother's training had been too deeply instilled to be ignored.

'Thank you, my lord, but certainly no great notice was ever required. I am always at home and happy to receive visitors. And you did advise my father of your intention to call, so I am not at all put out.'

It was a most gracious acceptance of his apology, and

David bowed again, admiring the finesse with which she had handled his momentary lack of civility.

Here, then, was the woman he hoped to marry, the lady his uncle had referred to as a dark horse, and whom society deemed a mystery. How ridiculous, he thought contemptuously. There was nothing in the least dark or mysterious about Nicola Wyndham. She was unaffectedly gracious and warm, yet possessed of a lively good nature which would make for the kind of companion David could imagine spending the rest of his life with. And, most assuredly, in the fetching silk gown which suited her complexion and richly coloured hair to perfection, she was as lovely as he could have wished.

'Well, now that the pleasantries have been exchanged, I shall leave the two of you alone,' Lord Wyndham announced into the silence. 'Don't need me at a time like this, eh, what?'

Impulsively, Nicola reached up to press an affectionate kiss to her father's cheek. 'On the contrary, I shall always need you, Papa.'

The earl's eyes softened as they rested on his daughter's face and he reached out to stroke a shiny lock of her hair. Then, giving her an encouraging wink, he turned on his heel and walked out of the salon.

Left alone with her guest, Nicola offered him a tentative smile. 'May I offer you some refreshments, Lord Blackwood?'

'Thank you, Lady Nicola, but no. I have just enjoyed a glass of your father's most excellent wine.'

'Then, will you sit down?'

Her voice was pleasantly low-pitched, with a slightly husky overtone that settled well on David's ear. It made a welcome change from the high-pitched giggles and titters that seemed all too prevalent in the drawing rooms of London.

'Actually, I should prefer to stand given the nature of what I am about to say. You, however, may wish to be seated.'

'As you like.'

With an unhurried movement, Nicola settled herself on the rose-coloured sofa and smoothed the skirts of her gown around her. She had taken a little longer with her toilette this afternoon and was glad that she had, if for no other reason than to lend herself extra confidence. She knew that the gown of Pomona green silk was the most flattering she owned, and that it became her very well. Even the thick, russet-coloured hair, which was so often the bane of her existence, toned perfectly with the shade. 'I am listening, Lord Blackwood.'

'Thank you, Lady Nicola. I suppose I should begin by saying that, even though our acquaintance has been of relatively short duration, and our time spent in conversation even shorter, I have come to admire you greatly. Your ease in social situations, your manners, and your sense of dignity, are all qualities I am looking for in a…lady.'

Nicola allowed herself a brief smile at his hesitation. It seemed that the word *wife* did not come easily to the tongue of the bachelor Marquis of Blackwood. 'Thank you, my lord.'

'As for myself, I fear I may not be as…entertaining as some of the gentlemen with whom you have been keeping company—'

'I have not been keeping the company of gentlemen,' Nicola felt obliged to point out. 'Having observed an extended period of mourning for…members of my family, I have been removed from Society these past two years.'

There wasn't a trace of self-pity in her voice and, knowing how hard her mother's death had been for her, David's admiration for the young lady rose. 'It is never easy to lose a parent,' he agreed sympathetically.

Nicola sighed. 'No, but then, I am sure you know how that feels. I understand that you were very close to both your mother and your father, Lord Blackwood.'

By this time, David had his emotions fully under control, and he was able to respond to her in a calm and steady voice. 'I was indeed. But life goes on, and we must make the best of it. My father would have wished me to marry and start a family of my own, and I know that Lord Wyndham is hopeful that you will do the same. And that is why I have come to see you today.' David cleared his throat and took a deep breath. 'I have already spoken to your father and received his blessing. And so I should now like to ask *you* to do me the very great honour…of becoming…my wife.'

It was hardly a romantic proposal, Nicola reflected. Yet how could it be when they had spoken to each other only a few times over the past two months?

'My lord, before I answer that, perhaps you would be so good as to explain why you wish to marry me.'

There was a very brief, but very meaningful pause. 'I…beg your pardon?'

'Well, as I am no doubt older than the ladies with whom you would have been keeping company, I simply wondered why you would not have asked a younger lady to be your wife. At five-and-twenty, most would say that I am on the shelf and have been for some time.' Nicola raised questioning eyes to his. 'Would you not agree?'

Her candour startled him. As did the deep, emerald-green of her eyes. David could not recall having seen such a remarkable shade before. And was that, possibly…a freckle on the tip of her daintily rounded nose?

He quickly marshalled his thoughts and returned to the matter at hand. 'I wish to marry *you*, Lady Nicola, because I have no desire to tie myself to a green girl fresh from the school room. I cannot imagine that we would have anything in common, nor have I any intention of wasting time trying to find out if we had. What I seek is a woman of breeding. A woman who knows how to conduct herself in Society, and how to manage a household effectively. Several households, in fact. And I hardly think an eighteen-year-old Bath Miss is likely to possess the degree of maturity necessary.'

'Is not the vitality of youth suitable recompense?'

David shook his head. 'Not to me. With youth comes giddiness, frivolity and a tendency towards unacceptable behaviour. Conduct I cannot condone in the future Marchioness of Blackwood. I have a duty to my family. To my name.'

'Ah, I see.'

Well, he was certainly setting it out plainly enough, Nicola reflected. Whosoever married the Marquis of Blackwood would be doing so with her eyes wide open. There would be no misunderstandings, no false expectations, and no grand delusions of love. Not exactly the type of proposal she had been dreaming of all her life, Nicola acknowledged wryly.

'In return, the lady who becomes my wife will wear the coronet of a marchioness,' David continued. 'She will be the mistress of two of the finest country homes in England, as well as an elegant town house in London, and will have jewels, carriages and servants at her disposal. She will enjoy the respect due to her position in Society, and will want for nothing.'

Nicola knew she shouldn't have, but she could not prevent a tiny smile from lifting the corners of her mouth. 'Is that all, my lord?'

'Is that all?' David looked down at her in astonishment. 'Is that not enough? Surely I have offered you all that is good in life?'

'Well, yes, you have, but—'

'But what?'

Nicola risked a quick glance upwards, about to explain to Lord Blackwood exactly what was lacking in his proposal, when the look on his face stayed the words on her lips and gave her the answer she was looking for.

No, love was clearly not a requirement in the marquis's choice of a wife. It would be too...unpredictable, too quixotic an emotion. It would spawn erratic behaviour and, instinctively, Nicola knew that such spontaneity would have no place in the life of the very proper Marquis of Blackwood. *Or* in that of the marquis's very proper wife.

'I take it my proposal is not to your liking, Lady Nicola?' David asked, as the silence between them lengthened.

'On the contrary, it is a very flattering one indeed,' she said, regretting that he had misinterpreted her hesitation. 'It is just that I am somewhat...surprised by the manner in which it was delivered.'

'Ah, yes.' David smiled sardonically. 'You were expecting something more romantic, perhaps. A proposal inspired by the honeyed words of Byron himself.'

'Not at all. I do not expect you to profess love where you feel none. That would be hypocritical indeed.'

'Then perhaps it is myself you find lacking,' David countered, trying to determine the source of her indecision. 'I have not led a very domestic existence to this point, nor will I try to make you believe that I have. But

you need not fear that you will be making a dreadful
mistake by marrying me. You will be given a free hand
with regard to the running of my homes and be treated
with the respect that is your due. And, in time, hopefully
there will be children for you to care for.' David stopped
and glanced at her quickly. 'You do like children, Lady
Nicola?'

Nicola's face lit up. 'Oh, yes, of course, I adore them.
Don't you?'

'To be honest, I have never given it much thought. I've
always considered it my duty to assure the continuation
of the line, of course—'

Nicola's feathery brows rose in surprise. 'Is that how
you look upon children, my lord? As a duty?'

'I suppose that is how I look upon a number of things,'
David replied slowly. 'In a position such as mine, freedom
of choice must often be compromised for the good of the
family. Surely you understand that?'

Nicola shifted her gaze and focused it on the painting
behind Lord Blackwood's head. 'Yes, I understand,' she
said softly. And she did. She understood that the most
important thing in Blackwood's life *was* his duty. Duty to
his name and to his family. He would put that before
everything—including love. That explained why there had
not even been a pretence of affection in his proposal. And
since he had chosen her to be his wife he obviously believed that she could deal with his offer on those same
terms. But could she? Hadn't she, like most young
women, harboured dreams of being loved for all the right
reasons? Of being told that she was the only woman in
the world who could make him happy?

Of course she had, and Nicola knew that she would be
a fool indeed if that was what she believed she was being
offered here. What she was being offered was a life of

supreme comfort, in exchange for her presence at the head of his table and her willingness to fill his nursery with children. That was what the Marquis of Blackwood was offering. And, just as Nicola was about to tell him that it simply wasn't good enough, Blackwood himself threw her into confusion.

'Forgive me, Lady Nicola. I don't seem to be doing a very good job of this,' he admitted as he sank down onto the sofa beside her. 'Perhaps because I have always believed marriage to be such…a serious business.'

The unexpected admission, humbly offered, caught Nicola totally unawares and she faltered. 'Well, yes, of course marriage *is* a serious business. But surely there can be reasons besides duty and obligation for wishing to marry someone.'

'I would like to think that there are, but I also think that you and I are mature enough to understand that none of those more…sentimental reasons come into play here,' David said quietly. 'Like you, I do not look for shallow declarations of love simply because they are expected. I believe that such a great depth of emotion can only develop over time, as two people come to know and to understand each other. But I would hope that we could deal intelligently with each other, and perhaps with affection. Most importantly, I will honour, respect and revere you, Lady Nicola,' David said softly. 'That much I *can* promise you, from this day forward.'

David wasn't sure who was more surprised by his admission—Lady Nicola, or himself. He couldn't remember ever having spoken so openly to anyone before. But she wasn't to know that he had been suffering pangs of conscience ever since she had asked him if he liked children, and his answer had made him sound like an insensitive boor. Of course he liked children; he always had. Why, then, had he made it sound as if it was only duty that made him consider having them?

David studied the lovely face beside him, and offered her a game smile. 'Well, I think that is all I have to say. Perhaps you would like some time to think it over? A few more days before I call again for your answer? Unless…you are sure of your answer now.'

Nicola lifted her head to look at him, and marvelled at how fickle the human heart could be. She had just received a proposal of marriage from one of the most eligible gentlemen in London—one whom most would have accepted before his final words were out—and now he was offering her time to consider an answer which, until a few short moments ago, would have been the same in a week's time as it would have been today.

Until a few short moments ago…

'No, I do not need more time, Lord Blackwood,' Nicola replied. 'What more could a lady ask than to be given the assurance that she will be well taken care of, and blessed with a family to love and to care for? Yes, I will marry you.'

David stared at her. 'You will?'

'Yes. And I thank you for asking.'

It was not until that moment that David realized how much he had been hoping that Nicola would agree to his proposal. So much so that, when he smiled, Nicola caught her breath at the change it wrought in his appearance. It made him appear younger, and so much more… approachable. She was hardly to know that it was a smile which only a few close friends and family members were ever privileged enough to see.

'I think it is I who should be thanking you…Nicola,' David whispered. He leaned forward to brush a kiss against her cheek, and noticed, for the first time, how very sweet was the fragrance that surrounded her. 'You have made me a very happy man. And now shall we call your father back in and give him the news?'

'Wait...before you do, there is...something I should like to ask you.'

'You may ask of me anything you wish, my dear.'

The endearment caused the strangest flutter in the pit of Nicola's stomach, but she forced herself to concentrate on what she had to say. 'My lord, I was wondering...how do you feel about...animals?'

Chapter Two

Animals? David glanced at Nicola sharply as a memory of her father's earlier words about the mighty buck suddenly sprang to mind. 'I take it you are referring to… pets.'

Nicola paused for a moment. Was she? In truth, Alistair was as endearing as the two black puppies, so she was not telling him a complete falsehood. And Guinevere was extremely well behaved…for a falcon.

She smiled with what she hoped was conviction. 'Yes, I suppose I am.'

'Then rest assured I have no objection to your keeping pets,' David said as the vision of the mighty buck was replaced by that of a small, fluffy lap-dog. 'In fact, I have several dogs of my own.'

Nicola's smile faded. 'Foxhounds?'

'Sheepdogs, actually. Big, lumbering brutes, but as gentle as kittens. Have you a dog of your own, perhaps, that you would like to bring to Ridley Hall?'

'I recently acquired two puppies,' Nicola told him, avoiding, for a moment, any reference to the other members of the menagerie, 'which I believe to be about six weeks old.'

'And you would prefer not to leave them here.'

'I confess, I have grown rather attached to them.'

'Then by all means bring them along. They will make admirable company for my own. What breed are they?'

'Spaniels.'

David began to smile. 'Didn't get them from old Lord Hartley by chance, did you?'

Nicola shook her head sadly. 'I found them down by the river. I was...too late to save the rest of the litter.'

'Too late to—' Abruptly, David broke off as he realized what she was saying. 'Oh, I see. Not purebred, then.'

Nicola raised wide green eyes to his face. 'No, they are not, but surely that is no reason for doing away with them in such a cruel and heartless manner.'

'It would be to a man like Hartley.'

Nicola flinched at Blackwood's offhand reply. 'Would it be reason enough for you, my lord?'

David hesitated, sensing the need to tread carefully with his new fiancée on what was obviously a very delicate subject. 'I have never been one for the indiscriminate taking of life, Nicola, but I can understand the rationale behind a man taking certain precautions to ensure the purity of the line.'

'Then I suggest he should have taken more care in the breeding of the dog in the first place,' Nicola said heatedly, well aware that animal husbandry was an inappropriate subject for a gently reared lady to be discussing.

It seemed that Lord Blackwood was in complete agreement. 'Well, I think that is enough said about the subject. You are welcome to bring the dogs along, Nicola, whatever their...parentage. Now, shall we call your father in and give him the good news?'

There was a slight reserve to his tone and, realizing that it would serve no useful purpose to protest further, Nicola graciously acquiesced. She did not wish to anger David over someone else's shortcomings, nor did she see that there was anything to be gained by doing so. It was enough that he was agreeable to her bringing her puppies along. And so, with a smile upon her face, Nicola rose with David to greet her father and to share their happy news with him.

It was not until some time later, as Nicola watched her fiancé disappear down the drive in his gleaming black and gold carriage, that she had time to think back over the events of the past hour and to marvel at how significantly her life had changed. She was now the fiancée of the Marquis of Blackwood. Quite an achievement in a society where matches were made solely for the betterment of financial or social standing.

But what kind of life had she committed herself to? Nicola wondered silently. She was not in love with David, nor he with her. But her father approved of the match, and she respected Lord Blackwood for the man she knew him to be. Was that not reason enough to accept his offer?

Not really, Nicola admitted to herself on a sigh. And she wouldn't have, had it not been for that brief and totally unexpected moment of softening, when David had spoken to her with humility in his voice and just a trace of wistfulness in his eye. Almost as though he regretted that theirs would not be a marriage of two hearts.

That was what had changed her mind about Lord Blackwood, and made her look at him differently. Maybe he did care about the importance of feelings between two people, Nicola decided charitably. Maybe he wasn't the staid, reserved aristocrat that most people accused him of being. Maybe it was simply that no one had ever taught the very upright Lord Blackwood how to laugh.

* * *

The announcement of the engagement of the Marquis of Blackwood to the Lady Nicola Wyndham duly appeared in *The Times* the following week, and, as Sir Giles had predicted, there arose from the marriageable ladies of the *ton*—or, rather, from their mamas—a sigh of disappointment that could be heard from one end of London to the other. From one drawing room in the country, however, there was only the sound of delighted laughter as the good news was received and celebrated.

'Well, my dear, you have certainly achieved the match of the season!' Glynnis, Lady Dorchester, told her niece in a tone of supreme satisfaction. 'And I, for one, could not be happier. I had begun to despair of Blackwood ever settling down. Lord knows, he has been as slippery as an eel these past few years. But, without even trying, you have caught him in your net and brought him home. Well done, my dear, well done!'

'Thank you, Aunt Glynn, although I don't know that he is any the less elusive now,' Nicola told her aunt with a smile. 'He merely slipped in long enough to propose before slipping right out again. I have not seen him this sennight.'

'Well, that is not such a bad thing,' said Lady Dorchester complacently. 'Absence makes the heart grow fonder, you know.'

'Perhaps, but it would have been nice had Lord Blackwood stayed around long enough to give me something to grow fond of,' Nicola observed dryly. 'I can hardly miss a man I know nothing about.'

Lady Dorchester glanced at her niece shrewdly. 'I take it this is not a love match, then?'

'Oh, dear, no, far from it.' Nicola laughed as she recalled the wording of the marquis's proposal. 'Lord Blackwood was very straightforward when it came to tell-

ing me exactly what he expected in the future marchioness.'

'And that is?'

'A sensible woman not prone to giddiness, frivolity
or…unacceptable behaviour I believe was how he phrased
it. He also assured me that he would be a good husband
and father, and that I would want for nothing.'

'Admirable sentiments, to my way of thinking.'

'And Papa believes it to be an advantageous match.'

'And so it is, my dear!' Lady Dorchester agreed whole-
heartedly. 'Lord Blackwood is one of the wealthiest men
in London, not to mention one of the most handsome. I
admit, he may not be as light-hearted as some of the gentlemen his age, but then, he has always been something
of a serious lad, and he grew even more so after his dear
mother died. He never really took to his father's second
wife, you see. Rumour has it that he blamed her for his
father's death.'

'Oh, dear, I had no idea,' Nicola said, biting her lip.
'But I know so little of Lord Blackwood.'

'Which is hardly surprising, given your extended absence from Town,' Lady Dorchester said. 'However, we
cannot overlook the fact that you have been extremely
fortunate, Nicki. And I feel sure that once Lord Blackwood is happily married you will see a considerable
change in his disposition. So, when and where is the wedding to take place?'

'I'm not sure. Lord Blackwood mentioned having the
ceremony at the family chapel at Ridley Hall, but I rather
had my heart set on St Andrew's, where Mama and Papa
were married. Unfortunately, he had to return to London
before we were able to come to a decision.'

'Well, no doubt you shall be able to settle it the next
time he comes to Wyndham. Now, we must start making

plans for your betrothal ball. And I will not take no for an answer,' Lady Dorchester said firmly, as Nicola went to object. 'Your father and I have already discussed it, and he has assured me of his complete cooperation. That is why we are going to hold the ball at Wyndham rather than here at Doring Cross. Given the number of people I intend to invite, Doring would hardly be large enough.'

'But it is such a lot of work, Aunt,' Nicola said guiltily.

'I am well aware of that, my dear, but, in truth, I am looking forward to it. I was not fortunate enough to have children of my own, and if I cannot do something like this for my own daughter, at least let me do it for my sister's child. I know this is what Elizabeth would have wanted for you.'

It was probably the best argument she could have employed, and thus appealed to, Nicola could not find it in her heart to say no. 'Well, if you are sure, but—oh, upon my word! Champagne?' she exclaimed as the door to the drawing room opened and the butler came in with a silver tray.

'Well, of course. It isn't every day my favourite niece becomes engaged to the Marquis of Blackwood, and I think such a momentous occasion warrants a special celebration. Besides, I have had precious little else to celebrate these last few months.'

Nicola's green eyes softened and, impulsively, she leaned forward to kiss her aunt's smooth, unlined cheek. 'Dear Aunt Glynn. You really should start moving about in Society again. Uncle Bart has been gone these three years, and you are far too lovely to shut yourself away. I know that you could find another husband if you only set your mind to it.'

'In all honesty, I am not sure that I wish to, Nicki.' Lady Dorchester's expression grew suddenly wistful.

'Your uncle and I were together for over fourteen years, and, frankly, I am not sure that I could adjust to having a new gentleman under foot—if I could even find one who would have me. A younger man will be looking for a woman to give him sons, whereas an older man will be looking for a pretty young thing to parade about Town on his arm. And at six-and-thirty I am neither one nor the other. I seem to fall into that…grey area in between.'

'Fiddlesticks. You are far too young and lovely to think of yourself as part of any *grey* area,' Nicola scolded her aunt affectionately. 'And I know that any number of gentlemen would tell you so, if you were but willing to listen.'

Lady Dorchester patted her niece's hand. 'You are a dear child, Nicola. And I would be lying if I said there were not certain things I miss about being married, especially to a man one is truly in love with.' Her eyes crinkled around the edges. 'The Duchess of Basilworth is forever telling me that I should take a *chèr ami*.'

Nicola gasped, and then started to laugh. 'Never!'

'Oh, yes. And she is quite serious.'

'No doubt she is. The duchess has been known to make some outrageous statements. But would you really consider doing such a thing, Aunt?'

Lady Dorchester looked thoughtful for a moment, and then shook her head. 'I think not. As exciting as the idea may be, one seldom finds happiness with such a man. They are usually either married, or considered too much a rake or roué to be so, and I, for one, have no desire to throw my heart away on someone I can neither have nor trust. Oh, dear, have I embarrassed you?' Lady Dorchester asked, noticing the sudden rosy hue in her niece's cheeks.

'Not at all.' Nicola was quick to assure her. 'I was

merely thinking about something I overheard at Lady Rumbolt's soirée the other evening.'

'Dear me, it must have been something very interesting to make you blush so.'

'Yes, it was.'

Lady Dorchester waited expectantly, then prompted, 'Well?'

Nicola bit her lip. 'I am not at all sure it is an appropriate topic for me to be discussing.'

'Why don't you tell me and allow me to make that decision?'

Nicola laughed self-consciously, then said, 'Very well. Is it true, Aunt, that…a married lady should not mind if her husband goes elsewhere for…well, that is, for his—?'

'Thank you, Nicola; I think I can figure the rest of it out,' Lady Dorchester said abruptly, even as her blue eyes began to sparkle. 'My word, that was *quite* a conversation you overheard. However, I will give you the benefit of my opinion, by saying that, yes, a wife should most definitely mind if her husband looks elsewhere for his…pleasures. Love between a man and his wife can be a wonderful thing, Nicola. And, if you are fortunate enough to really love your husband, the thought of his going elsewhere will cause you more misery than you can imagine. Unfortunately, all too often, women look upon…certain aspects of marriage as an unpleasant task, a duty that must be borne stoically and in silence, refusing to believe that, with a little effort on their part, they could actually come to enjoy it. And I'll wager you'll not hear *that* whispered in the drawing rooms of Society,' she added dryly.

Nicola looked thoughtful for a moment. 'Then such

feelings can exist within a marriage, if one but makes the effort.'

'Oh, yes, indeed. Mark my words, Nicki: if you want a happy marriage, make the effort to please your husband,' Lady Dorchester urged her. 'I give you my promise, it will be well worth it in the long run. For both of you!'

In London, David attended to the business of his upcoming nuptials with the same efficiency that he employed in matters concerning the running of his estates. He spent an afternoon with his secretary, dictating letters and issuing instructions, and generally whittling down the pile of correspondence which had accumulated during his brief absence. The pink, highly scented letters from his mistress he burned without reading. He had warned Yvette time without number not to address correspondence to his home, but she had not paid him the slightest heed.

Probably because it was not intellect the darling Yvette was renowned for.

Fortunately, his desire for the pretty ballet dancer had long since begun to wane—as had his interest in any kind of casual encounter—so it was not with a deep feeling of regret that David left her cosy little house that night, after bidding her a final adieu. In spite of the tears, he had no doubt that she would recover quickly from her grief. In fact, he fully expected that she would have a new gentleman in her bed by this time tomorrow night.

From there, he headed to St James's to enjoy a few quiet hours at his club. He was not at all surprised to find his uncle already reposed in a comfortable chair by the fire, a glass of port in one hand, a copy of *The Gentleman's Quarterly* in the other.

'Evening, Uncle Giles.'

Sir Giles looked up, and his face brightened considerably. 'David, my boy, thank God you're back. Place has been as quiet as a tomb without you.' The baronet folded his paper and signalled to the waiter for another glass. 'So, tell me, how did Lady Nicola react to your proposal? Did she say yes right off?'

David settled back into the comfortable leather armchair next to his uncle, and crossed one ankle over the other. 'Not exactly. As it turned out, she had a few questions of her own.'

'Did she indeed? Brave girl. I doubt many others would have had the courage to quiz you about anything other than how soon you would start showering them with the fabulous Blackwood diamonds.'

David chuckled softly. 'I admit, I was slightly taken aback when she asked me why I wanted to marry her.'

'The devil! And what did you tell her?'

'That I was looking for a sensible woman, and that in return she would want for nothing.'

'Did she think that an appropriate reply?'

'She must have. She agreed to marry me.'

Sir Giles studied his nephew thoughtfully. 'I wonder if she will not be quite as biddable as you think, David.'

Briefly reminded of the flash of determination in Nicola's eyes when she had asked about bringing along her river-salvaged pups, David couldn't help but wonder himself. What would she have said, he wondered, had he refused to allow her to keep the mongrels?

But then, recalling the look of pleasure on her face when he had sat down beside her, and the way her eyes had fluttered closed when he had kissed her cheek, he wondered whether the other was all that important. While he wasn't looking for an argumentative wife, neither did he wish to spend his life with a whey-faced young miss who would bow to his every whim. A certain amount of spirit was admirable. A *certain* amount.

'No, all things considered, I think Nicola and I shall suit,' David said, surprised at how content the statement made him feel. 'Time I gave up this bachelor existence anyway.'

Sir Giles's lips twitched. 'All of it?'

'*All* of it. I have given Yvette her *congé* in the form of a flashy ruby bracelet—'

'Which no doubt helped to ease the pain of parting.'

David laughed. 'No doubt. And I sent a note round to Belle, advising her of my intentions to marry.'

'Ah, yes, the fair Arabella.' Sir Giles hesitated, wishing to phrase his question diplomatically. 'Do you think she will be disturbed by the news?'

'I see no reason why she should be. Belle was kind enough to act as my hostess when I required one, and I was grateful for her efforts, but I hardly think she will feel put out when she learns that she is to be displaced by the woman I rightfully intend to marry!'

'So, Blackwood is finally planning to wed, eh?' the rotund Lady Fayne commented as she accepted a cup of tea from her hostess. 'About time too, if you ask me.'

Lady Mortimer sniffed disparagingly. 'Should have married years ago. Doesn't do to keep so many young ladies holding out hopes. Know anything about the gel?'

Arabella Braithwaite stirred a small spoonful of sugar into her tea and then sat back against the richly uphol-stered cushions of the gold damask settee, her lovely fea-tures arranged in a mask of amiability. 'Not really, other than that she spends a good deal of time in the country.'

'Lovely girl, though,' Mrs Harper-Burton put in kindly.

'I recall seeing her at Almack's years ago. They made almost as much fuss over her come-out as they did yours, Belle.'

'Still, the announcement must have come as something of a shock,' the Duchess of Basilworth said loftily. She smiled at the beautifully gowned woman across from her with a modicum of pity. 'I suppose you will have to resign yourself to playing a much smaller part in Lord Blackwood's life from now on. He will hardly need you acting as his hostess when he has a wife of his own.'

'Perhaps, but just because Lord Blackwood has a wife does not mean I shall no longer have occasion to see him, Your Grace,' Arabella said sweetly. 'We are cousins after all, and no doubt his wife will appreciate my being there to help smooth her transition back into London Society. I understand that she has been keeping a very low profile since putting off her blacks.'

'Oh, Belle, how generous of you,' Mrs Harper-Burton said. 'I thought you might have been…well, resentful of another woman taking your place.'

'Taking her place. Really, Clara!' the Duchess of Basilworth snapped. 'How can Arabella be resentful of someone taking a place which was never hers to begin with?'

'Indeed,' Arabella said lightly. 'I merely came to Lord Blackwood's aid at a dinner party, and, much to my surprise, he asked for my help at his next one. I really just…slipped into the role.'

'Well, you are just going to have to slip right back out of it again,' the Duchess said smugly. 'I am sure the future Lady Blackwood will not be looking for assistance in domestic matters. I understand she is a sensible young woman. No doubt she will be able to hire a competent staff to attend to such matters.'

Arabella's smile never faltered. 'Yes, I am sure she will. More tea, anyone?'

The conversation moved off into other areas and the topic of Lord Blackwood's upcoming nuptials was forgotten. But as soon as the ladies took their leave and Arabella was left alone the scowl which had appeared on her face upon receiving her cousin's note abruptly reappeared, wiping out all traces of her earlier complacency.

How could David spring the news on her like that! He had never even made mention of the fact that he was thinking of getting married, and here he was, engaged to some country chit, without so much as a private word to her beforehand. Did he care nothing for her feelings?

Arabella stood up and began to pace the room with the fury of a caged tigress. It was simply too galling! True, there had never been anything of a romantic nature between them, but Arabella had always hoped that, given time, their relationship might develop into something... warmer. But that wasn't likely to happen now. Because David was replacing her with a wife. His politely worded letter, thanking her for everything she had done, and assuring her that they would continue to see each other on a social basis, did nothing to lessen her humiliation. She had not just imagined the pity in the Duchess of Basilworth's beady eyes this afternoon. It had been there, as plain as day. The old biddy had been laughing at her; enjoying her fall from grace, as it were.

Well, David wasn't married yet, Arabella reminded herself, and, until he was, she intended to make very sure that she did not slip quietly into the background. Her cousin was a stickler for propriety, and he would expect his wife, as the future marchioness, to behave in a no less honourable fashion—the way Arabella herself had taken pains to behave every time she had been in his company.

Duty meant everything to David and, given that Arabella had heard some very interesting stories about the late Countess of Wyndham, and about the daughter who was rumoured to have inherited some of the mother's more eccentric qualities, Arabella decided that she would be well advised to stay close to the proceedings. If Nicola Wyndham put a foot wrong, Arabella wanted to be there to point it out.

She wasn't going to lose David without a fight. And she intended to make very sure that the ladies all laughed on the other side of their faces before this was over!

Chapter Three

At long last, the day of Nicola's betrothal ball arrived and, with it, the agreement that Lady Dorchester had outdone herself. The servants had been kept busy from morning till night, polishing and dusting, fetching and carrying, and helping to transform the ballroom at Wyndham Hall into a glittering fairy-tale forest, complete with bubbling fountains, miniature trees, and endless pots of white and pink roses which lent their colour and delicate perfume to the exquisitely decorated room.

Lady Dorchester herself had supervised the creation of Nicola's new wardrobe, and had taken her to her own modiste for the selection of the magnificent gown Nicola would wear on the night of the ball.

'You simply cannot be seen wearing anything that is not strictly *au courant*, my dear,' Lady Dorchester had informed her as the modiste had brought forth yet another bolt of exquisite material. 'This is the beginning of your new life. You must start as you mean to carry on.'

But as she studied her reflection in the cheval-glass on the night of the ball Nicola was not sure that she was making quite the right statement. 'Is it the fashion to be so revealing, Aunt?' she asked in dismay, eyeing the outrageously low décolleté of the gown and feeling that there was considerably more flesh above the neckline than below it.

'My dear girl, as the Marchioness of Blackwood, you will set the fashion, not follow it,' Lady Dorchester told her confidently. 'I only wish your dear mother could have been here to see you. She would have been so very, very proud. But we mustn't stand here dithering. I am sure Lord Blackwood is anxiously waiting for you to appear.'

As it happened, David was in the hall when Nicola and her aunt made their descent down the grand staircase. He had purposely arrived early in the hopes of spending a little time alone with his fiancée before the arrival of their guests, since there was one more thing he wanted to do before making their betrothal official. But as he stood and watched Nicola walk down the staircase towards him, looking a vision in a magnificent gown that flattered every sensuous curve of her body, he almost forgot what he had come early to do.

'You look...stunning,' he said quietly and with complete sincerity. He raised her gloved hand and pressed his lips warmly to the back of it. 'I am honoured to be at your side this evening, my lady.'

Nicola blushed prettily at the charmingly old-fashioned gesture, and then withdrew her hand. 'Thank you, my lord. I am delighted by your approval. I wonder, are you acquainted with my aunt?'

'I most certainly am,' David said, turning now to bow towards Nicola's aunt, who was equally resplendent in a gown of emerald-green satin. 'It is a pleasure to see you again, Lady Dorchester. And, may I say, looking every bit as radiant as your niece.'

There was a twinkle in Lady Dorchester's eye as she curtsied and said, 'And you are every inch as charming as I remembered, Lord Blackwood. My niece is a lucky young lady indeed to have secured the affection of such a gentleman. But then, I believe *you* to be even more fortunate in having secured hers.'

David chuckled deep in his throat. 'Indeed I am, Lady Dorchester, and, if I may be so bold, I would like to have a few minutes alone with Nicola before the evening gets underway. There is something I should like to give her.'

Lady Dorchester beamed. 'I would not mind at all. As long as you promise to have her back in time to greet your guests.'

'I give you my word.'

Thus assured, David took Nicola by the hand and led her through the house to the conservatory, which was located well away from all the hustle and bustle of the festivities.

'My lord, what is this all about?' Nicola asked when they stood alone in the middle of the spacious, plant-filled room.

About to make the formal presentation of the ring, David turned towards her, and then abruptly went silent. The room was illuminated by nothing more than the glow of the full moon shining in through the glass windows, and by the flickering light of the candles in the sconces lining the walls. Even so, it was enough to show him how truly beautiful was the woman he had asked to be his wife. In the shimmering silk gown, with the high-waisted bodice delicately beaded and hugging a creamy expanse of bosom, and the skirt falling in gentle folds to reveal tiny feet shod in dainty satin slippers, Nicola's loveliness nearly took his breath away.

And then there were those eyes. Deep-set and fringed with the most impossibly long, gold-tipped lashes he had ever seen, they were eyes that stirred the passion in a man's heart and coaxed the soul from his body. Eyes which, in the soft light of the moon, glowed a deep, luminous green.

Witch's eyes.

'My lord?'

'Mmm?'

'You're staring at me.'

'Am I?' David shook his head, wondering at the turn of his own imagination.

Witches indeed!

'Forgive me, Nicola, I fear my mind must be wandering tonight.'

'Well, I think even the great Marquis of Blackwood should be allowed to daydream once in a while. Don't you?'

David smiled to himself. What would she say, he wondered, if she knew exactly what he had been daydreaming about? He quickly thrust such frivolous thoughts aside, and said, 'I wanted to have a moment alone with you to give you something.' He drew forth a small velvet bag from his breast pocket and tipped a ring with a magnificent square-cut emerald surrounded by sparkling diamonds into his hand. 'I chose it with your eyes in mind.'

Nicola gasped as she caught the flash of diamonds and gold in the pale moonlight. 'Oh, my! This is…for me?'

'It is.' Slowly, Blackwood reached for her hand and reverently slid the ring onto her slender finger, knowing that it was only the first of many such heirlooms he would bestow upon his new marchioness. 'Now we are officially betrothed.' Then, to Nicola's astonishment, he bent his head and kissed her full on the lips.

Nicola had not been expecting his kiss, nor was she prepared for the devastating effect it had on her senses. As his mouth moved gently over hers, teasing her with its warmth, a strange new excitement began to stir within her body. She felt his arm close firmly around her waist and pull her close; so close that she could smell the clean masculine fragrance of his soap and feel the warmth radiating from his body. Goodness, no one had ever told her that a kiss could be like this, and, flustered, Nicola drew back.

David drew back too, though he didn't release her hand. He continued to gaze down into her face, committing to memory the elegant line of her nose, the feathery curve of her eyebrows and the intoxicating dimple at the left side of her mouth, and felt an inexplicable tightness in his chest. 'Does that please you, Nicola?' he whispered hoarsely.

'Y-yes. It was…very pleasant indeed.'

'Was?' Puzzled, David paused for a moment. Then, realizing what she was saying, he began to chuckle softly in his throat. 'I was referring to the ring, my dear.'

Nicola was eternally grateful for the darkness which hid her blushes. What a widgeon he must think her. Of course he was referring to the ring. He would hardly need question the expertise of his kisses.

'It is…truly beautiful, my lord,' she said, glancing down at her hand to avoid the dark, probing eyes.

'I am very glad to hear it. But, now that we are officially betrothed, do you think you could bring yourself to call me…David?'

It was such a silly oversight that Nicola started to laugh. 'Oh, dear, yes, I think I most probably could…David.'

And so, in a spirit of mutual charity, and much pleased with the events of the last few minutes, Nicola accompanied her fiancé back to the ballroom to await the arrival of their guests.

* * *

It did not come as any surprise to David that the evening—and Nicola—were a complete success. Chatting easily as the seemingly endless flow of people made their way down the reception line, David watched his future bride smile and greet their guests, and knew that he had not been mistaken in his assessment of her abilities. The confidence and the poise with which Nicola carried herself would have made any man proud, and, indeed, a duchess could not have been more dignified.

'Well, David, I am delighted to see you looking so settled,' the regal Duchess of Basilworth said, breaking into his reveries. 'And not before time either. I was beginning to wonder whether the fifth Marquis of Blackwood was not destined to become the *last* Marquis of Blackwood.'

'I assure you, Your Grace, I had no intention of allowing anything of the kind to happen,' David said, turning to offer her a warm smile. 'I was simply waiting until the time was right. *And*, of course, for the right lady to come along.'

'Yes, well, I am sure you aged most of the mothers in this room waiting for just the right time and the right lady,' the Duchess chided him affectionately. 'I know of at least five young ladies who turned down estimable proposals on the off chance that you might favour them with yours.'

'Really? I cannot think why. I am hardly such a worthy catch as all that. And I am old enough to be a father to some of these girls.'

The Duchess tapped him lightly on the arm with her fan. 'I assure you, there was nothing paternal in the way any of them viewed you. Still, I am glad that you have made your choice, and that you have chosen so wisely. Lady Nicola is a sensible young woman with the manners of a queen. Look at her dealing with that odious mush-room, Mrs Bonguard. One would never know that she was anything but delighted to be talking to her.'

'Perhaps she is.'

'Fustian, how could she be?' the Duchess disclaimed. 'The woman is married to a Cit and thinks that by virtue of her husband's wealth she is entitled to an entrée to Society. I wonder that someone hasn't put her in her place.'

David tactfully hid his amusement at the Duchess's re-mark. 'I am sure someone will, Your Grace.'

'Perhaps, but I fear it will not be your future bride. Too nice for her own good. Speaking of which,' the Duchess said, her sharp gaze returning to Blackwood's face, 'have you seen Arabella Braithwaite this evening?'

'Only in the receiving line,' David replied. 'I intended to speak with her later, though.'

'Yes, do that, David,' the Duchess advised. 'It would be wise for you to settle things between the two of you as quickly as possible.'

'Settle things?' David's brows knit together in confu-sion. 'I do not see that there is anything to settle, Your Grace. The day before the announcement appeared in *The Times*, I sent Arabella a note, personally informing her of my intention to marry so that she would be advised be-forehand.'

'And have you had word from her since?'

'No, but—'

'I thought not. I am going to give you a piece of advice, my boy, and you would do well to mind it.' The Duchess leaned forward and lowered her voice. 'Watch her care-fully.'

David looked at the woman in surprise. 'Nicola?'

'Gudgeon! Arabella. She has enjoyed playing the part

of the Marchioness of Blackwood, and she don't like being displaced,' the Duchess told him bluntly.

If he hadn't been so surprised, David would have been tempted to laugh. 'Nonsense! She can hardly be displaced from a position she never held.'

'No, but you had her act as hostess at your dinner parties, did you not?'

'A few, but—'

'And she saw to the arranging of your receptions and to various other sporting functions, did she not?'

'Again, yes, but—'

'Then what would you call that, if not playing the part of your wife?'

'I would call it lending assistance as a friend,' David replied calmly. '*And* as a relation. Need I point out that Arabella is my cousin?'

'Yes, and one ill-content to be so. Oh, come along, David, everyone knows that cousins marry, and pray do not attempt to appease my sensibilities by pretending they do not. I am telling you that Arabella had it in her mind to become the next Marchioness of Blackwood, and if you paid any mind to Society gossip at all you would have known that.'

Uncomfortably reminded of his uncle's words, David frowned his displeasure. 'I do not care for rumours and speculation, Your Grace, as I think you know. It is enough for me that Arabella helped me when I asked her to. I am sure she has no amorous intentions towards me, and I can assure you that I have none towards her. Our relationship has never strayed beyond the walls of the dining room, if you follow my meaning.'

'I know precisely what you mean, Blackwood,' the Duchess commented dryly, 'and I am not trying to ascertain whether your conduct towards your cousin is, or was in any way lacking. All I am saying is that spurning an ambitious woman can sometimes lead to trouble. It is entirely up to you whether you heed the warning or not. Now, having said that, I must go and have a word with Lady Fayne. She still owes me fifty pounds from our game of whist the other evening. No doubt she has forgotten again, poor dear. Mind like a sieve. I shall see you at supper, David,' the Duchess said, before moving away like a regal battleship at full sail.

David watched her go, surprised and not a little troubled that she could have misjudged his cousin so. Arabella jealous? Impossible. There had never been anything in her conduct to suggest that she was in the least interested in him romantically. In fact, David was sure that, when they had last ridden together, Arabella had expressed an interest in Lord Wickstead, a prominent peer with extensive holdings in Kent and a reputed income of some fifteen thousand a year.

'You look very deep in thought, David. Thinking about your new lady love?'

Startled out of his deliberation, and by the very person he had been thinking about, David turned to see Arabella wearing a gown of dark maroon silk, and looking as beautiful at eight-and-twenty as she had as a bride of eighteen. As the widow of a wealthy man, she could hardly lay claim to the mannerisms of a blushing bride, but there was still a touch of coquetry in her ways that a number of gentlemen found attractive.

To David, however, she was just his cousin Arabella, and he smiled at her accordingly. 'As a matter of fact, I was thinking about you, Belle. You are looking exceedingly lovely this evening.'

'I thought it only fitting that I look my best for my favourite cousin's betrothal ball,' Arabella replied in a carefully nonchalant voice. 'So, you have finally decided to settle down and marry. I am happy for you, David, and delighted that you have found someone with whom to share your life. After all, is that not what we all look for?'

'It is, and I am pleased to hear you say so, Belle. I would not wish to offend you in any way.'

'Offend me! My dear man, how could I possibly be offended?' Arabella said, her laughter just a shade too bright. 'You have always treated me with the utmost courtesy, and it has been a pleasure to preside over your various functions. But I am well aware that it was only a temporary measure until you found someone who could do it on a more…permanent basis. Which you now have. I just hope you won't cut me from your life altogether.'

'Of course I do not intend to cut you,' David told her, wondering at her making such a remark. 'We are family, after all. And as an old married man—'

'You will never be an old married man,' Arabella said fervently. 'You will always be my dearest cousin David.' Then, fearing that she may have sounded a trifle bold, she added quickly, 'Now, why don't you bring your lovely fiancée here? I should like very much to spend a few minutes chatting with her, and getting to know her better.'

'I am sure Nicola would enjoy that,' David said, turning to look for Nicola. Unfortunately, a quick search of the room failed to reveal the whereabouts of his Titian-haired beauty.

'How strange,' he said after glancing around the room. 'I can't imagine where she would have gone. Excuse me for a moment, will you, Belle?' Moving away, David did a quick circuit of the room, but to no avail. Nicola was simply nowhere to be found.

'Lady Dorchester, have you seen Nicola?' he asked, coming upon her aunt a few minutes later.

'No, Lord Blackwood, I have not. At least, not for a little while. The last time I saw her she was sipping champagne with old Lord Wexler.' Lady Dorchester glanced around the room and then suddenly began to frown. 'Oh, dear, you don't think the odious man has run off with her, do you?'

A faint smile briefly ruffled David's mouth. 'At sixty-eight, I doubt Wexler's heart would stand the strain. Funny, though, her disappearing like this. Perhaps I should take a look outside.'

'Yes, do that, Lord Blackwood,' Lady Dorchester said, glancing around the room again. 'I shall look for her father. Perhaps the two of them have gone away together for a talk. It would not be the first time.'

Little did either of them know, however, that at that precise moment the young lady in question was neither chatting to her father nor enjoying a stroll around the gardens. She was standing in the middle of the darkened billiards room, an expression of deep concern marring the tranquillity of her lovely features.

'And you are sure you saw her fly in here?' Nicola asked the young lad standing nervously beside her.

'Aye, m'lady. Saw it as plain as the nose on me face.'

'But how did she get out of the cage?'

The boy, who looked to be about eleven years old, fiddled anxiously with the cap in his hand. 'I just turned me back for a minute to get the piece'v meat Cook give me, and when I turned back round there she was—gone!'

'Oh, dear, this really is most inconvenient.' Nicola cast anxious eyes towards the ceiling. 'The wing was not set nearly well enough for her to fly. I am surprised she made it this far.'

'I did see 'er go down once, m'lady,' the lad admitted, 'and then she kind of 'obbled, like.'

'But how did she get in here?' Nicola murmured, moving slowly about the room. 'The windows are all closed.'

'Aye, but the windows in the one next to this one aren't. I saw 'er fly in there and I climbed in after 'er. Then, when she came in 'ere, I shut the door and nipped out to let Mr Trethewy know.'

'Well, I am very glad you thought to get word to me, Jamie,' Nicola said kindly. 'Now, listen carefully. I want you to run down to the kitchen and tell Cook to give you a length of old linen. Ask her for as much as she can spare. Then bring it back up here as quickly and as quietly as you can.'

'Aye, m'lady, I'll do that!'

The young lad dashed away, stopping only long enough to close the door behind him. As soon as he was gone, Nicola resumed her search for the injured falcon, all the while chewing nervously on her bottom lip. This couldn't have happened at a worse time. What ever must David be thinking? Surely he had noticed that she was gone. And poor Guinevere; she must be scared half to death. The sooner Nicola got her safely back into her cage, the better for all concerned.

She was just on her way towards the door, when a shuffling sound drew her attention towards the far corner of the room.

'Guinevere?' Slowly moving forward, Nicola raised the lamp, directing the light towards the corner—and saw the falcon wedged in between the two armchairs. 'Oh, Guinevere, you naughty girl. You have given me such a dreadful fright!'

Just then, the door opened and Jamie reappeared with a length of kitchen linen piled over his arm. 'Is this 'nuff, m'lady?' he asked anxiously.

At a glance, Nicola could tell that it was not, but there

wasn't time to send him back downstairs now. 'That will do fine, Jamie. Now, off you go and bring Guinevere's cage back here as quickly as you can.'

'Yes, m'lady.'

After he'd dashed out again, Nicola put the lamp down on top of the table where Jamie had left the linen, and then removed one of her long silk gloves. Starting at her wrist, she began wrapping the linen around her arm, making sure that the skin was covered all the way up to her elbow. She worked quickly, aware that with every passing minute her absence from the ballroom would grow more noticeable, until, finally, David would be forced to come in search of her. And heaven only knew what he would do if he found her playing nursemaid to an injured falcon.

Wrapping the last few inches of fabric around her arm, Nicola secured the makeshift bandage with a knot, and then pulled it tight. It wasn't nearly as thick as she would have liked it to be, but at least it would offer her some protection from the falcon's razor-sharp talons. If for any reason the bird panicked, those claws would slice through Nicola's soft skin like hot knives through butter. Finally, picking up the lamp, Nicola drew a deep breath and then turned to confront the injured bird.

'All right, Guinevere, you're going to be fine. But I need to have a better look at that wing.'

So saying, Nicola slowly raised the lamp—and then groaned. The broken wing was visibly hanging away from the bird's body. All that hard work for nothing.

'Well, it looks as though we are going to have to start all over again,' she said on a sigh. 'Now, if I can just get you safely back into your cage.'

As if listening, the falcon's dark eyes blinked at her and the hooked beak opened and closed. But Nicola didn't draw back. She had to get Guinevere back into her cage and out of the room before she did the wing, or herself, any more harm. For that reason, she continued to inch her way forward, closing the distance between them, and all the while uttering soft, soothing sounds so as not to frighten the falcon.

It took a while, but, eventually, the bird responded to the familiar sound of Nicola's voice. With an awkward hop, she jumped onto Nicola's arm, her talons sinking deep into the linen as they found a secure foothold. Nicola was glad that she had thought to make the bandage thickest in the area close to her wrist. Even so, she winced as the sharp talons sank through the layers of fabric and pierced the soft skin below. Now, if Jamie would just return with the cage—

Suddenly, Nicola froze. Someone *was* coming—but it wasn't Jamie. From beyond the door she could hear the unmistakable sounds of people. Of voices, male and female alike, raised in laughter. And they were coming in this direction!

'Oh, no!' Nicola murmured, her eyes glued to the door. This was the worst possible thing that could happen. If they came in now, Guinevere would take fright and try to fly away. As it was, she was already starting to flap her wings. Her talons were getting tangled in the linen and Nicola winced as they cut through the flimsy bandage and found the unprotected skin below again. At this rate, Guinevere was going to do them both an injury!

'Guinevere, please don't try to fly!' Nicola whispered as she backed away from the door, willing the crowd to pass.

But they didn't. The door-handle started to turn. The voices and the laughter grew louder.

Guinevere uttered a piercing cry and Nicola closed her eyes—

'*Wait*, m'lord, don't open the door!' a frantic voice called out amidst the peals of laughter. 'You can't go in there! Please, don't let them go in!'

Nicola's eyes flew open. Thank goodness Jamie had arrived!

Unfortunately, so had her father!

'What do you mean, we can't go in?' Lord Wyndham demanded. 'What's the meaning of this, lad? And what on earth is that cage for?'

'It's for the bird, m'lord.'

'What bird?'

'Gwenevere. She sent me to fetch the cage!' Jamie said frantically.

'What the devil—who sent you to fetch a cage?'

'Lady Nicola.'

'*Lady Nicola!*'

Nicola's eyes focused on the door and her heart plummeted.

The search was over. David had found her!

'Aye, she escaped when I were trying to feed 'er, m'lord,' Jamie said breathlessly, 'and I followed 'er in 'ere. Then I sent word to 'er ladyship.'

'And her ladyship came?' David enquired in a tone of stunned disbelief.

'Aye. I told Mr Trethewy to tell 'er what 'appened. And just now, she sent me to fetch the cage. But you daren't go in, sir, or she'll take fright fer sure! Gwenevere, that is.'

'All right, lad, we won't all go in,' Lord Wyndham said brusquely.

Nicola heard her father hushing the crowd and asking everyone to step back. Then, slowly, the door began to open. A hand holding aloft a candelabra appeared through the crack, and a voice called softly, 'Nicola?'

Nicola swallowed. 'Yes, Papa?'

'Is everything all right, my dear?'

'Yes, Papa.'

The door opened a little wider, and two men stepped forward. The light from the candles in their hands fell upon Nicola, silhouetting her against the window. Her back was turned towards them, her arm held slightly in towards her body, offering what protection she could to the frightened bird.

'Nicola, are you all right?' This time, it was David who spoke, though in a voice much sterner than her father's had been.

Nicola turned her head in his direction, and saw that the doorway was crowded with people all anxiously peering in. 'Yes, my lord, I'm fine. But I am afraid Guinevere is a little the worse for wear. Jamie, are you there?'

'Aye, m'lady,' came a shaky voice from somewhere in the depths of the crowd.

'Bring the cage in and set it on the table,' Nicola advised. 'Move slowly, now. We don't want to frighten Guinevere any more than she already is.'

The crowd reluctantly parted and Jamie's anxious face appeared in the doorway. He started to move forward, encumbered by a large wooden cage that was fully half as big as he was, and awkwardly set it on the top of the billiards table. Only then did Nicola turn round, exposing, to the eyes of her guests, the sight of the majestic falcon sitting proudly on her arm.

A gasp of astonishment rippled through the assembly.

Nicola raised uncertain eyes to her fiancé's face and saw the unmistakable look of shock and disbelief written all over it, and wondered how in the world she was going to explain this. Unfortunately, she didn't have time to worry about it now. She had to get the falcon back into the cage.

And so, with what looked to be half the people at her betrothal ball in attendance, Nicola slowly began to walk towards the cage.

'Nicola, your arm!' David said abruptly.

For the first time, Nicola glanced down at her arm, and inwardly caught her breath. It was not a pretty sight. Splotches of bright red stained the bandage in a number of places where the falcon's talons had pierced through to her skin. All she could do was try to laugh it off as she reached the cage and carefully placed her arm through the opening. ''Tis nothing, I assure you. Guinevere just became a little excited when she heard the voices. There now, Guinevere, back you go.'

Nicola tilted her arm and waited for the bird to move. It was only then she realized that one of the falcon's claws had become hopelessly entangled in the loose threads.

'Oh, bother! Jamie, will you help me with my other glove, please?' Nicola said, extending her left arm. 'Guinevere's leg is caught.'

But it was not Jamie who slowly stepped forward to remove the glove.

'I'll do that,' David said curtly.

Nicola held her breath as their eyes met and she held her arm out towards him. It was all she could do not to flinch as his fingers brushed the soft warm flesh above her elbow. She watched him roll down the glove and then slowly pull it free of her fingers, in a gesture that was so intimate, so...familiar that it brought the colour surging to her cheeks. She didn't say a word, however, as she took a deep breath and slowly put her bare hand into the cage, carefully untangling the threads that held the falcon captive. If Guinevere snapped at her fingers now, the resulting injury would be far worse than anything her claws had inflicted thus far.

Fortunately, whether from exhaustion or some sixth sense that Nicola was trying to help her, the falcon merely tipped her head and watched what was going on. Moments later, when both of her feet were free, she obligingly hopped forward onto the perch and allowed Nicola to remove her arm and close the door.

Guinevere was safely home once more!

'There we are, Jamie,' Nicola said weakly. 'Take her back down to the pen and feed her. And this time *do not* open the cage door for any reason.'

'I don't need no second warning about that, m'lady,' the boy said jauntily, now that the crisis was over. 'Come on, then, Gwenevere.'

The crowd hastily stepped back as the boy carried the cage and its occupant out into the hallway and towards the closest door. When he had gone, all eyes turned back to Nicola, standing in the middle of the room, her one arm bare, the other covered in a blood-spattered bandage.

The silence seemed to drag on for ever.

'Well, I think that is quite enough excitement for one night,' Lord Wyndham said brusquely. 'Ladies and gentlemen, why don't we all return to the ballroom?'

'Yes, that would be a grand idea,' Lady Dorchester added, promptly stepping forward to take charge. 'Come along, everyone, back to the ballroom if you please. I shall see to Lady Nicola. You need not stay either, Lord Blackwood.'

David stood by Nicola's side, his eyes fixed on the length of linen now liberally spotted with blood, and marvelled at the spectacle he had just witnessed. Had he really seen his beautiful, genteel fiancée parade around the billiards room with a hunting falcon on her arm, and a stable boy for an accomplice?

'Are you sure you're all right?'

'Perfectly, my lord,' Nicola said, with as much calm as she could muster under the circumstances. 'It looks much worse than it is.'

'Nicola, I must insist—'

'Blackwood, perhaps you'd care to have a drink with me before rejoining your guests,' Lord Wyndham offered hastily, sensing that this was neither the time nor the place for the inevitable confrontation to take place. 'Nicola will return to the ballroom, uh…directly.'

David glanced from one to the other, and then nodded. 'Very well. But I hope you will be good enough to give me an explanation for this at the earliest opportunity, Nicola.'

Nicola sighed. He was furious and doing his level best not to show it. 'I shall be happy to, my lord, but for now I would ask that you go back to the ballroom with the rest of our guests. I shall return shortly.'

David sketched her a quick bow, disapproval evident in every line of his body. Without another word, he turned and left the room. Only after the door closed behind him did Lord Wyndham venture a faint chuckle. 'I don't think Blackwood was very pleased at the sight of you with that bird perched up there, Nicki. Put the wind up him, seeing your arm all bloodied like that.'

Nicola began to unwind the blood-stained bandage from her arm, taking care not to get it anywhere near her gown. 'There was absolutely no reason why it should have alarmed him, Papa. Poor Guinevere was the one at risk, not me. Besides, it was my own fault for not ensuring that I made the bandage thick enough.'

'Unfortunately, that is what comes of keeping exotic pets.'

'Yes, well, under the circumstances, I think it better that Lord Blackwood not hear about…Alistair and the others right now,' Nicola muttered.

'I thought you were planning on taking your menagerie with you when you married?'

'I was,' she confessed. 'And I did tell Lord Blackwood about the puppies, and he said he did not mind my having pets. I just haven't found the right moment to tell him about…the others.'

'Well, I would advise you to do it soon, my dear,' Lady Dorchester said as she carefully took the soiled bandage from her niece and handed it to Trethewy who had magically appeared in the doorway. 'I doubt the marquis's perception of *pets* is going to be the same as yours, and he will hardly be expecting his future marchioness to be a gamekeeper! Now, come along upstairs, and let me have a good look at that arm!'

Chapter Four

The image of Nicola standing in the darkened billiards room, with a hunting falcon perched proudly on her arm, and blood staining the flimsy layer of cloth with which she had wrapped it for protection, stayed with David for a very long time. In fact, it made for an extremely restless night.

What the devil had she been thinking of? Imagine trying to rescue a bird that could just as easily have…ripped her to shreds as look her in the eye! It was commendable, yes. And brave, certainly. But, as the future Marchioness of Blackwood, it was hardly appropriate behaviour. Especially occurring right in the middle of their betrothal ball as it had.

Well, it would no doubt make for an interesting topic of conversation later in the day, David reflected as he stood in the guest bedroom at Wyndham Hall the next morning and painstakingly arranged the folds of his cravat into a perfect Mathematical. And for some clever explanations on the part of his fiancée, to be sure!

By the time David reached the breakfast parlour—his appetite having been considerably whetted by the tantalizing smells issuing from it—he was ready for a hearty repast. The fact that he would likely be enjoying it alone did not trouble him unduly. He knew that Lord Wyndham was not partial to breakfast, having oft heard him refer to it as a singularly uninspiring meal, and, as he knew that it was not the custom for well-bred young ladies to rise early following a night of dancing and revelry, David had no reason to suspect that Nicola would put in an appearance much before noon.

But then, he'd had no reason to suspect that she would treat him to a display of falconry in the billiards room last night either. Which was probably why, when he entered the breakfast parlour to find his fiancée already seated at one end of the long mahogany table, her plate generously heaped with curried eggs and toast, and her attention riveted on the pages of the romantic novel in front of her, he was not overly surprised.

'Good morning, Nicola,' he said laconically. 'Interesting book?'

Nicola's head shot up, her eyes widening in dismay as she realised that, once again, David had caught her doing something that wasn't quite appropriate. She quickly closed the book and offered him what could only be called an apologetic smile. 'David, pray forgive my abominable manners. Miss Withers would have had apoplexy if she'd caught me reading at the table, but, in truth, I did not expect to see you downstairs until much later.'

'*Later?*' David propped his back against the edge of the door and remarked in some surprise, 'Do I strike you as such a layabout, then?'

Catching the subtle inflection, Nicola hastened to reassure him. 'Not at all. It was simply my understanding that fashionable gentlemen preferred to keep to their beds in the morning. Unless they were partaking of some early morning sport, of course.'

'Of course.' Tempted to inform her that the only kind of sport that would keep him abed of a morning included the willing participation of a certain kind of lady, David instead said, 'I was under the impression that fashionable young ladies did exactly the same thing.'

'Well, yes, I believe they do. But then, I do not aspire to be a lady of fashion,' Nicola told him with an unaffected smile. 'At least, not in the truest sense of the word. There is precious little need for that when one spends most of one's time in the country.'

She might not aspire to be a lady of fashion, David thought, but one would never know it by her charming appearance this morning. In the fashionable white muslin gown, delicately embroidered with sprigs of pale blue flowers around the square neckline and hem, Nicola presented a very pretty picture indeed. Her hair was caught up in a charming cluster of curls, through which a ribbon the same colour as the flowers on her dress had been wound, while a few stray tendrils hung loose against the curve of her neck. It was only the fact that she was clearly enjoying a rather hearty meal, *and* that she had probably risen earlier than most of the household, that lent credibility to her statement at all.

'I take it from the fact that you are already well along with your breakfast that you are in the habit of rising early?' David enquired mildly.

'Oh, yes, most assuredly. Morning is my favourite time of the day.'

'How unusual. A lady who professes no concern as regards to maintaining a fashionable appearance, and who prefers the quiet, restful hours of a country morning. I would venture to say, my dear,' David said with a meaningful glance, 'that you are not at all typical of the rest of your breed.'

'No, so Papa has often told me. No doubt that is why I have been spared the attentions of the young tulips and dandies of London Society. I can neither match them in appearance, nor keep up with their nocturnal habits. Indeed, were I to marry such a man, I dare say we should see precious little of each other of a day.'

David's mouth twitched, but he stubbornly refused to smile. He wasn't yet ready to forgive Nicola for her behaviour of the previous night. 'Should I be offended that you do not consider me such a paragon of gentlemanly fashion?'

'Ah, but you are, my lord,' Nicola assured him in a most serious tone, even as her eyes sparkled. 'You are a pattern card to many a young sprig of fashion. But not, I fear, to the fribbles and dandies who would wear their collar points so high as to restrict movement of the head, or don waistcoats so bright that they are painful to the eye. Those are definitely not the type of gentleman who would emulate your considerably more…refined sense of style.'

She was bamming him, David acknowledged ruefully, and with a deftness that was making it dashed hard for him not to laugh out loud. He had not expected to find such a lively wit dwelling behind those enchanting eyes, nor such a conspicuous lack of arrogance in her character. Until now, those were qualities which he had found sadly lacking in the females of his acquaintance.

He pushed himself away from the door, and set about examining the tempting array of hot and cold delicacies displayed in silver platters upon the sideboard.

'I hope you are recovered from the events of last evening,' he remarked idly, selecting, amongst other things, a slab of freshly cured ham, a morsel of rare steak, two poached eggs and three slices of toast.

Having decided early on to be as optimistic as possible about what had happened in the billiards room last night, Nicola offered him a dazzling smile. 'I am suffering no ill effects whatsoever. In fact, I am not in the least tired, even considering all the dancing—'

'It was not the dancing I was referring to,' David said, cutting across her spate of cheery words. 'I was referring to that little episode with the bird.'

Nicola's smile dimmed a little. 'Oh, that.'

'Yes, that.' David nodded briefly in the direction of a footman, who scurried from the room in search of fresh coffee. 'I notice that you have covered your arms today. Are your injuries so grievous that you need to hide them from me?'

Nicola glanced up at him with an expression of genuine surprise. 'They are not grievous at all, it is merely the style of the dress. I have many others like it. Besides, as I told you last night, the bandage made the injuries appear far worse than they really were.'

'Indeed.' David turned back to the sideboard. 'What I should like to know is what a falcon was doing in the billiards room in the first place. And why *you* were the one trying to capture it.'

'Actually, I was…rescuing her.'

'I beg your pardon?'

'I was rescuing Guinevere. She belongs to me, you see,' Nicola explained. 'I found her in the woods some weeks ago.'

David turned to stare at the elegant young lady sitting so calmly at the table in front of him, and said, in disbelief, 'You found a wounded falcon…and brought it home?'

'Well, yes. She had injured her wing and I knew that

she was unlikely to survive the night, so I brought her back here and began nursing her back to health.'

'Nicola, we are not talking about a pretty little finch here. We are talking about a bird of prey, traditionally used for the hunting of small vermin and rodents. You can't just…take it in and treat it like a pet.'

'Guinevere is very gentle and exceedingly well behaved—'

'Yes, I saw how well behaved she was last night,' David drawled. 'So well that, even with a broken wing, she flew out of her cage at the first opportunity.'

'She merely slipped out when Jamie was feeding her,' Nicola replied in the bird's defence. 'It should never have happened.'

'And it wouldn't have, had you had sense enough not to keep the bird in the first place!'

'She would have died without my care!'

'That is the law of nature, Nicola. In the wild, only the strong survive. You cannot take it into your head to rescue every wounded bird you come across. My God, we should be overrun! Or over flown,' David muttered under his breath.

'I am hardly keeping a flock, my lord,' Nicola said, crossing her arms in defiance. 'I merely rescued one injured falcon.'

'I understand that, but has it not occurred to you that you might have been injured last night? What if that damn bird had gone for your face?'

'Oh, David, there was never any danger of that,' Nicola said, her tone evidencing a complete lack of concern. 'Guinevere was simply frightened by all the noise. You saw how docile she became when everyone quietened down.'

'And the injuries to your arm?'

'Were my own fault for not ensuring that the bandage was made thick enough.'

'But surely you realize—'

'My lord, would you care for some of Cook's home-made apricot jam?' Nicola interrupted, as the door to the parlour suddenly swung open and the footman returned carrying a fresh pot of coffee. 'She is renowned through-out the county for the recipe. I think you will find it goes very nicely on your toast.'

Forced by the rules of etiquette to comply, David smiled, and duly accepted the pot of jam Nicola held out to him. It wasn't the thing to be seen arguing in front of servants, and he waited until the young man had resumed his place by the door before continuing in a much softer voice, 'Nicola, I understand that you wished to help the bird, and I certainly cannot fault you for that. But I must insist that, from now on, if you happen to find any injured birds lying in the field, you leave them where they are. You will be far too busy attending to your duties as the Marchioness of Blackwood to trouble yourself with every debilitated bird you come across.'

'Can I keep Guinevere until she is well enough to fly?' Nicola asked, pouring herself a cup of tea.

David spread a generous helping of apricot jam over his toast. 'I cannot make any promises.'

'Then, unfortunately, my lord, neither can I.' Nicola spooned one small teaspoon of sugar into her cup and stirred it around. 'My mother was passionately concerned about the welfare of the birds and animals in the woods surrounding Wyndham Hall, and I share those concerns. And if I am to be your wife you will have to understand that there are some fundamental differences between us when it comes to matters of…nature. Or perhaps,' Nicola said, dropping her voice to a level that was barely audible, 'you would prefer to withdraw your offer of marriage altogether.'

David stared at her in astonishment. 'Withdraw it? What the devil do you—?'

'Edward, would you be so good as to have Cook prepare some fresh eggs for Lord Blackwood?' Nicola interrupted hastily. 'I do believe these have gone cold.'

'Yes, my lady.'

The footman hastened to remove the offending platter, while David sat choking on his reply. He barely waited until the door had closed behind the young man before proclaiming, in a voice that left Nicola in absolutely no doubt as to his feelings, 'I do not intend to withdraw my offer, Nicola, and let that be an end to it. The fact that you are even *suggesting* such a thing—and all as a result of some stupid bird—is quite ridiculous.'

It was Nicola's turn to be surprised, and she hastily dropped her eyes. She could hardly tell him now that she had only been teasing about the possibility of his withdrawing the proposal. He would likely find it a very poor joke indeed. But what was she to make of his violent opposition to her suggestion? Was his disapproval an indication that he was beginning to have feelings for her? Or was it simply a case of knowing that a certain amount of embarrassment would attach itself to the broken engagement that had caused him to speak out so fervently?

Sadly, Nicola tended to think it was the latter.

'Yes, it is ridiculous,' she said at length. 'And for that reason I propose that we speak no more about it. What happened last night is over and done with, and nothing can be gained by dwelling upon it any longer.'

'Nicola—'

'And, now, as it is such a lovely morning, why don't we finish our breakfast and then take a stroll through the gardens? I am most anxious to show you Papa's new ornamental pond. And to discuss topics of a more pleasant nature.'

'Such as?' David enquired suspiciously.

'Such as our upcoming wedding,' Nicola said, with a smile that she hoped would distract him. 'And precisely when and where it is to take place.'

News of the Lady Nicola's daring rescue of the injured falcon in the billiards room at Wyndham Hall spread through the drawing rooms of the *ton* like wild fire. It elicited a startling number of reactions, ranging from wide-eyed astonishment and grudging admiration to out-and-out ridicule for what was perceived to be, by some, extremely unladylike conduct.

For his own part, David was forced to endure a certain amount of good-natured ribbing from his cronies, most of which he managed to take in his stride. Nevertheless, he couldn't help but be nonplussed by the sudden interest Nicola seemed to have generated amongst the gentlemen who had paid her precious little attention before.

'Can't understand it,' David commented to Sir Giles as they sat enjoying a game of cards at his uncle's house one evening the following week. 'Rather than thinking it an unladylike pastime, they all seem to admire her for it.'

'Well, you have to admit it does take a certain amount of courage to toy with a falcon barehanded,' Sir Giles pointed out. 'Good friend of mine used to hunt with them, you know, and he never went near them without protective gloves. Jolly brave girl to approach a frightened falcon with all that bare skin and nothing but a flimsy length of linen wrapped around her arm as protection.'

'I am well aware of the courage demonstrated by my fiancée's actions,' David drawled. 'What I cannot understand is why she felt compelled to keep the damned bird in the first place.'

'I understood she was…nursing it back to health,' Sir Giles said, picking up a card and then, with a frown, casting it back onto the pile. 'Rather admirable thing to do, to my way of thinking.'

'It might be admirable, but it is hardly suitable behaviour for a future marchioness,' David complained. He picked up the card his uncle had discarded, slipped it into his hand, then set down his cards with a marked lack of enthusiasm. *'Vingt-et-un!'*

'What, again? Dash it all, David! I don't know why I bother playing cards with you any more!' Sir Giles exclaimed in frustration. 'I can't wager a farthing, and even if I could I'd still be out of pocket given that you beat me every time.'

'Never mind, Uncle, you know what they say. Lucky at cards, unlucky at love.'

'Humph! Easily enough said by one who's lucky at *both*,' Sir Giles grumbled. 'Still, if I could only choose one, I know which one I should rather be.'

'A wise man uses his head at both,' David cautioned.

'Then in such matters let me be a fool. Speaking of wise, do you still think you've made the right decision in choosing to marry the rather unpredictable Lady Nicola?'

'Of course I do,' David said without hesitation. 'I have no reason to believe that the incident with the bird was anything but an isolated occurrence, and I feel confident that it is one which will not be repeated. Nicola and I came to a clear understanding about that before I left Wyndham… Another hand?'

'Might as well; it's too early to go to bed. But as regards the lady, perhaps you are forgetting the nature of her upbringing,' Sir Giles said, his eyes twinkling as he picked up the cards and deftly began shuffling them. 'Her mother was something of a crusader when it came to the welfare of birds, and animals too, and there's no denying that Lady Wyndham had some rather remarkable skills in that area. Perhaps the strain is buried deeper than you think.'

David picked up his cards and leaned back in his chair. 'I appreciate your concern, Uncle Giles, but, I assure you, I am not in the least concerned. I made my feelings of disapproval over the situation very clear to Nicola, and I feel confident that, from now on, she will give me no further cause for concern whatsoever!'

After a brief discussion, it was decided that the wedding would take place at St Andrew's, the beautiful old church where Nicola's parents had been married, and where she herself had been christened, rather than in the private chapel at Ridley Hall.

Nicola had been pleasantly surprised by her fiancé's willingness to accommodate her wishes, and, in return, had agreed to a few of his own. Namely that they spend the winter in the country, and then return to London in January for the opening of Parliament. As this meant that Nicola would be able to spend Christmas with her father at Wyndham before travelling to London, it was certainly not a request she had been unwilling to grant.

The wedding itself was to be quiet. Sir Giles had agreed to stand as David's groomsman, and after a mid-morning service the couple and their guests would return to Wyndham Hall for an elaborate *déjeuner*. David had suggested that they travel abroad for their wedding trip, but when Nicola had pointed out that a slightly warmer time of the year might be more conducive to all the sightseeing she wished to do he had reluctantly agreed. Hence, they had decided to spend two or possibly three weeks at Ridley, enjoying the relative peace and tranquillity of David's sprawling country home.

As for the creation of her wedding gown, Nicola had decided to have it made by Madame Valois, the same modiste who had overseen the preparation of her new wardrobe. Madame Valois was a favourite of the *ton*, so it was hardly surprising that on the same afternoon that Nicola and her aunt chanced to be in the bustling shop selecting fabrics Arabella Braithwaite also arrived for a fitting of a new gown.

Nicola knew who Arabella was, of course. David had briefly introduced them at their betrothal ball, and, although she and Arabella had not had much opportunity to converse, Nicola knew that she was David's cousin. She was aware that Arabella had acted as David's hostess on more than one occasion, and that she was as refined and sophisticated as she was beautiful. What Nicola was not sure of was whether there was anything more to their relationship than that. Rumour had it that theirs was a strictly platonic association, and on the few occasions that David had spoken about Arabella it had been in such a casual tone of voice that Nicola had not felt even the slightest twinge of jealousy.

Why, then, did she feel so uncomfortable now, upon conversing with the woman in person?

'My dear Lady Dorchester, how lovely to see you again. I cannot tell you how much I enjoyed the evening's entertainment,' Arabella crooned in that distinctively husky voice of hers. 'And Lady Nicola, I do hope you are recovered from that dreadful incident with the bird. Everyone is talking about it, my dear. Saying what a brave young woman you were.' Arabella placed a gloved hand lightly upon Nicola's arm and lowered her voice. 'It was a harrowing experience, was it not?'

Nicola wasn't sure how Arabella managed to make a compliment sound so patronising, but certainly she had never heard one to its equal. Nevertheless, she forced a smile to her lips, and replied in as cordial a manner as possible, 'I assure you there was nothing brave about my behaviour, Mrs Braithwaite, nor harrowing about the situation. I knew what I was doing, and there was never any danger.'

'But you were injured, my dear!'

'A few scratches, nothing more. It was my own fault for not ensuring that the padding around my arm was made thick enough. I was far more concerned with the welfare of the falcon than I was with my own.'

'Well, whatever the reason, it made for quite a spectacle,' Arabella replied with a smile. 'You looked quite like Diana the Huntress with the bird poised on your arm like that. I am sure I could never have looked so valiant. And I could see that David was similarly…impressed.'

The subtle hesitation was long enough to convince Nicola that, in Arabella's opinion, it was certainly not admiration David had been feeling at the time.

'Shall we see you at the meet on Tuesday?' Arabella enquired now. 'I am sure you must be an avid hunter, with your father being Master of the Hunt, and David such an accomplished sportsman.'

'Actually, I prefer to have nothing to do with the hunt, Mrs Braithwaite.'

'Really?' came the startled reply. 'Why ever not?'

'Because I believe it to be a cruel sport which does little to prove a man's—or a woman's—mettle,' Nicola replied quietly. 'Chasing a fox on horseback and hunting it to the point of exhaustion is an exercise in barbarism as far as I am concerned. However, I am well aware that my opinion is more the exception than the rule.'

Arabella's aloof smile served as smug agreement. 'Pity. David is *extremely* fond of the sport, you know.'

'Yes, so I understand.'

'And very good at it too.'

Nicola refused to be drawn. 'Yes, I am sure he is.'

'But, then, as his cousin, I have spent so much time with David that I am well versed in what he does and does not like,' Arabella said carelessly, her smile suddenly reminding Nicola of a cat who had just eaten the family's canary. 'I would be happy to share that information with you, my dear, to help ease you over the early days of married life, if you wish.'

Unconsciously, Nicola stiffened, experiencing, for the first time in her life, a totally unexpected stab of jealousy. The sly look in Arabella's eyes hinted at something other than help being offered, and Nicola began to wonder whether the general belief that Arabella's relationship with David was strictly platonic might, in fact, be false.

'Thank you, Mrs Braithwaite, but, as I shall be spending the rest of my *life* with Lord Blackwood, I am sure there will be plenty of time for me to learn what he does and does not like. Good afternoon.'

Nicola quickly turned and walked out of the shop, thankful that she and her aunt had concluded their business with Madame Valois. She hadn't missed the sharp gleam of dislike which had flashed in Arabella's eyes when she had declined her offer of assistance, but neither could she allow herself to be troubled by it. Arabella was the one who had overstepped the mark, not she. And it was clear that her aunt was in total accord.

'Too coming by half!' Lady Dorchester exclaimed as she and Nicola waited for the servants to finish loading their parcels into the back of the carriage. 'Imagine saying that she would be happy to share what she knew of Lord Blackwood with you. I am very glad that you spoke your mind to her, Nicola.'

'I am afraid I was quite unable to stop myself,' Nicola admitted, still smarting from the encounter. 'I really could not see myself accepting help from another woman regarding what my fiancé does and does not like, even if she is his cousin.'

'Nor should you! What passes between you and Lord Blackwood is no business of Arabella Braithwaite's, and you did well to put her in her place,' Lady Dorchester pronounced. 'Insufferable chit!'

Surprisingly, the outrage in her aunt's voice helped to alleviate some of Nicola's own anger, and at length she merely sighed and said, 'Perhaps, though, I fear I may have done myself more harm than good. Arabella was not at all pleased at what I had to say, and she is David's cousin after all.'

'Well, I should not worry about it, my dear.' Lady Dorchester patted her niece's hand reassuringly. 'Rumour has it that Arabella enjoyed playing the part of Lady Blackwood, and no doubt with you coming along she is afraid of being ousted from the inner circle altogether. Mayhap she is just trying to inveigle her way into your good graces.'

Well, she certainly wasn't going about it in the right way, Nicola reflected silently. While her anger over the woman's effrontery had eased, her resentment towards her had not. It was clear that Arabella Braithwaite did not like her, and, if the truth were known, Nicola had to admit that she didn't much care for Mrs Braithwaite either. Nor could she bring herself to trust her. She had no doubt that the *help* Arabella had so generously offered would have amounted to little more than a blatant attempt to prove to Nicola just how well she knew her cousin—something that Nicola suddenly had no desire to hear, or to acknowledge!

Chapter Five

Feeling it incumbent upon herself to play hostess to some of the company with whom she would associate following her marriage, Nicola arranged an at-home for the following Sunday afternoon. She wanted to assure anyone who had doubts that she was perfectly aware of what constituted acceptable behaviour for a newly engaged young woman. She also wanted to assure David that he had not made a mistake by honouring her with his proposal. And in a pretty new gown in a soft shade of lilac cambric, which flattered her slender figure and accentuated the coppery warmth of her hair, Nicola knew that at least he would be unable to find fault with her appearance.

A soft scrabbling near the window interrupted her musings and drew Nicola's attention away from the cheval-glass. 'Arthur?'

The scratching continued at a more frantic pace, and Nicola's expression softened as she moved towards the cage. 'Feeling a little restless today, are you, pet?'

The question was addressed to a tiny brown and white field mouse who stood on its hind legs, its whiskers quivering, as Nicola unfastened the door and put her hand inside. 'All right, then, out you come. But only for a moment. And then I must be away to greet my guests. Now, let us have a look at that ear.'

Upon careful examination, Nicola decided that the torn ear was looking much better, though the ragged edge would probably always remain. Pity, Nicola reflected. He was such a handsome little fellow otherwise. She ran her finger over the smooth brown fur on his back and smiled at the comical way he twitched his nose at her.

Nicola had never been afraid of mice. When she had found this one at the bottom of a barn pail, little more than a baby, and with its ear torn and half starved because it couldn't climb back out, she had quickly smuggled it away and hidden it in her room. Her father had found out, of course, because somehow he always did. But he hadn't been angry. While he had refused to let Nicola give the mouse the run of her room as she had asked, he had agreed to allow her to keep him in a small cage on the table by the window.

Fortunately, Arthur seemed perfectly content to watch the world go by through the fine mesh walls of his cage. He was occasionally given the freedom of Nicola's room while she was in it, but he was just as likely to end up sitting on her shoulder, nibbling at a piece of cheese she had smuggled from the dinner table, as he was to go anywhere else.

'Nicki, are you ready?' Lady Dorchester called through the closed bedroom door. 'I believe a carriage is making its way up the drive.'

'Yes, coming, Aunt Glynnis.'

Nicola hastily returned Arthur to his cage and closed the door. 'I daren't let my aunt see me carrying you around in my hands, Arthur. The poor woman would likely have fits!'

Turning away from the cage, Nicola quickly dabbed her

wrists with sweet-smelling rose water, and then gave her appearance one last check in the cheval-glass. She was just about to leave when her maid entered the room through an adjoining door, bringing Nicola's favourite French shawl with her.

'I've seen to the tear, my lady,' the girl said in her soft Irish brogue. 'And I think you'll be pleased.'

'Oh, Maire, you are a dear,' Nicola said, stopping to take the garment from her hands. 'And very clever. Indeed, I cannot even remember where the tear was. Thank you, I shall wear it this very afternoon. Oh, and if you have time, would you check the hem of my new carriage gown?' Nicola said, slipping the newly mended shawl about her shoulders. 'I noticed a piece of lace hanging loose, and I feared perhaps I had caught it on something. It is not like Madame Valois to be careless.'

'I'll have a look at it, my lady,' the maid said.

'Thank you, Maire. Now, don't forget to close the door tightly when you leave,' Nicola cautioned with a secretive smile. 'We wouldn't want anyone catching sight of my little pet, would we?'

The maid—who, unlike her mistress, was definitely not enamoured of furry rodents—risked a dubious glance at Arthur and bobbed a curtsey. 'No, miss, I'm quite sure we wouldn't.'

It was a lovely day for visiting and, not surprisingly, quite a number of people called. Most had come intent on expressing their congratulations to Nicola on the news of her recent betrothal, and on wishing her well for the future. Some, however, came strictly out of curiosity, anxious to ask questions, and to view the grievous injuries inflicted by the injured falcon. Wisely, Nicola chose to play the episode with Guinevere down. She preferred not to be reminded of her 'inappropriate behaviour', as David had so eloquently termed it, and tactfully diverted the conversation to other topics whenever possible.

Unfortunately, talk of it kept cropping up like a bad chestnut in a roasting pan. Especially when Nicola found herself in the company of Arabella Braithwaite, her good friend Mrs Harper-Burton and Miss Ruby Stanton, a young lady who had been jealous of Nicola's good fortune in attaching the handsome marquis to begin with.

'Dear me, Lady Nicola, I must say I had nightmares when I learned of it,' Mrs Harper-Burton claimed dramatically. 'I hear the dreadful bird quite tore your arm to pieces.'

Nicola laughed softly, and held out her arm for all to see. 'As you can see, there is little enough damage, Mrs Harper-Burton. I fear whoever recounted the tale to you did so with a good deal of embellishing.'

'I understand that Lord Blackwood was not at all amused,' Ruby said smugly. 'In fact, I hear he was livid.'

Nicola's smile remained firmly in place, though the expression in her eyes cooled. 'Lord Blackwood was more concerned than he was annoyed, Miss Stanton. He feared the injuries to my arm were a good deal more serious than they actually were.'

'Yes, but then, Lord Blackwood has very definite ideas about what a lady should and should not do,' Arabella remarked smoothly. 'No doubt he felt Lady Nicola's display of falconry to be inappropriate entertainment for the billiards room.'

The other ladies tittered, forcing Nicola to conceal her annoyance behind a carefully affected nonchalance. 'It was not meant to be witnessed, Mrs Braithwaite, and had our guests remained in the ballroom, rather than traipsing *en masse* to the billiards room, no one would have been any the wiser.'

'I believe you consider the bird something of a pet, Lady Nicola?' Ruby continued derisively. 'Is that not rather unusual?'

'Not when you consider that her mother was rumoured to have kept a pet badger at one time,' Arabella put in slyly.

'Oh, yes, I heard about that,' the ingenuous Mrs Harper-Burton piped up. 'Apparently, it was quite remarkable the way she handled it.'

'A badger!' Ruby's eyes grew round as saucers, so caught up in the story that she failed to notice the arrival of a newcomer into their circle. 'Is that what gave rise to the rumours that she was a wit—?'

'Run along, Miss Stanton,' interrupted the Duchess of Basilworth frostily. 'I do believe I hear your mother calling.'

Ruby blushed hotly. 'But my mother isn't—'

'Off with you, child!' the Duchess commanded imperiously.

Ruby wisely disappeared while Nicola stood rooted to the spot, her cheeks pale. 'My mother was not a witch!' she whispered, for the benefit of Arabella Braithwaite and Mrs Harper-Burton.

'Of course she wasn't,' the Duchess of Basilworth proclaimed with a contemptuous sniff. 'Never did listen to any of that nonsense. Gossip spread by fools, and nothing more.'

'She *was* seen feeding a wild buck, Your Grace,' Mrs Harper-Burton offered tentatively.

'And that makes her a witch? Stuff and nonsense!' The Duchess snorted. 'Elizabeth Wyndham was as sensible a woman as m'self. I simply cannot think where people get these ridiculous ideas.' She pinned Arabella with her sharp-eyed gaze. 'I hope you do not suffer from such similar misconceptions, Mrs Braithwaite?'

Arabella's reply contained just the right amount of deference to pacify the aggravated duchess. She was far too shrewd to risk alienating one of the most powerful women at court. 'Like you, Your Grace, I have never been one to suffer fools gladly. It is most unfortunate,' she said, with a sympathetic glance in Nicola's direction, 'that Lady Nicola has been forced to.'

Nicola smiled, but refused to meet Arabella's eye. It was quite clear that the woman was enjoying a laugh at her expense, but there was nothing Nicola could do to retaliate. Arabella was too cunning.

'Lord Blackwood and Sir Giles Chapman,' Trethewy announced from the doorway.

Nicola turned, both surprised and relieved by David's timely arrival. They had not parted on the best of terms last week, and she had been hoping that he might call today. Now, excusing herself to the Duchess and Mrs Harper-Burton, and smiling coldly at Arabella, Nicola gracefully crossed the room to greet her fiancé. 'David, I am so pleased to see you. I was not sure whether you would be able to attend this afternoon or not.'

Her expression was clear, but as David gazed into her eyes he saw that something was definitely amiss. 'Is everything all right, Nicola? You seem troubled.'

Annoyed that she had allowed her irritation with Arabella Braithwaite to show, Nicola quickly shook her head. 'Not at all, everything is going splendidly. As you can see, we have gathered quite a crowd this afternoon. Even the Duchess is in attendance.'

Relieved to know that he had only imagined the shadows in her eyes, David smiled. 'Good. I was hoping that

it was not my arrival which had discomfited you. But I
did want to come. I wasn't happy about the way we parted
last week, Nicola, and I was anxious to set things straight
between us. I fear I spoke out somewhat…precipitously.'

Nicola's cheeks coloured in a most becoming fashion.
'I think you were still understandably upset by my behaviour in the billiards room. And I *was* being rather pe-
dantic about the falcon,' she admitted with a gentle laugh.
'I hope we may put that unfortunate episode behind us.'

'I should be only too delighted to, my dear.'

Accompanying David's admission was a smile of such
tenderness that Nicola felt the strangest constriction in the
area of her heart. Dear me, but the gentleman could be
charming when he wanted to be. No wonder she found it
hard at times to equate this warm, caring man with the
distant, reserved one who had proposed to her a few
weeks ago.

'Nicola, I would like to introduce my uncle, Sir Giles
Chapman. Uncle Giles, my fiancée, Lady Nicola Wyndham.'

Nicola had heard David speak of his favourite uncle
before, but she had not had the pleasure of meeting him.
A debilitating bout of the toothache had prevented him
from attending their betrothal ball. Now, however, as she
gazed up into eyes that twinkled back at her like those of
a sprightly gnome, and saw a smile that was as warm as
it was genuine, Nicola suddenly felt her good spirits suitably restored. 'Sir Giles, I am so pleased to finally make
your acquaintance. David has spoken of you often, and I
was sorry that you were unable to attend our betrothal
ball. Are you fully recovered from the toothache?'

'I am indeed, Lady Nicola, though at the time I was
ready to pull the dashed thing out myself,' the debonair
baronet admitted.

'Yes, I can imagine. I have only suffered with the tooth-ache once, but it was enough to make me hope that I never know such pain again.'

'Nicola, dear, I wonder if you—? Oh, forgive me, Lord Blackwood, I didn't notice you standing there,' Lady Dorchester apologised quickly. 'How delightful to see you.'

'I am delighted to be here, Lady Dorchester,' David said, with a gallant bow. 'Are you acquainted with my uncle, Sir Giles Chapman?'

Lady Dorchester turned to regard the distinguished gen-tleman standing beside Blackwood and suddenly began to smile. 'Would this be the same Sir Giles Chapman ru-moured to have such a marvellous collection of antique snuff boxes?'

The look of surprise on Sir Giles's face was almost comical. His bushy white eyebrows rose so high that they all but disappeared into the thick shock of silvery white hair. 'It is indeed, dear lady, but…how did you know?'

'Are you familiar with the Society for the Preservation of Mid-European Artefacts, Sir Giles?'

Sir Giles thought on that for a moment, and then slowly shook his head. 'Sadly, I am not.'

'It is a small but select group of ladies who are inter-ested in anything to do with ancient Greek and Roman artefacts. Our members meet twice a month, at which time we discuss any new and interesting finds of an archaeo-logical nature.' Lady Dorchester's blue eyes sparkled. 'Your sister, Hortensia, is one of our most active mem-bers.'

The penny dropped, causing a deep groove to appear between Sir Giles's eyes. 'Oh, dear. Then I fear I might as well leave now, if your knowledge of me is as a result of anything my sister may have said. No doubt she has declared me unfit for polite company.'

'On the contrary, she holds you in higher regard than you think,' Lady Dorchester said, laughing at the expression of dismay which had appeared on the baronet's face. 'It is merely your propensity for…games of chance to which she takes exception.'

'Ah. Then I may possibly consider myself spared,' Sir Giles said cautiously, 'for I assure you that any such weakness has been thoroughly expunged from my system.' He paused for a moment, observing the lady in front of him with more than a casual interest, and said, 'I wonder, Lady Dorchester, if we might speak about this… society of yours at some other time and in greater length? I find that I am suddenly most interested in learning more about what my sister amuses herself with—and with whom.'

The colour deepened noticeably in Lady Dorchester's cheeks. 'I cannot promise you as illuminating a discussion of the society as you might have with Hortensia or some of our other members, Sir Giles, as my involvement has not been of such long duration.'

'I can assure you, Lady Dorchester, a moment spent with you would be as fine as an hour spent with anyone else,' Sir Giles replied gallantly.

The extravagant comment earned the elderly peer a startled glance from his nephew and a delighted one from Nicola. Lady Dorchester, however, only laughed softly. 'I fear your sister did not make mention of the extent of your charm, Sir Giles, but I thank you for the most gracious compliment. And, yes, I would be pleased to acquaint you with the workings of our society.'

Sir Giles swept her a courteous bow. 'I am honoured, my lady.'

'At the moment, however, I must ask both of you to excuse us,' Lady Dorchester said, encompassing Lord Blackwood in her glance. 'Lady Fayne is most anxious to speak to Nicola about—'

The rest of the sentence was abruptly cut off by the sound of a high-pitched shriek that shattered the afternoon's quiet.

'Good God, what was that?' David exclaimed.

'I can't be sure,' Sir Giles said, turning in the direction of the noise, 'but there seems to be some kind of commotion over in the corner.'

All eyes turned towards the far corner of the room, where a group of ladies had risen in panic from their chairs and were holding their skirts as high as they dared, given the proximity of gentlemen whose eyes had dropped to the sight of neatly turned ankles.

'What on earth is the matter?' Lady Dorchester demanded in evident concern.

'I have no idea, good lady, but it looks as though—ha! Yes, indeed, it would appear we have a mouse loose in the drawing room,' Sir Giles said, with a hearty chuckle.

Lady Dorchester paled. 'A mouse!'

Nicola's reaction was nowhere near as calm. 'Dear heavens! We must catch him!' she cried aloud, before adding to herself, *Please don't let it be Arthur!*

The commotion was growing louder by the minute as one group of ladies after another picked up their skirts and headed for the safety of the nearest chair, table or whatever else they could find to perch themselves upon.

'Ladies, please be calm, he will not harm you!' Nicola shouted, trying to make herself heard over the din. Really, all this fuss for one tiny mouse. 'My lord, I wonder if I might appeal for your assistance in this matter?' she said, finally turning to her fiancé for help.

'Yes, of course,' David replied at once. 'I shall have Trethewy bring a shovel—'

Nicola gasped. 'That was not the kind of assistance I was looking for.'

'Then what—?'

'I would simply like you to help me corner him,' Nicola explained, already moving in that direction. 'Arthur is bound to be—'

'Arthur?' The single word rang with disbelief. 'Pray do not tell me that this is yet another of your…pets, Nicola?'

'Yes, I am afraid it is.'

'And just as well behaved as…what was that damn bird's name?'

'Guinevere,' she supplied helpfully.

'Yes, of course. And I suppose Sir Lancelot is waiting in the wings? What in God's name, is he? A frog?'

Nicola drew herself up stiffly. 'Don't be absurd, David. Everyone knows you can't train a frog! Oh, look, there he is! Quick, after him!'

The next ten minutes were possibly the worst of Nicola's life. Between ladies swooning, dandies smirking, and obliging gentlemen rushing in to do their all, Nicola could hardly keep her wits about her. Especially with David glaring at her all the while.

Eventually, however, calm was restored. The gentlemen were persuaded to return to their tables, and the ladies, more reluctantly, to their chairs. But not before the entire assembly had seen Nicola scoop the frightened little mouse up in her bare hands and carry him off to the nether regions of the house.

'By Jove, your bride-to-be is turning out to be an endless source of amusement, David,' Sir Giles chuckled when the furore had finally died down. 'What can we expect to see next? Bare-back riding on a pony that does tricks?'

When his light-hearted jibe met with stony silence, Sir Giles hastily cleared his throat. 'Yes, well, didn't mean that, precisely, my boy. Dashed unusual girl, though, what with wayward birds and misbehaving mice. Seems she has more of the mother's gifts than we originally believed.'

Unfortunately, ever since Nicola had claimed owner-ship of the errant mouse, the same thought had been run-ning through David's mind too. What in the world had she been thinking of? Well-bred young ladies simply didn't behave in such a manner. They were supposed to be afraid of mice—not enamoured of them!

But what, then, was he to do? He had seen the expres-sions on the faces of Nicola's guests before they had po-litely turned away, and he knew exactly what they had been thinking. They had been laughing at her; ridiculing the woman he had chosen to marry. And the most unfor-tunate part of it all was that Nicola had brought it all on herself. For the second time in as many weeks, she had exhibited extremely unbecoming behaviour for a woman who was to be the next Marchioness of Blackwood. For the second time in a row, she had disgraced herself in the eyes of the *ton*.

Dare he risk a third?

Chapter Six

Two days later, Nicola sat with her aunt in the cosy yellow salon and tried to focus her concentration on the intricate piece of embroidery in her hands. Her slender fingers worked the needle with unerring precision, yet her attention was as far removed from the piece of needlework as heaven was from earth.

The at-home had been a disaster; there was simply no other way of putting it. Even after Arthur's capture, her guests had taken their leave with disturbing alacrity, suddenly recalling other places they had to be. And, not surprisingly, no further callers had stopped by that afternoon. More bothersome than that, however, was the dismal certainty that she had incurred David's displeasure for the second time in as many weeks. Nicola had seen the look on her fiancé's face when she had picked Arthur up and borne him swiftly away—a look composed of shock, of displeasure, and, most definitely of disappointment. She had heard the titters and the whispers when she had returned to the salon shortly thereafter. And she had seen the look of compassion on her aunt's face, compassion which had done little to lessen Nicola's feelings of intense humiliation over the scandalous scene she had inadvertently created.

'Have you heard from Lord Blackwood yet?' Lady Dorchester enquired gently.

Despondently, Nicola shook her head. She had heard nothing at all from David since he had left the house on Sunday afternoon, and the knowledge that she had disappointed him yet again was causing her more grief than she could have possibly imagined.

'Well, never mind, dear, it is not worth such a long face as all that,' Lady Dorchester said, in yet another attempt to comfort her. 'People were just a little...taken aback.'

'They were horrified,' Nicola muttered, finally setting aside the tambour in disgust. 'Did you not see their faces when I picked up Arthur? Gracious, one would have thought I was handling a viper rather than a harmless little field mouse.'

'Unfortunately, to most of the ladies present I do not suppose there is a great deal of difference,' Lady Dorchester pointed out as delicately as she could. 'I have to admit I was rather surprised myself when I saw you pick the little fellow up and carry him off. And *I* know more than most what to expect from you.'

Nicola frowned. 'Arthur would not have hurt anyone.'

'That was what you said about the falcon.'

'Guinevere would not have hurt anyone either. The fact that I received injuries was entirely due to my own negligence,' Nicola maintained stubbornly. 'I should have sent Jamie back for more linen.'

'Well, I shouldn't worry about it, dear. I am sure Lord Blackwood understands all of that, and that he will be paying you a call in the very near future to assure you of it. He has, after all, many things to occupy his time.'

Either that, Nicola admitted ruefully, or he was avoiding her. And knowing David's feelings about duty, and his rigid observance of the proprieties, she had a feeling that his absence stemmed more from that than it did from any kind of…preoccupation.

'Do you think I should try to contact him, Aunt?'

'Perhaps it would be better if you waited for him to call,' Lady Dorchester suggested. 'After all, you know how men are.'

'No, actually, I do not,' Nicola admitted as she picked up her tambour and tried to concentrate on her work again. She had absolutely no idea *how men were*. How could she, when she'd had precious little exposure to any gentlemen other than her father?

And if she didn't know how to deal with normal men, how on earth was she to deal with the mercurial Marquis of Blackwood?

The suspense came to an end much sooner than Nicola had anticipated.

David paid her a call that very afternoon.

She was in the drawing room when he arrived, having just returned from the garden with an armful of flowers for the table. She was busy arranging them in a large silver vase when Trethewy tapped on the door and announced Lord Blackwood's arrival.

Nicola gasped. 'He's here? Oh, dear! I mean, yes, do show him in, thank you.'

As soon as the butler left, Nicola dropped her scissors on the table and ran towards the fireplace to check her appearance in the mirror above it. Oh, dear, this was definitely not how she wished David to see her looking. She should have run upstairs and changed the moment she had come in from the garden, but it was too late for that now.

As it was, she barely had time to smooth down the wispy
strands of brandy-coloured hair that had escaped from the
confines of her cap, and to wipe a smudge of dirt from
the end of her nose, before Trethewy announced, 'Lord
Blackwood, my lady.'

Nicola gamely fixed a smile on her face and turned to
greet him. 'David, I am…so pleased to see you,' she said,
faltering slightly at the sternness of his expression. 'Won't
you…sit down?'

As always, David was impeccably dressed. His jacket
of dark green superfine fitted to perfection over a pair of
close-fitting, fawn-coloured breeches, and his Hessians
were polished to such a shine that Nicola could see her
face in them. His dark locks were arranged *à la Brutus*,
his snowy white neckcloth was tied in the intricate Mathematical, and his manner was that of a man completely
in control of himself and of the situation.

For once, Nicola felt herself to be at a distinct disad-
vantage.

Fortunately, David knew that his arrival had caught her
unawares. The colour in her normally cool white cheeks
was unusually high, and the front of her gown was liberally spotted with water. But it was the look of apprehension in those clear green eyes that told David how
truly unprepared she was for his visit. She was both
watchful and uncertain, reminding him of a deer caught
in the hunter's sights.

He found it was not an association he cared for.

'You sound more alarmed than you do pleased, Nicola,'
David said as he crossed the width of the room and bent
to kiss her cheek. 'Surely I am not as fearsome as all
that?'

'Of course you are not fearsome. And, yes, I am…very
pleased to see you,' Nicola admitted hastily. 'It is simply

that…I have not heard from you these past two days, and I thought perhaps you were still angry with me over the incident with…Arthur.'

'Ah, yes, the Camelotian mouse,' David mused as he strolled towards the fireplace and leaned one arm against the mantel. 'I suppose you have as logical an explanation for that as you did for the presence of the falcon in the billiards room?'

'Yes. And it is most unfortunate, of course, but I suppose I…did not fasten the cage door securely enough when I put Arthur away,' Nicola said with a hesitant smile. 'And then when my maid inadvertently left the bedroom door open—'

'You keep the mouse in your room?'

'He is only a very little mouse, my lord.'

David's eyes narrowed. 'I see. And was he also… injured and in need of a home?'

'As a matter of fact, he was. I found him in the bottom of a barn pail when he was little more than a baby. You may have noticed how badly tattered his poor ear was.'

'Actually, no. Can't think how I missed that.'

Nicola flushed at the sarcasm, but wisely made no rejoinder. Whilst she was relieved that David did not sound as angry as she had expected him to, there was still a wariness in his eyes that told her all was not forgiven. She felt her knees go a little weak beneath her, and slowly sank down onto the gold and white striped settee. 'Are you…very angry with me, my lord?'

'Angry?' David stared down at the beautiful woman in front of him, aware that she had pushed him to the very limits of his patience and as a result of situations which, a month ago, he would not have believed possible, and wondered why, in truth, he was not more angry with her. On more than one occasion, Nicola had demonstrated behaviour highly unbecoming for a future marchioness. She had argued with him, contradicted him, and even disobeyed him, without, it seemed, so much as a second thought.

And yet, as he looked down at her now, there was something about that innocent face and that sweet smile that made it impossible for him to feel anger towards her. How could he reproach her when her motives were so noble? And her beautiful green eyes so beseeching?

And her appearance this afternoon so adorably... *déshabillé*.

'No, I'm not angry, precisely,' David told her truthfully.

'Disappointed?'

'Perhaps.'

'Surprised?'

'A little. Though I know I should not be, given what I have heard of your mother.'

Instantly, Nicola's look of contrition vanished. 'I beg your pardon, sir, but what precisely have you heard about my mother?'

'Rest assured, Nicola, I was not about to criticize her,' David said gently. 'I am well aware that I would run the risk of alienating both your father and yourself were I to do such a thing. I simply meant that I have heard about your mother's uncanny ability with animals, as well as her compassion for them, and I am not surprised that such a trait has manifested itself in you. However,' David continued, his expression changing to one which was somewhat more stern, 'I cannot continue to condone this type of behaviour in the woman who is to be my wife. Surely you understand that?'

'I did not set out to embarrass you, my lord,' Nicola felt obliged to say.

'And I am not for one moment saying that you did. I understand that your actions were motivated by the most noble of reasons and are, therefore, entirely beyond reproach. But I am sure you can see that as the Marchioness of Blackwood you will be expected to set a certain standard of behaviour. There will be expectations you will be required to meet, along with obligations you will be required to fulfil.'

'Are you beginning to doubt my ability to fulfil those obligations, my lord?'

'Not in the least. I only ask, Nicola, that you be aware of the responsibility you now bear. Ours is a noble name—one of the few, perhaps, that remains untarnished by scandal or disgrace, and while I am willing to overlook these two rather...unusual incidents, by putting them down to the generosity of your nature, I must insist that, from now on, you refrain from any such displays of heroism. I cannot have people thinking I've married the Pied Piper of London.' A boyish smile tugged at his lips. 'Is that too much to ask, my dear?'

A fleeting image of Alistair danced in Nicola's head, and she toyed with the idea of telling David about the fox then and there. But then, as she thought about it a little more, Nicola realised that it would really serve no useful purpose. She had already decided not to take Alistair to Ridley Hall with her, but rather to leave him here at Wyndham. Or, even better, to try to return him to his home in the wild before she left. And, that being the case, where was the logic in disclosing to her fiancé something that was far more likely to incite his anger than to discourage it? Especially when it seemed that David was so willing to forgive the embarrassment she had already caused him.

'No, David. It is not too much to ask, and I am grateful

for your patience,' Nicola said sincerely. She rose to her feet and impulsively pressed her lips to his cheek, surprising David *and* herself by the spontaneous gesture. 'I can assure you, you will have no cause to chastise me again.'

An invitation to the Duchess of Basilworth's ball was one of the most sought-after tickets of the social season. For those who received the heavy, gold-embossed invitation, it was a symbol of acceptance; a recognition of one's standing in the community. For Nicola, it was an opportunity to redeem herself in the eyes of the *ton*, and, more importantly, in David's. And she set out to do just that.

She wore the most stylish of her new gowns, a breathtaking slip of Indian muslin that floated around her body like a misty white veil, and had Maire arrange her glowing curls in an elegant style that flattered the smoothness of her brow and the dark curve of her brows. She even had her darken the underside of her eyes with kohl so that she presented a more dramatic and sophisticated appearance—an appearance which was well worth the trouble of achieving, judging by the startled look on David's face.

In truth, David *was* taken aback, and he made no attempt to conceal his admiration from Nicola as she gracefully descended the staircase with her aunt at her side. He knew that she was trying to please him, and, in the low-cut gown which displayed most provocatively the sensuous curves of her figure, she had surely done that. But tonight it was more than just Nicola's physical appearance that brought him pleasure; it was the expression in her eyes. Gone was the haunted look which had so disturbed him the last time they had been together, leaving her eyes a deep, clear green, untroubled by anxiety or doubt.

'I cannot find the words,' David breathed as Nicola stopped before him and offered him her hand. He tried not to let his eyes linger on the creamy expanse of neck and shoulders visible above the low *décolleté* of her gown. 'You look…breathtaking.'

A faint blush stained the delicate pastel of Nicola's cheeks. 'Thank you, David. And I do apologise for keeping you waiting, but I fear I was at a loss to…find my gloves.' Her voice was a trifle unsteady, but it was hardly to be wondered at. The sight of David in formal attire was enough to make even the crustiest of dowagers sigh, let alone a young woman who dared to have feelings for him.

'I would have waited all night for the pleasure of strolling about the room with you on my arm,' David assured her softly. 'If only to watch the other gentlemen glower at my good fortune.'

An enchanting dimple appeared at the corner of Nicola's mouth. 'I don't know that too many other gentlemen will be thinking you are fortunate to be escorting me, my lord, but, hopefully, I will not cause you any manner of fresh embarrassment this evening.'

David's slow smile was reassurance enough. 'I am sure we will have no cause for worry. Unless you happen to have secreted Arthur in your reticule.'

'You need have no fear of that. Arthur is securely fastened in his cage upstairs. And I saw to the closing of the bedroom door myself.'

'I am relieved to hear it. Lady Dorchester, you are a vision this evening,' David said, turning to greet Nicola's aunt, who did indeed make a striking appearance in a shimmering gown of violet gossamer satin. 'One could almost mistake you for Nicola's sister.'

'Her *older* sister, no doubt,' Lady Dorchester replied, though her eyes glittered as brightly as the magnificent necklace of amethysts and diamonds which circled her throat. 'But flattery is always most welcome, Lord Blackwood, and I must admit both you and your uncle have an uncommon talent for it.'

'Ah, but it is not mere flattery, Lady Dorchester, and I know that my uncle would agree. He was much taken with you the other evening.'

'Was he, indeed?' Lady Dorchester chuckled softly as she turned to allow David to place an evening cape over her shoulders. 'I admit, I found him quite charming, and not at all like Hortensia had described.'

'There has never been any love lost between my uncle and his eldest sister, Lady Dorchester,' David advised her. 'Even as children, they fought like cats and dogs.'

'So I gathered from Hortensia. Although I believe that much of her antipathy stems from his unfortunate penchant for gambling.'

'Agreed. As I understand it, my uncle spent considerable time in gaming hells when he was a young man,' David told her. 'Rouge-et-noir was his particular favourite, and, from what I have heard, he was uncommonly good at it—most of the time. Unfortunately, *most* of the time is not good enough when one is playing for large sums of money.'

'No, it is not. I confess to having enjoyed betting on a few hands of whist myself,' Lady Dorchester admitted, 'though never to any financial detriment. Playing for pennies with the ladies on Thursday afternoons is hardly ruinous to one's fortune. But, as for Sir Giles, is it true that he has now cured himself of the vice?'

'Oh, yes. Aunt Hortensia does not make idle boasts, and when she threatened the much beloved snuff-box collection my uncle was, shall we say, forced to comply.'

Lady Dorchester laughed softly. 'Well, if it has cured

him of the desire to gamble, it will have been well worth the trouble. Indeed, he should be thanking her for her efforts, rather than condemning her. Is he to be in attendance this evening?' she enquired casually.

'Sadly, no. I fear his social standing is not quite up to snuff for the Duchess of Basilworth. However, he does send his most sincere regards, and bid me take very good care of two such beautiful ladies. Naturally I assured him of my total and most willing cooperation.' David smiled warmly at Nicola, and then offered each of the ladies an arm. 'Shall we go?'

To say that the Duke and Duchess of Basilworth's house was large was to liken the Elgin Marbles to a nice collection of stones. The great, fortress-like structure—set amidst seven hundred acres of parkland, with a lake and four acres of formal gardens, and with bedrooms to accommodate seventy-five—was an architectural marvel. It had been built in the early fourteen hundreds, and added on to by successive generations of Basilworths—some of whom had possessed a singular lack of good judgement—resulting in a house that was garish, rather than gracious. Fortunately, the interior of the monstrosity had been decorated with a good deal more taste than had the exterior, and as Nicola walked into the Great Hall she was startled by the opulence of the hangings and the exquisite furnishings which graced it.

'My word!'

'Yes, it is impressive, is it not?' Lady Dorchester whispered in her niece's ear. 'And I understand that the collection of paintings in the gallery here is quite beyond compare.'

'Still, I can see why the duchess prefers the smaller house in Park Lane,' David commented dryly. 'Only think how long it must take a servant to deliver Her Grace's morning chocolate in a place this size.'

Nicola laughed behind her fan as they awaited their turn to be presented. 'No doubt it would be cold upon arrival.'

The party made their greetings to the duke and duchess in the receiving line, though there was little opportunity to chat. The line stretching out behind them was a long one, and as carriages continued to pull up to the porticoed entrance, dispensing yet more elegantly gowned ladies and their escorts, the line continued to grow. For that reason, David and his party proceeded directly to the ballroom, a magnificent salon, squarish in form, with long windows running the length of one side and beautifully frescoed panels decorating the other. The orchestra was discreetly hidden behind an ornamental screen at the far end of the room, while the flickering flames of a thousand candles shed soft light down on the beautifully gowned and bejewelled guests.

Nicola walked into the ballroom with her head held high, and her hand tucked securely into the crook of David's arm. She had already decided that she would not allow herself to be intimidated by any curious glances that might come her way, and took comfort from the knowledge that she was as well dressed as any of the ladies in the room tonight. Indeed, even now, a number of gentlemen were risking openly admiring glances in her direction. As were their ladies, though Nicola knew those had nothing to do with *her* appearance. It was far more likely the handsome man at her side whom they were admiring, or the magnificent diamond and emerald ring that sparkled on her hand, signifying her status as David's fiancée. Either way, Nicola knew that their arrival had been duly noted and commented upon.

'I told you the gentlemen would be envious,' David

suddenly whispered in her ear. 'In fact, Lord Fayne hasn't
taken his eyes from you since the moment we walked
through the door.'

Nicola smiled, and quickly turned away from the sight
of the fuzzy-haired Lord Fayne, aware that he certainly
was making no effort to conceal his observance of her.
'One would think that he had never seen me before.'

David glanced down at her sideways, enjoying the sight
of softly rounded breasts rising seductively from the bodice of her gown, and murmured, 'I would venture to say
that he has never seen you looking…quite the way you
do this evening, Nicola.'

Turning just in time to catch David's lingering glance,
Nicola felt the heat rush to her cheeks. 'Oh, dear. I wondered if perhaps the gown was too daring,' she said anxiously.

David raised her hand and pressed his warm lips against
it. 'You are a beautiful woman, Nicola, and other gentlemen are bound to admire you. Just so long as they do it
from afar, all will be well.'

Nicola glanced at him through her lashes. It was the
kind of compliment David had begun paying her recently,
and she couldn't help but wonder whether he wasn't starting to have some genuine feelings for her. Indeed, his
conduct throughout the entire evening was all that she
could have wished. He stayed close by her side through-
out, dancing attendance on her every whim, and kept her
entertained with a string of amusing anecdotes and hu-
morous tales that were guaranteed to make her laugh.

At supper, he put together a tempting collation of delicacies to tantalize her delicate appetite, and made sure
that her glass was never empty. And later on the dance
floor, with her hand resting lightly in his and his arm
around her waist, he whisked her away to the lilting

strains of a waltz, their bodies moving in total harmony as they spun in time to the music. It was almost as though they had been dancing together for years.

'Are you having a good time?' David said against her ear.

'I cannot remember when I have enjoyed a ball more.' Nicola glanced up into the handsome face that was so close to hers and smiled. 'As a rule, I cannot wait to make my escape from these tedious outings.'

'Well, it is still early yet,' David reminded her. 'When the room grows stiflingly hot and the candles begin to drip wax, and everyone takes on that slightly glazed expression from having consumed too much food and too much wine, you may still wish to flee.'

Only if you flee with me.

The unbidden thought brought the colour surging to her cheeks, and Nicola quickly dropped her eyes. Heavens, she would be foolish indeed to harbour such imprudent thoughts with regard to David. Had he not told her exactly what he had been looking for in a wife on the day that he had proposed? That they would deal intelligently with one another, and perhaps with affection, but that theirs would be a suitable match, rather than an amorous one.

Yes, Nicola remembered all that. But, oh, how she longed to forget it just for a while. To close her eyes and lean into his touch; to feel his arms close tightly around her, and to make believe, if only for a moment, that it was truly love which bound them together, rather than duty…

'I should like to know what prompted that little flurry of colour,' David whispered, stroking his finger over her warmly glowing cheeks. 'Dare I ask you to share it with me?'

'You m-may…ask anything you wish,' Nicola stammered, 'but it is up to me whether I answer or not.'

'And will you?' David held his breath, his finger still resting on the warm curve of her cheek. Her skin was as soft as velvet and he was sorely tempted to tip her head back and press his mouth to the tempting curve of her lips. But he sensed that such improper conduct would earn him a swift and well-deserved rebuke.

Sadly, it did. It seemed that, this evening, Nicola knew exactly what constituted acceptable behaviour—and what did not.

'I think I will not answer, my lord. Nor do I think we are behaving in a manner…suitable for the dance floor.'

David smiled, and dutifully resumed the proper position for the waltz. He would have liked to see, even a hint of encouragement in those marvellous green eyes for the kiss he had so dearly wanted to bestow, but, at the same time, he was pleased with Nicola for having rejected his advances. It was as though she was telling him, and anyone else in the room who might have noticed, that she was a lady, and that she knew *precisely* how to behave.

David could not remember when he had enjoyed an evening more.

Chapter Seven

The following afternoon, David and Nicola set out for a ride along the top pasture at Wyndham Hall.

It was a perfect day for a gallop. The sun shone gold from the heights of an azure-blue sky, while a pleasant breeze blew across the hills, ruffling the long grass and sending whispering fingers of crisp autumn air through the trees. And, indeed, but for the presence of Jenkins following discreetly behind, Nicola might have believed that she and David had the rolling countryside all to themselves.

David's black stallion was a magnificent creature, who pranced and pawed at the ground before bursting into a gallop that would have left one believing that the very hounds of hell were nipping at his heels. Nicola's dapple-grey mare was much more a lady. She blew gently through her nostrils at the stallion's flashy performance, and then, at the merest touch from her mistress's whip, stretched out her legs and moved gracefully into a gallop, quickly narrowing the distance between her and the mighty stallion ahead.

Fortunately, Nicola was not a timid rider. Her father had schooled her well in the equestrian arts, and, as a result, she was as much at home in the saddle as she was in the drawing room—perhaps more so. Her gloved hands kept a firm but steady pressure on the mare's mouth, and never pulled or sawed at the reins as so many less competent riders were wont to do.

David, of course, was a superb horseman. He rode as though one with the stallion, giving the magnificent animal plenty of freedom to run, but never pushing him too hard or for too long. When at last he reined in, Nicola promptly followed suit, pleased, as always, to see how quickly Nightingale responded to her command to 'walk'. Certainly a good deal faster than did the tempestuous Knight.

'He's rather full of himself today, my lord,' Nicola observed. 'I do not know that I would like to try to hold him in check for any length of time, but you make it look easy.'

David laughed, a rich sound that reflected his enjoyment of handling the spirited bit of blood. 'I would wager there's not many who could handle him. They warned me at Tatt's that he had a temper, but I like to think it's more spirit than meanness.'

Nicola admired the stallion's exceptionally fine head and darkly lashed eyes. It always amazed her that horses had such long, curling lashes. 'It is not a mean streak which sets him to dancing so, but rather a desire to run. No doubt he will settle as he ages.'

David cast her a curious glance. 'You sound as though you know well of what you speak.'

With a slow, secret smile, Nicola nodded. 'I do.'

'Would you care to explain how?'

'I don't know how I know. I just…do.' She flashed him a quick, dazzling smile before closing her eyes and breathing deeply the sweet country air. 'Oh, David, is it not a glorious day?'

David glanced down at her from the height of his saddle, and wondered if he had ever seen a woman look more beautiful. It wasn't just the cut of the stylish habit, or the veiled cap with its saucy spray of curling maroon feathers, that drew one's eye to Nicola. It was a brightness that radiated from within, as though all the joy and the passion she felt for life were reflected in her face.

'I think it must be, to hear you speak of it so passionately,' David said softly. 'Tell me, Nicola, is there anything in life which you do not approach with such enthusiasm?'

Nicola opened her eyes wide to look at him. 'It is not enthusiasm, my lord, so much as appreciation for the wonders of nature all around us. How can anyone look upon a newly formed rainbow without marvelling at the beauty of it, or not feel humbled by the tremendous force of a storm? These are things over which man has absolutely no control.' She sent him a teasing look through her dark lashes. 'Or are you one of those jaded London gentlemen who profess themselves bored by everything, and who find nothing of interest except in betting on, and indulging in, other entertainments?'

'I do not like to think of myself as being as shallow as all that,' David replied dryly. 'I simply do not look for complication in my life.'

'Do you call the glorious sight of a fiery sunset at the end of a day a complication?'

'No. I reserve that for the spectacle of wild creatures running amok in a drawing room.'

'Ah. Actually, I prefer to think of those as…unfortunate incidents to which you happened to bear witness,' Nicola said, her green eyes sparkling beneath the whisper-fine veil of net.

'Yes, I'm sure you would. But then, I suppose I shouldn't find that at all surprising, given the fact that unfortunate incidents with animals tend to run in your family.'

'I beg your pardon?'

'Your father once told me that your mother was seen feeding a huge buck by hand. Such a thing would require a rather...extraordinary talent, wouldn't you agree?'

Again, the slow, secret smile hovered about her lips. 'Are you asking me to confirm the rumours that my mother was a witch?'

'No. I am merely saying that if she *had* any unusual abilities I should not find it unusual that you would have inherited some of them.'

'Does that bother you?'

David slid her an oblique glance. 'Hard to say. It has already made for some very interesting situations in our life together, wouldn't you agree?'

They had reached the crest of the hill by now, and Nicola drew her mare to a halt. She glanced out over the gently rolling English countryside below, and breathed a sigh of utter contentment. 'I have always found life to be filled with...interesting situations, David. I suppose it is all in how you look at things.' And then, casting him what could only be called a flirtatious glance, Nicola urged her mare to a canter and disappeared over the top of the hill.

Caught completely off guard, both by the remark and by her unexpected flight, David threw back his head and laughed. Saucy baggage! She had deliberately thrown him a challenge and bolted, as though daring him to give chase. Well, far be it from him to disappoint a lady.

As he gathered the reins in his hands and sent the stallion flying down the hill in hot pursuit, David realized, with a growing sense of wonder, that he was actually looking forward to being married. Because there was one thing that he was suddenly very sure of.

Life with the beautiful Lady Nicola was going to be far from boring!

The air of accord which arose between David and herself in the days following the Basilworths' ball was an unending source of joy to Nicola. As was the fact that, with each day that passed, they seemed to grow closer together. While she could not say that David was precisely a loving fiancé, he was an extremely kind and considerate one, and the attention he began paying her, and the care he took when she was in his company, completely erased the unhappy memory of their earlier days together.

Others noticed their new-found closeness too, and it was during a lull in the dancing at the Haverstocks' rout two weeks later that Sir Giles commented to his nephew that things seemed noticeably more settled between the two of them.

'Indeed they are, Uncle Giles,' David replied with the air of a man well satisfied with life. 'Indeed they are.'

'I take it, then, that you have resolved the matter of the mouse and the falcon to your mutual satisfaction.'

David chuckled as he watched Nicola finish a country dance with Lord Alberton, a portly, middle-aged peer whose florid complexion had grown even ruddier with the lively pace required by the dance. 'The matter is resolved and forgotten. It would appear that I have become betrothed to a young woman whose heart is bigger than her pride, which is, in itself, something of a departure. However, I do not expect a repeat performance.'

Abruptly, Blackwood's eyes narrowed. Nicola had been

escorted from the floor by her partner and the music had begun again. But this time she was being squired back out by Humphrey O'Donnell—the young popinjay reputed to have been heartbroken at the news of her betrothal!

'Beg pardon?' David said, belatedly aware that his uncle was still talking to him.

'I said, I wonder if it runs in the family?'

'What?'

'This uncanny ability with animals. Wonder if the aunt possesses any traces of it?'

Intrigued by the tone of his uncle's voice, David asked, 'Do I detect an interest in the charming Lady Dorchester?'

When a flush darkened the baronet's cheeks, David began to smile in earnest. 'Upon my word, I believe I do.'

'Yes, and why should you not?' Sir Giles retorted. 'Damned fine-looking woman, that, and more my age than most of the young chits hereabouts. I'd have something in common with a lady like that.'

David risked a quick look across the room to where Nicola's aunt was talking to Lady Fayne—and trying very hard not to reveal her boredom at doing so—and said, 'Then why not take a few minutes to find out? If I do not miss my guess, Lady Fayne is talking Lady Dorchester's ear off about some tedious subject that no one could possibly be interested in, and I believe the lady would appreciate being rescued.'

Sir Giles's face brightened. 'Do you think so, dear boy?'

'Most assuredly.'

'Perhaps I should…ask her to dance?'

'It has been known to work in the past,' David replied with a perfectly straight face.

'What if she says no?'

'You'll never know until you try.'

Sir Giles straightened his white silk waistcoat and smoothed back the shining silver hair at his temples. 'Yes, well, in for a penny, in for a pound, I suppose. Wish me luck.'

David carefully hid his smile as Sir Giles moved off in search of a dance. He could tell that his uncle was nervous, no doubt as a result of having been a bachelor all his life, but he obviously cared enough to give it a go.

Thankfully the lady did not disappoint him. Lady Dorchester's face brightened immeasurably as she turned to greet his uncle, and after chatting comfortably for a few minutes the two moved onto the dance floor, leaving the deserted Lady Fayne to seek out other prey.

Chuckling over the possibility of a second wedding being in the offing, David turned to find his cousin Arabella standing directly behind him.

'And what has taken your fancy this evening, David?' she whispered huskily. 'Perhaps you will share it with me so that we may enjoy it together.'

David shook his head, though the smile lingered on his lips. 'I fear it would be unkind to relay the source of my amusement, Belle, as it would be at the expense of another.'

'Ah, but whom better to laugh at than other people, darling?' Arabella bantered lightly. 'Especially when they are not aware that they are being laughed at.'

For the first time, Arabella's words struck a discordant note, and David's smile cooled. 'I think it would be kinder to find something else to draw one's amusement from than this. Will you excuse me, Arabella?'

'Of course,' she said quickly, though the smile on her lips was purely mechanical. David had addressed her by her full name. Why? She was Belle to him, just as he was David to her. When had that suddenly changed?

The sound of gentle laughter drew Arabella's attention towards the dance floor, where the sight of Lady Nicola engaged in a dance with Humphrey O'Donnell caused her eyes to narrow into icy slits. *That* was when things had begun to change, she acknowledged bitterly. When the Lady Nicola Wyndham had cast her spell over David and begun to turn him away from her. From the moment David had first advised her that he was to be wed, in that cold and distant letter which Arabella had read and reread and then finally burned in a fit of jealous anger, his attitude towards her had been changing. He no longer had time to talk with her when they were at parties together, nor was she required to sit at his table and act as his hostess.

The fact that David had not done any entertaining since well before his betrothal mattered little to Arabella now. Or that they had never spent a great deal of time socializing in the first place. What mattered was that the woman who had turned her cousin against her was now jeopardizing the very foundations of that relationship. That countrified upstart, with her stupid animals and her ridiculous notions of behaviour, was beginning to create a distance between Arabella and the cousin she loved.

She must be a witch, Arabella decided wrathfully. Because David was not a man easily swayed to another's way of thinking. But *she* had done it. With all that flame-coloured hair and those evil green eyes, the witch of Wyndham Hall had beguiled him; seduced him. She had intruded into his life and turned it into a shambles.

More to the point, she had intruded into *their* lives, and undermined everything that Arabella had been working so hard to achieve. And that was a slight that she was not about to forget.

Or to forgive.

Oblivious to the malevolent looks being cast her way, Nicola competently executed the steps of the dance with Mr Humphrey O'Donnell and wondered if she had ever been happier. Not just because she was wearing a fine gown of glowing cream silk shot through with delicate strands of gold, its tiny puffed sleeves and low *décolletage* edged with gold embroidery. And certainly not because this evening the gentlemen were all paying her the most delightful compliments now that she was betrothed to the Marquis of Blackwood.

No, Nicola was happy simply *because* she was betrothed to the Marquis of Blackwood. And because, at some time during the past few weeks, her feelings for David had undergone a startling transformation. The warmth and tenderness with which she had always regarded him had suddenly grown into a much deeper and more abiding affection.

She had fallen in love with the man she was to marry. And she could not have been more delighted.

'Are you truly going to marry Blackwood and cast me into despair, Lady Nicola?' O'Donnell was saying to her now. 'Not so long ago, I had hoped that I might approach your father myself.'

Startled by the unexpected declaration, Nicola said quickly, 'I am flattered that you would care enough to do so, Mr O'Donnell, but, yes, I do intend to marry Lord Blackwood. And I am very pleased about it.'

'But how can you be pleased about such a dismal state of affairs.' The handsome young man's voice was filled with remorse. 'You are so young and beautiful, whereas Blackwood is so much older and more staid.'

'He is not that much older than myself,' Nicola replied staunchly. 'Or perhaps it is just that I am not that much younger. Have you forgotten that I am a few years older than yourself?'

O'Donnell flushed. 'Age means nothing to me; surely you know that! It is only your lovely face that I see, my dearest Lady Nicola!'

'Then perhaps it would be best if you were to see it from a distance, Mr O'Donnell,' a voice cut in ominously.

'David!' The pleasure in Nicola's voice was undisguised, and, hearing it, David felt a satisfaction entirely incommensurate with the level of affection he had come to expect of their relationship.

It was equally clear, however, that Mr O'Donnell was nowhere near as pleased. 'I say, Blackwood, if you don't mind, Lady Nicola and I were just enjoying a conversation during the privacy of our dance.'

'Ah, but I do mind, Mr O'Donnell. Because I do not approve of anyone having private conversations with my fiancée other than myself, and I would thank you to remember that. As for this being your dance, I think, if *you* don't mind, I shall cut in.'

The young man's face flushed an unbecoming shade of red. 'I beg your pardon, sir!'

'As well you should.' David's voice dropped to an ominous growl. 'Do not forget that it is *my* fiancée we are talking about, O'Donnell, and that I will do whatever necessary to convince *anyone* who doubts it of my sincerity in the matter. Do I make myself clear?'

'Perfectly,' O'Donnell said, belatedly aware that he might have pushed things a little too far. He had no desire to be called out by the Marquis of Blackwood. Everyone knew that the man was a dab hand with a foil, and a crack shot with a pistol. And he had energy and strength to spare, having lasted many a round in the ring with the Gentleman himself.

No, there was a time and a place for everything, O'Donnell decided wisely. And, judging from the thunderous look in Blackwood's eyes, this was definitely not it.

He stepped back and bowed stiffly towards Nicola. 'I regret that our dance had to come to such a precipitate end, Lady Nicola, but, I can assure you, I enjoyed every moment of it. I bid you a good evening.' And then, favouring Blackwood with as short a nod as he dared, the young man turned and briskly walked away.

Looking up into her fiancé's face, Nicola said, in a gently chastising tone, 'You really were too hard on poor Mr O'Donnell, David. He was not bothering me.'

'No, he was bothering *me*,' David replied calmly as he took Nicola's hand and resumed the steps of the dance. 'His manner was totally inappropriate towards an engaged lady.'

'But he is such a young man,' Nicola said, feeling suddenly very old and wise at five-and-twenty, 'and he was speaking from the heart. I am sure he did so without thinking.'

'Then perhaps he will think twice before speaking to you in such a manner again,' David said tersely. 'Because I can assure you, Nicola, that when I said I resented his familiarity with you I, too, was speaking from the heart. Or do you find that so difficult a concept to come to terms with?'

Nicola hesitated. She was not so naive as to think that David's behaviour indicated the presence of love, but there was no denying that he was softening. Or was it just that her own love for him made her vulnerable to every nuance in his voice, and every flicker in his eyes?

'I had no reason to suspect that…you would have cause to speak to me from the heart, my lord,' Nicola answered carefully. 'I am fully aware that ours is a match arranged for the benefit of both rather than as the result of any strong feelings of love. And if a relationship is predicated on feelings of mutual understanding and respect there would be no reason for me to believe that the heart would enter into it.'

It was as close to a rebuke as Nicola was likely to offer, and David knew it. He also knew that it was entirely justified, and, strangely, the knowledge irked him.

'Happiness has been found in such arrangements before, Nicola,' David said diffidently. 'As you yourself pointed out, people do marry for reasons other than duty and obligation. And if those more…estimable reasons are lacking at the beginning of the relationship, surely one could hope that they might develop over time?'

'It is to be so hoped.'

'Then, is it so unusual to hope that such reasons might eventually develop…in ours?'

Nicola strove for a tranquil expression. 'I certainly see no reason why they should not, my lord.'

'Good. Then it is all that I could wish for.'

And with those few simple words it became, for Nicola, another idyllic evening.

There were really only two components to country life which Nicola found distasteful—the first being the dreadful shortage of good-quality reading material to be found in the local circulating library, and the second—and certainly the more offensive of the two—the countryman's passion for fox-hunting.

To Nicola, it was a cruel and barbaric sport, indulged in by men and women who believed themselves keen sportsmen for being able to run a poor, unfortunate creature to death, and cheered on by the farmers whose poorly constructed hen-houses offered little resistance to the cunning of the wild creatures. With the holes to their dens stopped up with earth, and their every movement tracked by a pack of hounds, the foxes stood little chance.

It was about as sporting as shooting goldfish in a pond!

Unfortunately, given that her father was Master of the Hunt and that David was an avid hunter, it was impossible not to be aware of when and where the meets were held. Many of them, in fact, started at Wyndham Hall and took place in the countryside surrounding it. Still, that did not mean that she had to be there when the field set off.

And so, early on Tuesday morning, Nicola slipped down the back stairs and set off for the stables. She wore one of her older habits, but one to which she had always been partial. The dark green velvet jacket and skirt were as comfortable as they were stylish. Her glowing Titian hair was arranged in an elegant knot at the nape of her neck, and was topped with a rakish bonnet with a curled black feather and black netting, all of which became her very well.

The fact that no one was around to appreciate her efforts did not trouble her in the least, however, for she preferred to slip away without being seen. Even now, the gentry from the nearby houses would be assembling in the front courtyard of Wyndham Hall. Her father would be there, and the huntsman would be overseeing the gathering of the hounds in preparation for setting off. Then, once the fox had been drawn, the cry would issue, the hounds would be loosed and the field would follow, ready to set a cracking pace, and all in the name of sport.

David would be one of those people, Nicola realized sadly. Exceedingly handsome in his black jacket and white breeches, his top boots polished to a brilliant shine, his glossy black beaver pulled down low, he would cut a dashing figure to be sure.

Nicola had toyed with the idea of staying to see him off, but when the moment had come she had found it more than she could manage. She hadn't been able to face the sight of all those people anxiously waiting to set off. She hated the barbarism of it. The callous disregard for life.

But Arabella Braithwaite didn't hate it, Nicola reminded herself harshly. In fact, Arabella was one of the few women who—according to gossip—rode to hounds as well as or better than some of the gentlemen. She would be there this morning, looking as beautiful as she invariably did, and, in all probability, not too far from David's side.

Nicola slapped the whip against her leg, irritation evident in every impatient flick. She had tried very hard to keep thoughts of Arabella Braithwaite from intruding into her life, but she wasn't having much luck. Probably due to the fact that, all too often of late, Arabella seemed to be everywhere they were. No matter what soirée or function she and David attended, Arabella was there too. In fact, it had become so noticeable that Nicola had almost begun to wonder whether the woman didn't plan her social calendar specifically around what she and David were doing.

If that was the case, and Arabella *was* taking pains to attend many of the same functions, it certainly wasn't in order to further her acquaintance with herself, Nicola acknowledged ruefully. Arabella seldom spoke to her once the initial pleasantries were over. She moved away and lost herself in the crowd. But never so far away as to allow

Nicola a complete sense of freedom. She was always there, hovering in the background. Waiting. Watching. Almost as though she was expecting Nicola to do or to say something wrong.

'Here you are, m'lady,' Roberts, the head groom, said as he led Nightingale out. 'All tacked up and ready to go. Would you like Jenkins to ride out with you?'

Nicola shook her head. 'Thank you, Roberts, but I shall be fine on my own. I won't be venturing far.'

'Aye. Just far enough to get away from the crowd, I'll wager,' Roberts said with the familiarity of a long-time retainer. He cupped his hands together and bent to give Nicola a leg up. 'Widgin says they'll likely be heading for the high fields this morning, so you'll be wanting to stay away from there.'

Nicola smiled as she settled her right knee in the crutch and her left foot in the stirrup. 'Thank you, Roberts. I shall bear that in mind.'

Roberts touched his cap and then headed back into the stables as Nicola gathered the reins and turned Nightingale towards the path. Widgin was the oldest man still in service at Wyndham. He had been a groom in her grandfather's time, and still lived in a small room above the stables. He wasn't able to do much now beyond groom his beloved horses and see to their oats and water, but there was nothing the old man didn't know about the rolling hills and the forests which surrounded Wyndham Hall, or about the wildlife that inhabited them.

Nicola had often seen her mother and Widgin walking by the lake, their heads down as they slowly circled the wide body of water, and wondered what they were talking about. Were they exchanging stories about the creatures who lived in the forests? Comparing notes, perhaps, as to the best method of curing an ailing horse, or the most effective way to splint a broken limb? Certainly it was a possibility, because her mother had always believed that Widgin knew more about the ways of the forest and its creatures than anyone she had ever met.

In turn, Widgin had been her staunchest ally. He wouldn't hear of anyone maligning the beautiful Lady Wyndham. The stable boys went in fear of him, and if he heard so much as a whisper from the villagers—or even from the top-lofty visitors who called at the house—he would give them a dressing down they didn't soon forget!

Nicola smiled to herself. No wonder so many people went in fear of the poor old man.

As soon as they were clear of the yard, Nicola gave the mare her head. She was seldom happy with a staid, placid trot, and today she was even less so. She needed to feel the rush of the wind against her face, and to see the ground go flying past beneath her. Fortunately, Nightingale was fresh, and seemingly just as anxious for a gallop as her mistress. Her legs flew over the grassy turf, hooves pounding as they left the Hall behind, all the while making sure to stay well clear of the high pastures as Widgin had advised.

Finally, Nicola drew the mare to a halt at the site of one of her favourite places, and, freeing both her legs, lightly sprang down from the saddle. She tied the mare's reins to a nearby bush, and then made her way towards the gently meandering brook that wound its way through the entire length of the Wyndham property. Finding the flat black rock that jutted out over the edge of the water, Nicola carefully gathered up her skirts and sat down. She tossed a stone into the water and watched the rings radiate out and out until they finally brushed the grassy edge of the far shore and disappeared.

Not surprisingly, her thoughts turned to David as she

sat there, and, in particular, to the confusion which had lately begun to surround her relationship with him. In spite of what he had said to her the other evening, Nicola didn't believe that David's reasons for wishing to marry her had changed. It was true that he was as kind and considerate as she could have wished, and, granted, he had talked about the possibility of feelings developing between them, but who was to say that he wasn't just saying that to make her feel better about the situation which existed between them?

And, while it was true that his behaviour towards Humphrey O'Donnell had resembled that of a jealous man, perhaps it was just his droit du seigneur which had been challenged, rather than his romantic sensibilities. Nicola was his fiancée, which meant that in the eyes of the law she was his possession. Or, at least, she would be, once they were officially wed.

Still, she liked to think that his actions weren't entirely motivated by duty and obligation. He must hold her in some regard, otherwise he wouldn't have been so forgiving of her escapades with Arthur and Guinevere.

But was that regard enough to keep him by her side? Nicola pondered now. If the affection he felt for her was based purely on duty and obligation, would he simply produce the requisite heir, and then turn to another for his pleasures? To…Arabella, perhaps?

It was a depressing thought, and Nicola irritably threw another stone into the water. She knew that it was a common enough occurrence amongst the upper classes. Gentlemen took mistresses, and wives took lovers. It was an accepted mode of behaviour, so long as it was done with discretion and tact.

But it didn't *have* to be that way, Nicola reminded herself. Her aunt had assured her of that. '…if you are fortunate enough to really love your husband, the thought of his going elsewhere will cause you more misery than you can imagine.'

'Dear me, how very right you were, Aunt,' Nicola whispered softly into the breeze. She hadn't for a moment believed that she would fall so deeply in love with David. So much that the thought of his turning to another for *anything* was like the pain of a knife plunging into her heart. Mercy, was all this misery truly a part of loving?

Because, if it was, God help her once they were well and truly married!

At about the same time, David rode his black stallion into the courtyard of Wyndham Hall, and began searching for his beautiful, green-eyed lady. He had already told himself that it was highly unlikely that he would see her, given her antipathy towards fox-hunting, but he still found himself looking, holding out hope that she might have made an exception for him in light of their newly found closeness.

Regrettably, it seemed that she had not. Instead, it was his cousin Arabella who sought him out.

'Good morning, David,' she greeted him warmly. 'Still happily anticipating wedded bliss?'

Not surprisingly, Arabella was looking her early morning best in an exquisitely tailored habit of cherry-red velvet with hat, gloves and boots to match. She was as lovely as any of the freshest young faces at court. And yet, for the first time since he had known her, David found himself comparing his cousin's somewhat calculated beauty to Nicola's natural grace and loveliness.

'Very much,' he replied without hesitation. 'In fact, I intend to recommend it to all of my single friends.'

Arabella's smile was a pale imitation of his. 'How

nice.' Then, fearing that she was about to hear more of his delightful fiancée, she said quickly, 'Is it not a perfect day for the hunt?'

'It is indeed. You haven't seen Nicola, have you?'

Arabella's expression did not change, though her voice hardened slightly. 'No, but then, I would hardly expect to, my dear. Your lady does not approve of fox-hunting. In fact, she told me that she is quite dead set against it.'

'Yes.' David smiled fondly. 'She has expressed that opinion to me on more than one occasion too.'

'Pity, really,' Arabella said, trying to ignore the note of regret in David's voice. 'I've always thought it prudent for a husband and wife to enjoy the same things, especially when they are first married. Wouldn't you agree?'

'I am sure there will be many other things that Nicola and I will be able to enjoy together.'

Arabella laughed, a soft, throaty trill. 'Yes, perhaps the two of you can go falconing together.'

It was a mistake, and Arabella knew it the moment the words left her mouth. She saw David's mouth tighten into a hard, unyielding line, and realized that she had to make amends—and fast. 'Of course, I meant no slight—'

'I do not think there is any need to dwell on the subject further, Arabella,' David interrupted quietly. 'Nicola has already explained why she made the effort on the falcon's behalf. And, while I admit that tending an injured falcon is a somewhat unusual occupation for a well-bred young lady, I found that, given her reasons for doing so, I could not reproach her for it.'

Hating Nicola all the more for putting her in such an awkward position, Arabella said quickly, 'Nor am I, David. On the contrary, I have the *greatest* admiration for the girl. I simply thought it a rather…peculiar sight to see her standing there with a falcon on her arm. As was the sight of her picking up that mouse with her bare hands—'

'My fiancée is an unusual woman,' David said, sure that he had never uttered a truer word. 'And one who puts the welfare of others before herself. I find that in itself a refreshing and admirable trait, and one which requires no defence from me. Enjoy the hunt, Arabella.'

David briefly doffed his hat, and then, collecting his reins, headed into the field of riders, content to lose himself in the crowd—and to ponder the unpleasant conversation he had just had with his cousin.

To be sure, Arabella's words had rankled—even though he knew there was no reason for them to have done so. Nicola *was* unusual. She did and said things that were entirely out of keeping with the behaviour and habits of other gently reared young ladies. Never in his life, for example, had David met a young woman who truly cared about the well-being of the animals around her, whether they be domesticated stock or creatures of the wild. In this day and age such compassion was unheard of, and David knew that Arabella could really not be held culpable for pointing out those truths to him.

The problem was, the more time David spent with Nicola, the more he realized just how special and unique she really was. She hadn't a selfish bone in her body, and she was genuinely concerned about the welfare of those less fortunate than herself. Her trait of caring for wounded creatures was an endearing one, and, while he wouldn't have admitted it to anyone, and certainly not to Arabella, David almost found himself wondering what kind of amusing escapade Nicola was likely to get up to next.

Chapter Eight

At just gone half past ten, the bugle blew to gather the hunters. Not long after, amidst a frenzy of yelping and yapping, the pack was loosed. Noses to the ground, they searched the covert for signs of their quarry. Then, at last, there was a flash of red, and one baying cry went up, followed by another as the hounds and the huntsman set off, followed closely by a flurry of black- and red-coated riders.

The hunt was under way!

Riding along the valley road some distance away, Nicola heard the faint baying of the hounds, and abruptly pulled up on the reins. They were on the scent! Soon, they would be scrambling across the grassy fields and surging over stiles and fences, chasing the poor fox until at last, exhausted, it either went to ground or climbed a tree. Then…

Nicola shut her eyes at the gruesome picture. Thank goodness she had been able to spare Alistair that horrible death. Her little pet would never know the feeling of being driven to ground, running until he was too weary to go on. He was safe in his cage. She had checked on him before going to bed last—

'Good morning, Lady Nicola.'

The familiar masculine voice startled Nicola and caused her to cast a hasty glance back over her shoulder. Her eyes widened in dismay as she watched Mr Humphrey O'Donnell approach on the back of a fine bay hunter. She had been so wrapped up in her own thoughts that she had not even heard him approach. 'Mr O'Donnell!'

O'Donnell doffed his glossy black beaver with a flourish and a bow. 'What a delightful and unexpected surprise.'

Nicola politely inclined her head, feeling definitely surprised, and far from delighted. 'Are you not participating in the hunt?'

'Like you, I find the sport an unappealing one. I prefer to ride over the hills and hedgerows for pleasure rather than in search of game. And perhaps, to that end, you would allow me to ride with you for a while, since it seems that we are intent on the same purpose?'

'I do not think that would be a good idea,' Nicola said quickly. 'As you can see, I am unaccompanied, and it would be unseemly for us to be seen riding alone together.'

His smile was persuasive. 'I doubt there would be anyone of import to see us. The gentry are intent upon their hunt and we are some distance from the closest town. And I promise that I shall not repeat my foolish behaviour of the other evening,' Mr O'Donnell said humbly. 'I behaved badly, and I crave your forgiveness for my unpardonable conduct.'

In the face of such a genuine apology, Nicola was forced to relent slightly. To do otherwise would have seemed churlish. 'There is no need to take on so, Mr O'Donnell. I do not hold your behaviour against you. I realise that you spoke in the…heat of the moment.'

'I did indeed, my lady, and from my heart. However,' O'Donnell said, when he saw that Nicola was about to object again, 'you made your feelings known and I have no wish to jeopardize our friendship by compromising your wishes again. So, I hope that you will at least honour me with the pleasure of your company and allow me to ride with you for a little way. It is an uncommonly beautiful morning, after all.'

Nicola bit her lip, annoyed to find herself in something of a muddle. She should have listened to Roberts and allowed a groom to accompany her. It simply wasn't the thing for a lady to ride alone in the company of a gentleman, especially as she was now the fiancée of the Marquis of Blackwood. Society had its rules, and it was rigid in its observance of them.

Still, surely no harm could come of allowing him to ride only as far as Wyndham Hall with her, Nicola thought. It meant that she would have to return home sooner than she had planned, but that was of little consequence now. The field was far enough away from the house, and long before they returned she could have the carriage readied and drive into the village. She did need some new silk for her embroidery after all.

'Very well, Mr O'Donnell.' Nicola relented. 'You may accompany me as far as the turning for Wyndham Hall, but that is all. And we will stay to the main road, in plain sight.'

It was obviously enough for Mr O'Donnell, who obligingly doffed his beaver again and turned his horse beside hers.

They rode in silence for a few minutes, before Mr O'Donnell enquired idly, 'Have you ever hunted, Lady Nicola?'

'Indeed I have not,' Nicola replied with a shudder. 'Nor have I ever wanted to.'

'Is there a reason for your disdain?'

'It is not so much disdain, Mr O'Donnell, as abhorrence,' Nicola corrected him. 'When I was about ten, a friend of my father's came to stay with us. He was an avid hunter, like Papa, but, unlike my father, he was a cruel man, who loved to brag about all the game he had shot. I believe he had even been to Africa on a hunting expedition. Regardless, one day, when he came back from a meet, he had the…fox's tail. He was holding it in his hands as though it were some kind of…trophy. There was blood on the front of his jacket, and he was laughing and talking about it all at great length—' Nicola broke off, and shuddered again. 'I thought I was going to be ill.'

'Yes, I can see why you would have taken such an aversion to it. And I admit, I was not well pleased either the first time I was blooded.'

She glanced at him in surprise. 'Really?'

Mr O'Donnell nodded as a faint pink stain crept into his cheeks. 'My father was a great sportsman. Used to hunt with the Quorn, you know. And, of course, when I came of age, he decided that it was time for me to follow in his footsteps. Well, I was a lot younger then, and we were only out for some cubbing,' O'Donnell added quickly, 'but I hadn't spent that much time on a horse. So, it was hardly surprising when I came a bit of a cropper over a particularly nasty bullfinch.'

'Oh, dear.'

'Yes. Shook myself up a bit, bloodied my nose. Father said I looked a right clunch, but then he would, being the neck-or-nothing rider he was. And, to top it all off, I wasn't very good with that…bit at the end,' O'Donnell said, laughing self-consciously. 'All in all, not an experience I cared to repeat.'

'But you still like to ride?'

'Oh, yes. I'm always game for a canter, but I've no desire to take a flying leaper over fences in a mad rush to catch a fox.'

Nicola turned her attention back to the road ahead. Somehow, she wasn't surprised to learn that Mr O'Donnell didn't have the stomach for hunting. Nevertheless, it did allow her to think of him with a touch more charity than she had in the past.

Suddenly, Nicola started, and drew up on the reins. The baying of the hounds seemed alarmingly close by.

'Are you all right, Lady Nicola?' Mr O'Donnell enquired, seeing her concern.

'Yes, fine. I just never get used to the sound of the pack. Perhaps we should make haste to— Oh, no!' Nicola gasped as a flash of red streaked across the path ahead. 'Dear heavens, there's the fox!'

Feeling her heart leap into her mouth, Nicola followed the animal's progress with her eyes. He looked to be making for the road, but he was disoriented and unsure of himself. No wonder, Nicola thought, her heart hardening against the hunters. The poor little mite was probably terrified. She saw him break cover again and then pause in the middle of the road. He lifted his nose to test the air and took a tentative step forward, his front foot pausing.

A front foot on which was blazoned a rather large white patch of fur.

'Dear God!' Nicola gasped, momentarily forgetting herself. *'Alistair!'*

O'Donnell stared at her in bewilderment. 'I beg your pardon?'

Suddenly, as if only just alerted to the presence of the humans nearby, the fox turned—and Nicola blanched.

It *was* Alistair. She would have known that mischievous little face anywhere. *And* the patch of white on his foreleg. But how in the world had he managed to get out of the cage?

'Alistair!' she called.

Unfortunately, Alistair was far too frightened to make sense of anything that was going on around him now. The smell of the dogs had driven everything from his mind but the instinct to survive. Nature had taken over, and, in a flash, he was gone.

'Quickly, I must go after him!' Nicola cried.

'After him?' O'Donnell choked. 'But…I thought you said…you didn't care for fox-hunting.'

'I don't, Mr O'Donnell, but that wasn't just any fox. That was Alistair!'

Nicola pressed her heel into the mare's side and tore off down the road after her pet. She had to catch Alistair and get him back to the house. He wasn't strong enough to withstand the rigours of the hunt, and the pack were closing in. Thankfully, he had left the main road and was now running over a newly turned field where his bright red brush was easy to see. 'Alistair!' she called again.

The fox veered again, this time following a path on the diagonal. Nicola pushed her horse on, off the road now, mindful of the treacherous footing on the freshly turned field. If she went down now, Alistair would be lost for sure.

Suddenly, off in the distance, Nicola saw the first of the hounds break cover at the top of the hill. The rest of the pack couldn't be far behind, and after them would come the hunters.

And David.

The thought caused Nicola's stomach to lurch painfully. If he found her out here in the middle of a field trying to rescue the very fox they were hunting, there would be the devil to pay! Not to mention what he would say when he saw Mr O'Donnell with her—and not a groom in sight!

'Lady Nicola, are you…sure you know…what you are doing?' Mr O'Donnell shouted from behind, valiantly trying to keep up with her.

'Quite sure, Mr O'Donnell, but I think *you* had best return to the road as quickly as possible,' she threw back over her shoulder.

If he answered her, Nicola didn't hear it, and, loath to waste time, she didn't ask again. She spurred Nightingale on, fighting to keep up with the fleet-footed fox. Time was of the essence now. If she couldn't keep Alistair in sight, he would go to ground and then she might never be able to get to him. All she could try to do was get close enough to the terrified little animal to pick him up before the hounds closed in.

Unfortunately, it seemed that luck was not to be on her side today. Alistair disappeared into a thick clump of trees, forcing Nicola to rein in. Behind her, the pack drew ever closer, their excited barks getting louder as they sensed the proximity of their foe.

'Lady…Nicola, surely this is…madness?' Mr O'Donnell gasped, red-faced and breathing hard from his full-out gallop across the fields. 'You cannot possibly… find the fox before…the pack do.'

'I certainly intend to try, Mr O'Donnell. Find him *and* catch him.'

Nicola urged the mare onward, cautiously picking her way into the first of the trees. She knew these woods from having played in them as a child, but the footing was treacherous for a horse, and she went only as fast as she dared. 'Alistair?' she called out.

Nicola ducked down under the low-hanging branches, trying to keep her eye on the tangled undergrowth beneath her mare's hooves, and on the ground ahead of them. 'Alistair, where are you?' Nicola shouted into the woods. 'If you do not show yourself soon, it is going to be very difficult to— *Alistair*!'

She saw him then, standing by the base of a tree. His bright eyes were glazed and his sides were heaving painfully. But at least he had stopped. Obviously, the familiar sound of her voice had finally penetrated through his panic.

Slowly dismounting, Nicola gathered up her skirts and started towards him.

'Lady Nicola, for God's sake, get away from there!' O'Donnell shouted, watching her in disbelief. 'There is no telling what the creature will do!'

'I know what I am doing, Mr O'Donnell,' Nicola said quietly. 'Please be quiet or you will frighten him.'

Nicola continued her slow, careful approach. If Alistair bolted now, it would all be over. She couldn't possibly hope to get back on her horse and catch him in time. But he was terrified; she could see that. His body was trembling and he was panting heavily. Would he remember who she was, or had instinct taken over completely?

In spite of her own uncertainty, Nicola tried to remember everything her mother had taught her about dealing with an animal's fear. She cleared her mind, and concentrated on the fox. She lowered her voice to a quiet, soothing tone, the same one her mother had taught her to use, and called him again. 'Alistair.'

The fox stood stock-still, eyes fixed on her.

Nicola called his name again, purposely keeping her

voice to a low and calming level. If she truly did possess
any of her mother's skills, sweet heaven, she needed them
now!

'Come, Alistair. Come.'

The fox took a tentative step towards her, then hesitated, his body still quivering.

Nicola took a deep breath and walked another pace
closer. She was almost close enough to grab him—or to
lose him. The moment of truth had come.

She softly called his name one…more…time. 'Alistair.'

And, then, with a bound, he was in her arms.

Behind her, Mr. O'Donnell all but swooned. *'Sink me!'*

Mr O'Donnell's dismay was the least of Nicola's concerns right now. She pointedly ignored him as tears of
relief rushed to her eyes. She could feel the trembling in
Alistair's body every time the hounds barked, and she
desperately tried to soothe him. *'Oh, Alistair*, you naughty
boy,' she murmured into the silky fur. 'You had me so
worried. You mustn't run away again, do you hear?'

But what was she to do with him now? How could she
keep him safe from the dogs? She couldn't hope to outrun
them on foot; not when they were so close. Nor could she
get back on Nightingale and hope to be clear of the copse
before the first of the pack broke through. Which meant
that she had to find some kind of sanctuary here. She
gazed at the circle of brush all around her—and then saw
her answer in the clearing ahead.

The old oak tree! Of course! The one she had climbed
a hundred times when she'd been a little girl. The tree
with hand-holds and thick branches that would enable her
to climb high up into the sheltering leaves and hide there.
High enough to escape the dogs.

It was her only hope.

Not stopping to worry about the consequences of her actions, Nicola started running towards the massive tree. It was going to be awkward climbing with Alistair in her arms, but it was their only chance for escape. If she was still on the ground when the hounds broke through, there was no telling what kind of mayhem would ensue!

O'Donnell watched her in growing alarm. 'Lady Nicola, what are you doing?' He nudged his horse forward. 'Where are you going with that animal?'

'As high into that tree as I can get, Mr O'Donnell,' Nicola told him briefly. 'Could you lend me a hand, please?'

O'Donnell, his cheeks already pale, went even whiter. 'You *cannot* be *serious*!'

'I assure you, I am very serious. And, since you have decided to stay, I would very much appreciate your assistance in this matter.' Nicola turned towards her mare and whistled softly. Obediently, Nightingale trotted forward and came to a halt at her side, while Mr O'Donnell reluctantly trotted his horse towards the base of the tree.

'Now, I want you both to cooperate,' Nicola whispered to the horse and to the fox. 'Because if you do not we are all going to be in a great deal of trouble. Mr O'Donnell, would you kindly hold my mare's reins?'

Mr O'Donnell swallowed, distinctly uncomfortable with the part he was being asked to play in the proceedings. Nevertheless, he leaned down and took the reins from her. 'What shall I do now?'

'Nothing. Just ensure that Nightingale does not go anywhere.'

Moving as slowly and as carefully as she dared, Nicola set Alistair on the back of the mare, and prayed that he would neither jump nor slip.

Now, she had to make her own way up the tree.

She turned back to smile at Mr O'Donnell. 'Would you mind turning your head for just a moment, please, Mr O'Donnell?'

'I think it would be better if I were to keep my eye on you, Lady Nicola,' O'Donnell said dubiously. 'In case you begin to fall.'

'I do not intend to fall, nor have I time to argue. In order for me to climb, it will be necessary for me to adjust my clothing. Now, if you do not mind, kindly turn your head.'

Nicola could see that he was still reluctant to comply, and sighed in exasperation. 'Very well, I shall have to make my preparations and climb regardless.'

Mr O'Donnell gasped and quickly turned his head. 'I shall never forgive myself if you fall and I am not there to catch you,' he complained in a muffled voice.

'Rest assured, I shall not fall,' Nicola assured him as she hitched up her skirts to a most unladylike level and then placed her hands on the tree. 'I have climbed this oak a hundred times, and never once lost my balance.' And, so saying, Nicola began to climb.

It was slow going at first. Nicola struggled to find the old hand- and foot-holds, and she was more than thankful for the leather soles of her half-boots which gave her a relatively secure footing. Even so, it wasn't long before her arms began to ache from the strain of pulling herself up. Obviously she'd had a great deal more energy when she'd been a child of eight than she had now!

Then, in the distance, Nicola heard the sound of the bugle, and of the dogs baying in excitement. The end was imminent. The hunters were closing in!

The sound caused her to double her efforts, and she climbed with as much speed as she dared. Finally, when she was about seven feet off the ground, and breathing

heavily from the exertion, Nicola stopped. 'All right…
steady now, Nightingale. Please do not…move, Mr
O'Donnell. And please do not look!'

'Are you sure you are all right, Lady Nicola?' he enquired nervously.

'I am…fine, Mr O'Donnell, thank you for…asking.'

Taking a firmer grip on the branch, Nicola leaned over
and very carefully lifted the fox from Nightingale's back.
Thankfully, Alistair didn't squirm a great deal, and Nicola
was able to resume her climb with Alistair tucked firmly
under her arm. Also, the branches were closer together
here and offered her better footing. Finally, when she
looked to be about fifteen feet off the ground, Nicola
stopped and settled herself in the crook of a particularly
large branch, and glanced down. They were definitely
higher than the dogs would be able to jump.

For the moment, they were safe.

'All right, Mr O'Donnell, I suggest you either leave the
clearing altogether, or get away from the base of this tree
as quickly as possible,' Nicola advised.

Astonished, O'Donnell spun around on his horse. 'Lady
Nicola?' He looked all around, and then, hearing the rustle
of leaves above him, turned his eyes upwards. 'Oh, my
God! What in the—?'

'Get away from here, Mr O'Donnell!'

But it was already too late. Mr O'Donnell managed to
get about ten feet away before the first of the foxhounds
poured into the copse. Like a liquid stream of brown and
gold, the pack diligently followed the trail to the base of
the very tree in which Nicola sat, and then, realising that
they had finally located their prey, began to circle the base
of the tree, baying frantically.

Hidden in the branches, Nicola clutched the terrified
fox to her chest and watched in horror as the hounds

hurled themselves against the trunk in a furious attempt to get at them. She saw the snapping jaws and the wild eyes and tightened her grip, knowing that if Alistair jumped now it would mean certain death.

In the copse below, Nightingale whinnied nervously at the frenzied behaviour of the pack, while Mr O'Donnell, his face as white as a sheet, held on tightly to her reins. Minutes later, the first of the riders broke through—causing Nicola to gasp, as though a fist had landed hard in the middle of her stomach.

David!

She saw him glance in astonishment at the sight of Humphrey O'Donnell holding a riderless horse, and then saw his dark eyebrows rise as he realised it was a lady's mount.

'Well, well, Mr O'Donnell, I wasn't aware you were a sporting man,' David said in amusement. 'Though, judging from the saddle, I would venture to say it was a different kind of sport you were hoping to indulge in.'

O'Donnell's face went crimson, though whether it was through embarrassment or fear Nicola wasn't sure. 'Have a care, Blackwood. There is a lady present.'

'Yes, I fully suspected there was,' David drawled. 'And for her own safety I suggest that you tell me where she is as quickly as possible. This is no place for anyone, let alone a lady, to be walking about on foot.'

'The lady is not on foot, Blackwood. Take a look in front of you. And…up.'

Nicola saw David's look of amusement change to one of horror as his eyes moved quickly upwards from the pack of frantic hounds clamouring around the base of the tree to the sight of his fiancée sitting in the crook higher up. 'What in God's name—? *Nicola*, is that you?'

'Yes, David, but—'

'Never mind "but." What the *hell* are you doing up that tree?' he demanded. '*And* with the bloody fox!'

'There's no need to shout, David,' Nicola called down. 'Just please call off the dogs.'

'Never mind the dogs, have you taken complete leave of your senses?'

'Not yet, but I fear such a departure may be imminent if you do not get these hounds away from the base of this tree soon.'

Suddenly, another rider burst into the glade. 'Blackwood, what the devil's going on?' Lord Wyndham said, shouting to be heard above the frantic barking of the dogs. 'Where's the damned fox?' His eyes followed David's up the tree and into the branches above. 'What the—? *Good God! Nicola?*'

'Papa, please call the dogs away.'

'Dash it all, Nicola, you're not supposed to be holding our fox.'

'I am not holding your fox!'

'Then what do you call that creature in your arms?'

'It's…Alistair.'

David gasped. *'Alistair!'*

Nicola winced at her fiancé's strangled exclamation, but desperately appealed to her father for help. 'He obviously got out of his cage and came looking for me. And in doing so he became…mixed up in the scent of the other fox. I saw him dash across the road out by the Manse and followed him as best I could. That's how we ended up here in the woods. And when I realised that I wouldn't have time to get him safely away before the pack closed in I decided to take shelter in the old tree.'

'No. I don't believe any of this,' David muttered, more to himself than to anyone else. 'First a falcon, then a mouse, and now a bloody fox?'

'Nicola, you can't stay in that tree,' her father shouted over the din as another three riders burst onto the scene.

'No, but I can't come down with the pack madly running around either. Alistair's terrified as it is!'

It wasn't long before the entire field was gathered in the copse, turning it into a heaving mass of shouting riders, plunging horses and frantically barking dogs. Hoping to disguise her identity, Nicola drew as far back into the shelter of the leaves as possible. She could only imagine how bizarre she must look—an elegantly dressed young woman perched in the branches of a huge tree, trying to hold a fox that didn't know whether to snarl or whimper, beneath which clustered a bevy of angry hunters who held her responsible for the sad conclusion to a good day's hunting. Not to mention poor Mr O'Donnell who was staring at it all in utter bewilderment.

It was not an enviable position, to say the least.

It deteriorated even further with the arrival of the last rider. Arabella Braithwaite valiantly made her way through to the front of the riders and stared up into the tree. The mockery and ridicule in her eyes served as Nicola's final humiliation. Because if anyone had doubted the identity of the person hiding in the branches before, Arabella's startled exclamation served as undeniable confirmation.

'My word, David, your charming fiancée seems to have put an end to our sport. Upon my word, now she has even rescued the fox!'

And then, to Nicola's mortification, the woman began to laugh. Openly and without compunction, the sound echoing off the trees until it was picked up by every member of the field, and they were all laughing at her. Every one of them—with the exception of her father and David—laughing at the sight of the Lady Nicola Wyndham,

fiancée of the Marquis of Blackwood, sitting in the
branches of a tree; a woman who had rescued first a
wounded falcon, then an injured field mouse, and now a
fox.

It was the most humiliating moment of her life!

And it was far from over.

'O'Donnell?' Lord Wyndham barked, squinting his
eyes across the clearing. 'Is that you?'

'Y-yes, my lord,' the young man said miserably.

'What the devil are you doing here?'

'Yes, what are you doing here?' David asked sharply,
suddenly realizing that it was Nicola's horse that
O'Donnell had been holding when he'd first burst into the
clearing, and that it was his fiancée with whom O'Donnell
had been riding—alone and unchaperoned.

'I—I—'

'For God's sake, man, stop babbling,' Lord Wyndham
commanded. 'Bring Lady Nicola's horse here, will you?
Nicola, let the fox go and come down out of the tree.'

'Let him go?' Nicola stared at her father in horror. 'But
I can't!'

'Nicki, we can't get you down while you're holding the
fox in your arms. You're liable to fall.'

'I managed to get up here with Alistair in my arms and
I am not going to put him down now. He would be dead
in minutes.'

'Nicola, drop the fox! *Now!*'

Like the deafening crack of a gunshot, David's voice
ripped through the air, silencing the crowd, and causing
Nicola—who had never been spoken to like that by anyone in her life, and certainly not by the man she was about
to marry—to lift her chin in trembling defiance. 'No, my
lord, I will not. Papa, call off the pack.'

'Nicola!'

'Papa?'

'Oh, all right, all right. Haversham, get the hounds to-gether!' Lord Wyndham bellowed. 'Peters, lend a hand.'

The men quickly sprang to do the earl's bidding and within moments the last of the hounds were contained.

'All right, Nicola, the dogs are tied,' David said, in a voice that could have frozen the Thames. 'The animal will come to no harm. Now let him go and come down out of that tree!'

Nicola sent him a hostile glare. 'It is not my fault I had to climb up here. If you people would take your sport elsewhere—'

'Nicola, I am going to say this once, and once only,' David told her in a dangerously quiet voice that left no one in any doubt as to his feelings. 'Let the fox go and come down out of that tree, or so help me, God, I shall climb up there and carry you down myself!'

It was clear that Blackwood was trying to hold on to his patience, but it was equally clear that there was precious little of it left. Nicola might not know him well, but she knew enough of him to be sure of that—and to know that he wasn't making idle threats.

She glanced beseechingly down at her father. 'Papa, please—'

Her father looked up and sighed. 'Let the fox go, Nicki.'

'But—'

'Let…the fox…go.'

Nicola looked down at the dogs, their eyes filled with blood lust as they strained against their leads, and felt the tiny form in her arms shiver uncontrollably. If even one of them got loose…

'David?' Nicola cast one last desperate look at her fi-ancé, hoping to see even a trace of compassion in those

fine, dark eyes, but she might just as well have been looking down into the eyes of a stranger. He was coldly and
furiously angry, and he was not going to help her. And at
that moment, Nicola felt something precious shrivel up
and die inside her. Because, until that moment, she had
truly believed that they had a chance to be happy together.
That David might have been able to overlook his prejudices, and come to terms with her love for the creatures
that were so important to her.

Now, she knew better.

'Very well,' Nicola whispered, stung by David's bitter
betrayal. 'Would all of you be kind enough to turn away?'

Nicola waited until all of the gentlemen present—her
father and David included—dutifully turned their heads.
Then, with Alistair wedged firmly under her arm, she
slowly and carefully began to climb back down the tree.

Her father had been right about one thing, Nicola realized dimly. Working her way *down* the tree with a fox
in her arms was a great deal more difficult than making
her way *up* it had been. She only had one arm with which
to hold herself against the tree, and when she suddenly
slipped, and scraped the skin on her knee against a rough
piece of bark, it was all she could do not to cry out in
pain.

Even so, her grip on Alistair never faltered. She continued to move slowly and steadily down the length of
the trunk until, finally, she was only about six feet from
the ground. At that point, Nicola hooked her legs around
the base of a sturdy branch, leaned well over, and, taking
a last quick look to make sure that the dogs were indeed
in check, gently dropped the fox down the remaining three
or four feet to the forest floor.

He hit the ground running, tearing out of the copse as
fast as his little legs would carry him. Behind him, the

frustrated hounds set up a deafening chorus of yelps and howls, unable to comprehend why their foe had been allowed to escape so easily.

Fearing the worst, David turned around—and felt his heart leap into his mouth.

She was *hanging* from a branch. Literally…hanging there, her skirts around her knees, the tears streaming down her face as she watched the fox run away. If she slipped now and fell, dear God, she could kill herself…

'Nicola, jump forward and I'll catch you,' David said, moving the stallion into place. 'Your footing is poor the rest of the way down.'

Nicola stiffened at the sound of his voice. Like one in a dream, she turned to glare at him, her eyes seemingly oblivious to the stares of the gentlemen who had turned back to watch the proceedings—and who were clearly enjoying the sight of a pair of neatly turned ankles and shapely calves.

'Look away!' David barked.

As one, the gentlemen complied. But not before Nicola had seen the smirks upon their faces. Nor did Arabella Braithwaite look away. She sat quietly on her horse, her eyes raised to the sight of Nicola poised precariously in the tree, her skirts revealing far more of her legs than was seemly—and enjoyed every minute of the other girl's humiliation. For her, it was sweet retribution.

For Nicola, it was the final disgrace.

'Mr O'Donnell,' Nicola said in a flat, dead voice. 'Would you kindly bring my horse to the base of the tree?'

'Stay where you are, O'Donnell,' David snapped.

Nicola's eyes flashed green fire, but her tone did not change. 'Very well. Papa?'

Lord Wyndham shifted uncomfortably in the saddle. 'Nicola, this is no time to—'

'Papa, my horse, if you please.'

Nicola did not raise her voice, but the message was clear. She would accept no help from her fiancé.

And so, sending a resigned look towards the marquis, Lord Wyndham went forward to retrieve Nightingale's reins from Mr O'Donnell and led the mare towards the base of the tree.

The tightness in David's chest became almost unbearable. The sight of Nicola's tears and the coldness in her voice were tearing him apart. 'Nicola, for God's sake, let me help you!'

'Perhaps you would be good enough to make room for my horse, Lord Blackwood,' Nicola said expressionlessly.

For a moment, David said nothing, his icy blue eyes never leaving her face as he struggled to control the anger and despair that suddenly rose within him. Did the silly little fool not realize the danger she was in? Surely she didn't hate him as much as all that?

Perhaps she did, because it was clear that she had no intention of accepting help from him. And consequently, when David did finally speak, the force of his reply set those around him glancing at each other nervously. Even Arabella flinched.

'Very well. Since you do not require my help, I will take my leave.' He silently backed the stallion out of the way and turned to go as Lord Wyndham brought the mare forward. But just before he left he turned back, forced against his better judgement to watch as Nicola began the last part of her descent.

With a grace and agility he would not have believed possible, she swung her body around and then lowered herself into the saddle and secured her right knee. She did not look at him as she slipped her left foot into the stirrup and spread the somewhat tattered remains of her emerald skirt around her. In complete silence, she gathered the reins and turned her mare in the direction of Wyndham Hall.

She did not stop to look back at anyone.

Chapter Nine

Nicola waited by Alistair's cage until well past dusk. For hours, she watched the darkening fields, straining her eyes for some sign of her pet. But when at last the sun sank down below the horizon, and shadows began to gather, Nicola was forced to give up her vigil.

It was pointless, she knew that now. Alistair was gone. What had happened to him in the woods this morning had revived his instincts for survival and turned him into a wild creature once more. He would not be returning to his home at Wyndham Hall again.

On the way back to the house, Nicola stopped to check on Guinevere's progress. Thankfully, the falcon's wing was looking much better and Nicola even dared to hope that the young bird might fly again. Obviously, she had not suffered unduly for her brief brush with humanity. Nicola only wished that she could have said the same for Alistair.

'Ah, there you are, my lady,' Trethewy said with some relief as Nicola walked slowly into the front hall. 'Lord Wyndham has been looking for you these past two hours. He is in his study.'

'Is Lord Blackwood with him?'

'No, my lady.'

'Very well.' Nicola nodded wearily. 'Tell my father that I shall see him as soon as I have changed.'

As the butler went to relay her message, Nicola put her hand on the polished banister and slowly began to climb the stairs. Her body was aching and she was in no mood to see her father, but she knew there was no way of avoiding it. She had made a spectacle of herself this morning and would now be called to task over it. The only thing she could take some comfort from was the knowledge that David was not with him. She was so angry with him that she had no idea what she might have said—except that it would not have been kind.

Maire was waiting anxiously in Nicola's room for her mistress to return. 'Oh, thank the Lord you're finally home, miss,' the Irish girl said. 'I've been that worried about you. And just look at the state of your lovely gown.'

Nicola sighed as she turned to let Maire help her out of the sadly tattered skirt and jacket. 'Yes, I doubt I shall be able to wear it again. Pity, it was one of my favourites.' She paused for a moment, and then said, 'Did Lord Blackwood return to the house with my father this morning, Maire?'

'Aye, miss, but he left soon after. And with a fearsome scowl on his face, so the lads said.'

Yes, no doubt he did, Nicola thought. If she lived to be a hundred, she would never forget the look on David's face just before she had left the copse. She could well understand why he was held in such respect by his peers. But, for all that, she could not forgive him. How could he have just ordered her to abandon Alistair like that? To…drop him into a pack of snarling hounds, without a moment's guilt or regret? Had he learned nothing of the way she felt about animals in the brief time they had been together?

Obviously not. For his betrayal of her today had hurt Nicola more than she would have believed possible.

'Which gown shall I put out for you, my lady?' Maire enquired, crossing to the wardrobe.

'The pale blue one, I think,' Nicola said, knowing it was one of her father's favourites. But even as she tied a white lace fichu around her shoulders, and pinched her white cheeks to add a hint of colour, she knew that her looks were secondary.

The confrontation with her father would take place regardless, and she was not so naive as to believe that a pretty appearance would soften anything that he had to say.

Lord Wyndham was seated at his desk when Nicola arrived.

'You wished to see me, Papa?'

The earl glanced up at the sound of her voice, and then slowly put down his pen. 'Yes, Nicola, I did,' he said quietly. 'I was wondering when you would come in.'

'I…apologise for being late. I thought perhaps Alistair might come back.'

'And did he?'

Nicola shook her head, and dropped her eyes.

The earl breathed a heavy sigh. 'Oh, Nicola, you knew that this would happen one day. A fox is a wild creature. He cannot be domesticated like a dog or a cat. Sooner or later he was bound to return to his natural habitat,' her father said, with more patience than Nicola had been expecting. 'It is where he belongs. You should be happy about it, my dear, not sad.'

'I am not saddened by the fact that Alistair has returned

to the wild, Papa,' Nicola told him in a lacklustre voice.
'I always knew that, one day, his instincts would lead him
back there, and, indeed, I always hoped that they would.
What I am angry about is the manner in which I was
ordered to let him go.'

'By myself, or by Lord Blackwood?'

'By Lord Blackwood. You did not speak to me in such
a contemptuous manner. Indeed, I have never been spoken
to like that in my life,' Nicola said heatedly. 'He all but
commanded me to drop Alistair, and you know as well
as I what would have happened had I released him before
the dogs were restrained. He would have been torn to
pieces within seconds!'

Her father shifted uncomfortably in his seat. 'Yes, I
know that, my dear, but I do not think it was only the
matter of the fox which upset Lord Blackwood this afternoon. What in the world were you doing alone in the
woods with Mr O'Donnell, and without the benefit of either a groom or an abigail?'

Nicola blushed, but stood her ground. 'I was doing
nothing wrong, Papa. I was riding along the road out by
the Manse when Mr O'Donnell happened upon me and
asked if he could ride with me. I saw no harm in allowing
him to do so.'

'Do you really think that was wise?'

'At the time, I saw nothing wrong with it. I was on my
way home anyway, and, until I saw Alistair and gave
chase, we stayed to the main road. But Mr O'Donnell was
a perfect gentleman the entire time. Indeed, on the whole,
I think he acted a great deal more admirably than did Lord
Blackwood, who had no right to speak to me in such a
manner. He is not my husband.'

'Even so, being your fiancé does give Lord Blackwood
certain rights—'

'Which do not include humiliating me in public,' Nicola broke in. 'And as regards his blatant disregard for Alistair's welfare I can think of nothing at all to say that would excuse him.'

'Nicola, you must remember that Lord Blackwood is a member of the aristocracy.'

'And I am not?' Nicola retaliated.

'Of course you are, but you look at things differently. I have come to terms with your rather unusual…fondness for animals,' her father said, struggling to find the right words. 'I had to, given your mother's remarkable gifts. But Blackwood doesn't understand that. He sees you as the gently reared young woman he has chosen to be his wife, the woman who will bear his children and be the mistress of his homes. How do you think he felt at seeing his future marchioness perched up in a tree like that, and for all those people to see?'

'I really do not know,' Nicola replied mumpishly, 'nor do I care. He might at least have been civil.'

'I think he was as civil as the circumstances allowed him to be, my dear,' Lord Wyndham said judiciously. 'Certainly it was as civil as I would have been.'

Nicola started to reply, and then, realising that it would make little difference, sadly shook her head. 'Is what I am doing so wrong, Papa? Not with regard to Mr O'Donnell; I am willing to concede that I made a mistake there,' she granted. 'But am I wrong to want to help the injured creatures I find in the woodlands? Does it make me more normal to walk past a wounded animal and know that it will die from the wounds that other animals, or perhaps even men, have inflicted upon it?' she asked passionately.

Lord Wyndham got to his feet, and his heart lay heavy within his breast. 'No, not more normal, Nicki,' he said gently. 'Simply more acceptable. The laws of Society are harsh, my dear, and they are unforgiving. Whereas a man may be forgiven many things, a woman is pardoned considerably less. And while Society may find the new and unusual diverting for a while they soon tire of it and cast it aside. Unfortunately, while it will not be so easy to toss aside the wife of a marquis, they may find other ways of dealing with the problem.'

Nicola glanced at her father quickly. 'You mean…by cutting me?'

'Possibly. And in so doing they will be insulting the man who is your husband. A man to whom duty and honour are paramount.'

Nicola stared at the black outline of the hills beyond the study window and called to mind once again the words David had spoken to her on the day that he had asked her to marry him. She remembered them well, having gone over them time and time again in her mind. 'A woman who knows how to conduct herself in Society… Conduct I cannot condone in the future Marchioness of Blackwood. I have a duty to my family. To my name.'

Yes, he had a duty to his family, Nicola acknowledged sadly. To behave in a manner befitting his position and to keep free from scandal or disgrace the Blackwood name. Something that was in direct opposition to what she had done today. And, sadly, to what she had been doing all along.

'I think, Papa, that before I cause Lord Blackwood any further embarrassment it might be…best for all concerned if I…put an end to this engagement,' Nicola said quietly. 'I have come to the conclusion that…Lord Blackwood and I simply do not suit.'

Her father stared at her aghast. 'You cannot mean this, my dear. You are…overwrought.'

'Yes, a little,' Nicola admitted. 'What happened today would shake even the most stoical of dispositions. But I do mean what I say. I cannot believe that Lord Blackwood anticipated taking such a handful to wife and, in truth, had today's episode taken place before he had offered for me, I wonder whether he would have offered for me at all.' Nicola laughed sadly. 'Perhaps after today's debacle he will welcome the chance to end it gracefully.'

'But what of your own feelings in the matter?' Lord Wyndham asked gently. 'You are unlikely to achieve a match of this stature again. Lord Blackwood is a wealthy man and you would be a marchioness, with no worries to trouble you for the rest of your life. Are you so sure that you want to give that up?'

Nicola's smile was wistful. 'There is absolutely *no* chance of my contracting a marriage as advantageous as this one, Papa; you and I both know that. Given everything that has happened, I would say that the chances of my attracting *any* kind of man, let alone one with position or wealth, are virtually non-existent. However, I must also consider myself in this equation. I cannot ignore the gifts that my mother has given me, nor do I wish to. And I do not think I could tolerate living with a man who was so narrow-minded that he could not see those gifts for what they are worth. I will not live with a man such as that, Papa, whether he be a marquis—or not!'

A number of thoughts were running through David's mind as he sat in his study late the following evening, not the least of which was how he was going to handle his next meeting with Nicola. It would be a difficult encounter to say the least.

A fox! David marvelled as he stared into the brandy at

the bottom of his glass. He had thought the falcon and the mouse bad enough, but a fox?

And then there was the matter of O'Donnell, David thought darkly. What the hell was he to make of that? A woman like Nicola knew the hazards of riding out with a gentleman unaccompanied. The damage to her reputation could be irreparable. What on earth had possessed her to do such a foolish thing? Did she really care so little for what he thought?

Or…did she care more for what O'Donnell did?

As that unsettling thought began to creep into David's subconscious, an even deeper and more disagreeable emotion began to settle in too. Was it conceivable that… Nicola held O'Donnell in some kind of…genuine affection?

'Looking rather deep in thought, my boy,' Sir Giles said quietly. 'Matters of the heart weighing heavily upon the mind? Or have I got it the wrong way round?'

David glanced towards the doorway of the study and sighed. He wasn't overly surprised to see his uncle there. The man seemed to have an uncanny knack for knowing just when things were in a complete bumble.

'Evening, Uncle. I take it by your presence here that the latest scandalbroth has already circulated. Brandy?'

'A small one, thank you. And yes, I admit I did hear some rather interesting stories at the club this morning. And when I hear rumours like that I prefer to go to the source.'

'Dear me, that bad?'

'I fear they do rather leave the stories of the falcon and the mouse in the dust,' Sir Giles said dryly as he advanced into the room. 'Was she really sitting…halfway up a tree?'

David filled two glasses and handed one to his uncle. 'Like some beautiful, exotic bird.'

'And with…a fox clutched in her arms?'

'Indeed. But not just any fox,' David drawled, returning to his chair. 'Her pet fox, Alistair.'

'By Jove.'

'Yes, it seems that my fiancée is keeping quite a menagerie at Wyndham Hall.'

'Good Lord, do you mean to say…there are others?'

'I don't know.' David took a mouthful of brandy. 'I've not had the courage to ask.'

Sir Giles grinned. 'You might be well advised to do so before too much longer.'

'Rest assured, I intend to—after I get an explanation for what happened yesterday.'

'You've not spoken to Lady Nicola, then?'

David hesitated, remembering all too well the way Nicola had looked at him before refusing his help to come down the tree. It was a look that had been brittle with anger and resentment. And hurt, David realized sadly. She had been terribly hurt by what she perceived to be his betrayal of her. And it was that perception that bothered him more than anything else.

'No. She left the scene rather abruptly.'

'Yes, so I heard.' Sir Giles hesitated tactfully. 'I understand O'Donnell was there too.'

David's nostrils flared with anger. 'That young jackanapes. I intend having a word or two with him before this is all over. I'm simply biding my time until my temper cools.'

'Look, David, is everything all right between you and Nicola?' Sir Giles's light-hearted expression suddenly gave way to a much more concerned and serious one. 'Considering everything that's happened…'

'Everything is fine,' David replied brusquely. 'Nicola is just a touch more…headstrong than I had anticipated. She has very definite ideas about…how to go on, and she is…reluctant to take instruction.'

'Perhaps you need to take her more firmly in hand,' Sir Giles suggested casually. 'To remind her that the man is master in more than just his home.'

David swirled the golden liquid in his glass as a memory suddenly came to mind—that of Nicola's mouth softening under his the first time he had kissed her. He had kissed a good many women in his time, and certainly with considerably more passion than he had Nicola. And yet her kiss had been so very sweet. Her lips had tasted like wild-clover honey, and the touch of her mouth on his had warmed him to the core.

He had never felt about anyone the way he did about Nicola, and, not for the first time, David began to wonder whether he truly was bewitched. She was in all ways an exceptional woman. Her beauty, her graciousness, her capacity for love. Did he really wish to alienate such a gentle creature, and yet one who, at the same time, was blessed with such compassion and spirit, by laying down his hand as lord and master?

'No, I think not, Uncle Giles,' David said softly. 'Nicola is well aware of the correct mode of behaviour. She has demonstrated that to me on more than one occasion. But the problem—if it is a problem,' he acknowledged thoughtfully, 'is that she reacts to people and to situations on a purely emotional level. She looks to her heart rather than to her head for the answers.'

'A shortcoming I believe you once accused me of suffering from,' Sir Giles pointed out with a smile.

David grimaced, recognizing the irony in the situation. 'At least you do not act so openly upon your impulses.

Nicola does, and while it is that very spontaneity which sets her apart from every woman I've ever met it is also the means by which she will fail socially. That's why I am hoping that with a little guidance, and perhaps some gentle persuasion, she may yet conform.'

'To your expectations, or to Society's?' Sir Giles enquired, his smile broadening.

This time, David did laugh. 'I don't know that she will ever conform to Society's, Uncle, but if we can at least stop her from inciting a minor riot every time she comes anywhere near an animal I shall be happy.'

'End our betrothal!'

David stared at his fiancée as though she had suggested putting poison in the old King's wine. 'Nicola...I cannot believe that you are serious about this.'

Nicola sat in the brocade wing-chair in the yellow salon at Wyndham, her hands clasped primly in her lap, the skirts of her bishop's blue gown spread about her. The room was flooded with late morning sunlight which accentuated the deep copper highlights in her hair, and turned her eyes to emerald jewels. But its warmth could do nothing to penetrate the chill which surrounded her heart.

Her face was very pale, her manner composed as she returned her fiancé's direct regard and said, 'Yes, I am, my lord. I think that it would be...best for all concerned.'

'Nicola, there is no need for this!'

'On the contrary, after the events of recent days, I think there is every need,' Nicola said quietly. 'I have disgraced you, and you have humiliated me.'

'Humiliated you? How?'

'By showing a complete disregard for my wishes. By

demanding that I...forfeit the life of an animal in order to obey you.'

'I beg your pardon,' David said in astonishment. 'I did no such thing.'

'Did you not?' Nicola regarded him with eyes that suddenly turned cold. 'You demanded that I drop Alistair into a pack of frenzied dogs, and then ordered me to come down from the tree as though I were...a disobedient child.'

'I ordered you to come down because I was concerned for your safety. You could have fallen!'

'Nonsense. I was trying to tell you that I had climbed that tree any number of times when I was growing up. I was in no danger.'

'Yes, just like you were in no danger from that damn bird in the billiards room,' David ground out. He began to walk back and forth in front of her. 'Nicola, you were at least sixteen feet off the ground—'

'It was no more than ten—'

'You could have fallen while you were trying to hold on to that blasted animal! Damn it, you could have been killed!'

Nicola focused her gaze on his snowy white cravat, admiring the intricacy with which he had tied it, and shook her head. 'And so you thought to...save me by... ordering me to fling Alistair to his death instead?'

'I am marrying you, Nicola, not the blasted fox!' David said, his eyes shadowed and dark as they rested on her face. 'But it wasn't just the incident with the animal. Why were you riding with O'Donnell without the benefit of a chaperon?'

Nicola lowered her eyes. Her own emotions were so raw that she did not see the anguish in his. 'I was not riding with him.'

'The two of you were in the copse together.'

'I had gone out riding to avoid the hunt,' Nicola explained quietly. 'I was on the Manse road when Mr O'Donnell happened to appear. When he asked if he could join me, I told him, reluctantly, that he could accompany me as far as the turn-off for Wyndham Hall. It was shortly after that that I spotted Alistair on the road and gave chase.'

'And Mr O'Donnell felt obliged to follow you?'

'I have no idea what Mr O'Donnell felt obliged to do, Lord Blackwood,' Nicola said impatiently. 'All I know is that he followed me across the field and into the copse. I was far more concerned with Alistair's welfare than I was with Mr O'Donnell's.'

'Yes, I have no doubt of that,' David murmured, well aware that Nicola would put an animal's welfare before a human's in most instances. 'So, you are telling me that you did not purposely seek out the gentleman's company?'

Nicola stared at him in surprise. 'Of course I did not seek him out. I merely agreed to let him ride with me. Which I freely admit now was an error in judgement. However, that did not give you the right to shout at me in such an arrogant and high-handed manner.'

Distinctly relieved that his fears with regard to Nicola's possible affection for Mr O'Donnell were totally unfounded, David held out his hands, and asked quietly, 'Then what would you have had me do, Nicola? Should I just have…ridden on, and left you stranded in that tree?'

'Why not? I was perfectly capable of getting out of it.'

'But I had no way of knowing that. How do you think I would have felt had I ridden off, only to learn that you had fallen moments later?'

Nicola flushed. 'It would not have been your fault—'

'No, but did it ever cross your mind that I would have felt responsible anyway? You are my fiancée, Nicola. The woman I intend to marry. Your well-being is my concern, and it is my responsibility to ensure that you are safe at all times.'

'Oh, yes, your responsibility,' Nicola snapped, painfully reminded once again of David's dedication to duty. 'I appreciate the sentiment, Lord Blackwood, but it does not excuse the fact that you humiliated me in front of all those people. What do you suppose they were thinking when you shouted at me? Did you not hear your cousin Arabella laughing at me?'

'I don't give a damn what Arabella does, or what anybody else thinks!' David said harshly. 'How many times do I have to tell you—it was *you* I was worried about? Not O'Donnell, or Arabella, or the fox—'

'And that is another area where our unsuitability is evident,' Nicola interrupted. 'I have no desire to live with a man who has so little regard for life.'

'I have plenty of regard for life!'

'Human life, perhaps, but not any other kind. How can you say that when you so joyously partake of the hunt?'

'Hell and damnation, Nicola, every gentleman I know rides to hounds. Your own father is one of the most avid hunters of my acquaintance!'

'Yes, well I know it, sir, and much do I wish it were otherwise!' Nicola flung back at him. 'I am only grateful that my father has never compelled me to participate in the activities surrounding it. I find myself wondering if you would be so considerate.'

David's voice dropped to a dangerously low level. 'And exactly what is that supposed to mean?'

'As Marchioness of Blackwood, would you not expect me to host your hunt balls and breakfasts?'

'As my *wife*, I would expect you to perform whatever duties befell you, yes. I fail to see why you should take exception to that. Arabella was willing enough to do so.'

It was like waving a red flag in front of a bull. At the mention of the woman who had openly antagonized, belittled and then laughed at her, Nicola finally lost her temper. 'How dare you!' she said, rising slowly to her feet and glaring at him with cold, reproachful eyes. 'How dare you compare me to one such as Arabella Braithwaite? She is a rude, overbearing female, who I would thank you not to mention in my presence!'

'Oh, for goodness' sake, Nicola, I merely pointed out that Arabella has never found it difficult to act as a gracious hostess at my functions. You should not assume—'

'I assume nothing, my lord. In my mind, the other day was just another example of how poorly suited we are for each other. I recall very clearly your saying that you were looking for…a woman of breeding. A woman who knew how to conduct herself in Society, and who did not tend towards giddiness and…unbecoming behaviour. Well, tell me, David, in the brief time that we have been engaged, what have I evidenced *except* unbecoming behaviour?'

Nicola abruptly turned away, annoyed to feel hot tears trembling on her lashes. Dear Lord, this was so very hard… 'I said to my father that…if all of this had happened before you offered for me I wondered whether you would have…offered for me at all.' Nicola blinked rapidly, and then, glancing down at her hand, slowly began to pull the ring from her finger. 'I tend to believe that you would not.'

'Nicola—'

'But now that it has happened I think it only fair that I release you from your promise,' Nicola said, placing the beautiful emerald and diamond ring upon the table beside her. 'And now I would ask you to leave. I don't believe there is anything else for us to say.'

David stared at her back—and, for the first time in his life, found himself at a complete loss for words. There was so much he wanted to say; so much that he wanted her to hear. And yet, faced with that proud little back, and that unwavering resolution in her voice, he could think of nothing. The admirably self-assured Marquis of Blackwood had been humbled by a slender, five-foot woman.

'Is that your final word, Nicola?' David said hoarsely.

'It is.' Nicola closed her eyes, praying that he would leave before she broke down and took back every word. 'I think it is best—for both of us.'

A long, heavy silence dragged on. As the minutes ticked by, Nicola felt the thin edge of her control slipping away. Until now, she'd had no idea how much love could hurt; how devastating its loss could be. Finally, after what seemed like an eternity, David sighed.

'Very well, if that is truly what you wish. You may consider our betrothal…at an end. I shall have a retraction printed at the first opportunity.' He glanced down at the emerald and diamond ring on the table, trying to think of something—anything he could say that might make her change her mind, and then, sadly, realized there was nothing. He slowly retrieved the jewel and slipped it into his pocket. 'Good afternoon, Lady Nicola.'

By the time the first tears spilled over and rolled down Nicola's cheeks, David was gone, taking with him all of her hopes and dreams for a long and happy future together.

She sank down onto the chaise longue and whispered in a barely audible voice, 'Goodbye, Lord Blackwood.'

Chapter Ten

'My dear girl, are you quite sure you have done the right thing?' Lady Dorchester's eyes reflected the depth of her concern as she poured a cup of jasmine tea for her niece and handed it across the table to her. 'Perhaps you were a touch hasty in your decision.'

'I do not think that I have been at all hasty, Aunt Glynnis.' Nicola took the fine china cup and saucer and held it between fingers that were, to her own way of thinking, remarkably steady. 'I did what I had to do. Lord Blackwood left me little choice.'

'But breaking off your betrothal over a fox! What ever did Lord Blackwood say?'

'There was nothing for him to say. He could do naught but accept my decision.'

Lady Dorchester thoughtfully stirred her tea. 'Well, it is your decision to make, of course, but I cannot help but feel that you have been a trifle rash. Only think what people will say when word of this gets out.'

'I do not care what people say,' Nicola asserted glumly. '*They* do not have to live with Lord Blackwood, *I* do. Or, rather, I would have, had I been unfortunate enough to have married him.'

'Yes, well, I am sure there will be more than enough young ladies anxious to step into the position you have so thoughtfully left vacant,' Lady Dorchester murmured. 'However, if your mind is made up, I suppose there is nothing for it but to get on with things.' Setting down her cup, she reached for the invitation lying on the table beside her. 'I had not planned on attending Lady Ramsland's musicale, but given the circumstances I think it would be a good idea.'

Nicola frowned. 'Why? I thought you couldn't abide Lady Ramsland.'

'I can't, but by the time the musicale arrives news of your rift with Lord Blackwood will have circulated, and the gossip will be frightful. For that reason alone, it is imperative that you attend. People are always curious about this sort of thing, Nicola, and it is best that you be there to put on a brave face, rather than have them believe you are hiding out here at Wyndham.'

'Aunt Glynnis, I have already said that I do not care what Society thinks,' Nicola reiterated in a flat voice. 'It is entirely my business whether I choose to marry Lord Blackwood or not.'

'Of course it is, dear, but we cannot ignore the fact that, since you have chosen *not* to marry him, you are once again an eligible young lady, and one far too lovely to remain unwed. It is essential that you start circulating again.'

'I have no desire to circulate,' Nicola replied mumpishly.

'That is neither here nor there. People—especially gentlemen—must not be allowed to think that you are going into a decline.'

'But what if Lord Blackwood is in attendance?' Nicola

asked, not at all happy about this plan of her aunt's. 'Have you any idea how difficult that is going to be?'

Lady Dorchester shrugged, and set the invitation aside. 'So much the better. It will be good for your reputation if you can be seen to deal amicably with him. There will be speculation aplenty as to what went wrong, and there will be those hoping to see you go into that decline I just mentioned. But you must never let them know what you are feeling inside,' Lady Dorchester said, in as encouraging a tone as she could manage. 'No matter what the state of the heart, the smile must remain. Now, shall I tell Lady Ramsland that we will be two?'

'I say, David, steady on!' Sir Giles protested as his nephew tagged him yet again. 'I am not as young as you, and I was never as nimble. If you are going to play the game at this level, I fear I shall have to insist that you find a fitter and more agile opponent to do it with.'

David sighed, and guiltily lowered his foil. 'Sorry, Uncle Giles, didn't mean to wind you.' He slid the fencing mask back and ran his hand through the dark curls that were now glossy with sweat. 'I seem to be harbouring more aggression than usual. Can't think why.'

'Well, I can,' Sir Giles drawled, likewise removing his mask. 'You've been blue-devilled ever since Lady Nicola broke off your engagement—and don't try to tell me you haven't, because I know you too well. And I am telling you straight out, this simply cannot go on.'

'I have no idea what you're talking about,' David growled. 'I am not blue-devilled, and the fact that Lady Nicola has decided that we would not suit has certainly not given me cause for despair. In fact, I should be relieved at her crying off. I told you the reasons for my marrying, and it had nothing to do with falling head over heels in love. If Lady Nicola does not wish me for a husband, I shall find someone else who does—and who will meet my requirements a damn sight better than she did!'

'Then why aren't you socializing?' Sir Giles replied promptly.

'I am.'

'Balderdash! I am not talking about tipping your hat to ladies in the street,' Sir Giles said in exasperation. 'I am talking about attending elaborate social functions planned for the purpose of ensnaring eligible young gentlemen like you in the sticky nets of matrimony.'

David grunted, but made no reply.

'Very well, since it is obvious that I am going to have to force you into this,' Sir Giles said regretfully, 'you may as well know that I have told Lady Ramsland that we will be in attendance at her musicale tomorrow evening.'

'You did *what*?' A shadow of annoyance darkened David's face. 'You know very well that I cannot abide musicales *or* Lady Ramsland.'

'I know, but I did it for your own good, dear boy. And I shall make it easy on you,' Sir Giles added, by way of a compromise. 'You need not stay until the wee hours of the morning, nor do I ask that you speak to every eligible lady present. I merely ask that you attend.'

'Why?'

'Because there are all manner of rumours floating around with regard to what went wrong between you and Lady Nicola. Some are saying that *you* broke off the engagement out of embarrassment over her behaviour with the fox, while others are speculating that Lady Nicola chose to end it herself because you spoke to her so…'

David glanced at him sharply. 'So…what?'

'So…imperiously.'

'The lady was all but hanging from a tree! Can you blame me for speaking my mind in a somewhat…forceful manner?'

'That is not for me to say,' Sir Giles replied with equanimity. 'All I am saying is that, if you do not make an effort to show your face in Society, the stories that you are miserably pining away are going to receive more and more credibility. It is much like riding a horse, my boy. When you fall off, you get back on, and as quickly as possible—before the damage has a chance to set in.'

'Damage?' David frowned. 'What are you talking about, Uncle, what damage?'

'The damage this could do to your reputation.'

'My reputation? Surely you jest?'

'I assure you, I do not.'

'But…what possible impact could this have on my reputation? What are people saying?'

'Well, there are two factions, actually,' Sir Giles informed him. 'The one side are saying that you are nursing a broken heart as a result of Lady Nicola tearfully ending your betrothal—'

'The devil!'

'The other speculates that *you* were the one to call off the engagement as a result of the lady's unacceptable conduct, and that you are avoiding Society functions for fear of encountering Lady Nicola and being taken to task *by her* for what she considers to be unjust treatment.'

'The hell I—!'

'And *both* parties are speculating that neither you nor Lady Nicola will be able to conduct yourselves civilly upon the occasion of your first meeting.'

David's eyes widened in anger and disbelief. 'You can't be serious!'

'I believe the betting at White's has it two to one in

favour of the latter. Of course, not everyone is sorry to hear about the split,' Sir Giles added casually. 'I understand Humphrey O'Donnell is delighted.'

'O'Donnell!' Blackwood's dark brows snapped together in a fierce line. 'Well, we shall see about that. *And* about these ridiculous rumours. Not able to be in the same room as Nicola, indeed. I shall set them all straight in a very short time,' David growled ominously. 'What time are we expected at Lady Ramsland's?'

It was with considerable trepidation that Nicola climbed down from the carriage in front of the sprawling Elizabethan home of Lord and Lady Ramsland three evenings hence. She had not seen or heard from Lord Blackwood since the afternoon they had parted, and, while she had assured herself that she was neither expectant nor desirous of doing so, the tumultuous beating of her heart told her otherwise.

'Courage, Nicki,' Lady Dorchester said unexpectedly. 'Show them fear and they will feast upon it, but show them poise and they will stand in awe of it. As long as you have no regrets about your decision—'

'None whatsoever,' Nicola said defiantly.

'Good. Then you have nothing to worry about. Just hold your head up high, and look on this as one more tedious Society function which must be endured.'

At the same time, David was sitting back against the velvet squabs of his carriage as it rumbled towards Lord and Lady Ramsland's house on the outskirts of London, and wondering why he had agreed to attend the function in the first place. He didn't like musicales, and he liked Lady Ramsland even less. She had three exceedingly homely daughters, all of whom were still at home and all of whom were desperately seeking husbands. And Lady Ramsland had made him the target of her matchmaking attempts on more than one occasion. Which was why David usually endeavoured to avoid any and all functions at which he knew the Ramsland girls would be in attendance.

So why had he agreed to place himself in the heart of the lion's den now?

The carriage was not making record time, but for once David wasn't perturbed. It was probably better that he arrive late anyway. As this would be the first social occasion he had attended since he and Nicola had ended their betrothal, it was important that he not give people the impression that he was anxious to see her again. Conversely, he did not wish his tardiness to be interpreted as reluctance to meet with her either. He must be seen to be in total control of his emotions and of the situation. Which, he assured himself, he was.

Consequently, when he finally arrived at the Ramsland mansion and made his way towards his host and hostess, David pretended not to hear the murmur of surprise that rippled through the gathered assembly. Indeed, with a sardonic smile on his face, he strolled through the room as though nothing were amiss, greeting Lord Ramsland, and bowing over the hand of his hostess as though he hadn't a care in the world. 'Lady Ramsland, you are looking very well this evening.'

Realizing what a coup she had achieved by Blackwood's unexpected attendance at her gathering, Lady Ramsland's greeting was both effusive and prolonged. 'You are *too* kind, Lord Blackwood. And may I say what a *pleasure* it is to see you. I had hoped that you might grace us with your presence this evening, but, of course, given the variety of entertainments open to a gentleman such as yourself, one can never be too sure.'

'I was delighted to receive an invitation,' David lied blandly. 'Your daughters are all well?'

'All enjoying the most excellent health, thank you,' Lady Ramsland crowed, casting about for the whereabouts of her eldest daughter even as she spoke. 'Eudora will be delighted to see you. And I dare say you will scarce recognize our Clementia,' Lady Ramsland continued, well aware that it wasn't the thing to promote her youngest daughter over her eldest, except that, of the three girls, Clementia was the least homely and the only one likely to catch the eye of a nonpareil like Blackwood. 'She is as lovely and as prettily behaved as any mother could wish. I am sure I could find her for you if you—'

'Pray do not trouble yourself, Lady Ramsland,' David remarked urbanely. 'No doubt I shall cross paths with all of them throughout the course of the evening.'

David bowed and moved off, anxious to find more congenial company in which to spend the hour or two his uncle had required of him in the reclamation of his reputation. Or, as more accurately might be the case, in the convincing of Society that he was neither pining for nor going in fear of Nicola. Perhaps that was why he was perceived as being a touch more affable to the young ladies in the room than he had been known to be in the past. He circulated, as he was supposed to, he socialized, as he was expected to, and he smiled, when he chose to. Consequently, more than one doting mama was sure that she had observed Lord Blackwood spending a little extra time with her Dora, or paying prettier compliments to her Elizabeth, or her Mary.

Truth was, David had eyes for none of them. Because there was only one woman he was looking for. And when he finally saw her, standing against the far wall with Lady Dorchester, and looking, if possible, even more beautiful than he remembered, David knew that there could never be anybody else.

He also realized that he should never have come.

'David, my boy, glad to see you,' Sir Giles said, suddenly appearing at his side.

David quickly turned away from his study of Nicola, and affected a casual stance. 'Did you expect me to back down?'

'To tell the truth, I wasn't sure what you would do,' Sir Giles admitted. 'Since I know full well that I bullied you into coming tonight.'

A smile worked its way to David's mouth as he realized that his uncle was gruffly offering him an apology. 'You did not bully me, Uncle. What you did, you did out of concern for me. And you may be quite sure that, had I been totally dead set against coming, nothing you could have said or done would have made any difference.'

'You're probably right. Still, you're here now and that's the main thing. So, have you seen anyone of interest?' the baronet enquired casually. 'I thought Lady Warden's daughter was looking quite the thing tonight.'

'Yes, if only she didn't have that unfortunate tendency to bray.'

'Mmm, very apt description,' Sir Giles agreed. He rocked back on his heels and surveyed the room. 'The Ramsland girls are looking…better, don't you think?'

'Better than what?'

'Ah, just so,' Sir Giles agreed. He turned and made another leisurely perusal of the room, and then finally began to smile. 'So, she *did* come.'

'Who?'

'Lady Nicola. And in the company of her charming aunt. Shall we pay our respects and get it over with?'

David stiffened slightly. 'As you wish.'

Nicola sensed rather than saw David coming. There was a discernible drop in the level of conversation all around her, and she caught a number of surreptitious glances being cast her way. It seemed that the long-awaited meeting was about to take place.

Nicola glanced quickly at her aunt, saw her brief nod of encouragement, and then, with a practised flick of her wrist, opened her fan and turned to greet her former fiancé.

'Good evening, Lord Blackwood.'

'Lady Nicola.' David bowed formally from the waist. Her voice had been reserved but not cool. He decided to take that as a good omen. 'Lady Dorchester. May I say that you are looking exceedingly well this evening.'

'We both thank you for your kindness, Lord Blackwood,' Lady Dorchester said serenely.

Grateful that her aunt had included her in the response, Nicola turned to greet David's uncle. 'Sir Giles, how very nice to see you again.'

'The pleasure is all mine, Lady Nicola,' said Sir Giles. 'And my dear Lady Dorchester, what a pleasure to find you in attendance this evening. It is a crush, is it not?'

'I dare say Lady Ramsland has invited half of London,' Lady Dorchester agreed. 'But then, she usually does.'

David tried not to let his eyes stray back to Nicola, but found it was impossible not to. In a simple but elegant white gown she was, quite simply, breathtaking. Her complexion was pale, and there were faint violet shadows under those glorious green eyes, but to him she was still the most beautiful woman in the room.

'Did Lord Wyndham not accompany you this evening?' he enquired politely.

'Unfortunately not. Papa decided to stay at home, so Aunt Glynnis kindly invited me to stay with her at Doring Cross for the night, since it is closer,' Nicola replied with all cordiality.

'And who is looking after your pets?' Sir Giles asked innocently.

Nicola heard her aunt's gasp of dismay and saw the flush which darkened Lord Blackwood's face, but managed to say, with admirable calm, 'They are being tended by a most capable lad who is almost as attached to them as I.'

'Ah, that would be the young Jamie I heard mentioned in regard to…what was the falcon's name?'

'Guinevere,' Nicola replied weakly.

'Yes, that's right, Guinevere. Charming name. Is she on the mend?'

Nicola didn't know whether to laugh or cry. Surely Sir Giles was aware of the nature of the problem which had forced an end to her betrothal to Lord Blackwood in the first place? 'She is…coming along nicely, thank you, Sir Giles.'

Thankfully, it was her aunt who finally came to her rescue. 'I do believe the evening's entertainment is about to commence, Nicola. Lady Ramsland is signalling for people to move into the music room. Lord Blackwood, Sir Giles, would you excuse us?'

'By all means,' Sir Giles said with a definite twinkle in his eye. 'Can't have us monopolizing the two loveliest ladies in the room all evening, can we?'

Lady Dorchester valiantly hid a smile while Nicola vigorously applied her fan to her burning cheeks. She did not look at Lord Blackwood as they took their leave. When they were far enough away not to be overheard, however, she placed a gloved hand on her aunt's arm and whispered, 'Dear Aunt Glynn, thank you so much for coming to my rescue. I cannot imagine what possessed Sir Giles to bring up such a topic. Surely he must know of the trouble it caused between Lord Blackwood and myself.'

'I confess, I was rather surprised at his choice of subject,' Lady Dorchester agreed with a delicate frown, 'though I do not believe there was any malicious intent behind it. I think Sir Giles is simply an honest man who is sometimes lacking in diplomacy. I know he holds you in the highest regard, Nicola, and he did seem genuinely concerned about the welfare of your animals.'

'Yes. Pity his nephew does not share his sentiments,' Nicola replied distantly. 'Somehow I cannot see Sir Giles taking exception to my keeping a mouse in my chamber.'

'I should not push it *that* far, my dear,' Lady Dorchester said, laughing softly. 'After all, there are still rules which govern one's behaviour and—'

'Lady Nicola, excuse me, but…might I have a word?'

The interruption caused Lady Dorchester to frown, and Nicola to sigh. Was she not to have a moment's peace this evening?

'Good evening, Mr O'Donnell.'

'Lady Nicola, you look positively radiant this evening. Indeed, quite the most beautiful lady here,' O'Donnell said, then added, belatedly, 'Good evening, Lady Dorchester.'

'Mr O'Donnell,' Lady Dorchester said, her greeting noticeably less cordial than Nicola's had been. She glanced at her niece with a question in her eyes. 'Nicola?'

'You go on ahead, Aunt Glynn,' Nicola said, carefully concealing her impatience. 'I shall be along directly.'

'As you wish.' Lady Dorchester cast another less than

friendly glance in Mr O'Donnell's direction, but, knowing that it would make no difference, regally moved off to secure seats for the evening's performance.

The moment she did, Mr O'Donnell's smile grew more confident. 'My dearest Lady Nicola, I do hope you are recovered from that tragic incident in the woods. I have been so dreadfully concerned about you. Indeed, I thought to call at Wyndham Hall, but was not sure how I would be received.'

'I am quite recovered, thank you, Mr O'Donnell,' Nicola said, deciding not to venture an opinion as to the wisdom of his visiting, but heartily relieved that he had not. 'Though perhaps I should ask you the same. I am sure you did not expect to end up tearing across a field in pursuit of a fox when you asked if you could ride with me.'

'No, I admit, the ride didn't turn out quite as I had… anticipated,' O'Donnell acknowledged ruefully, 'but now, of course, I understand that it was all in a most worthy cause. Did…Adrian ever come back?'

'Alistair. And no, he did not,' Nicola said, suddenly wishing that Mr O'Donnell would go away and leave her alone. 'I fear the shock of being hunted by a pack of dogs brought his instincts for survival to the fore. No doubt he is long gone.'

'Ah. Well, yes, I suppose these things do happen,' O'Donnell said, avoiding her eyes.

Nicola waited, sure that Mr O'Donnell wished to express his feelings about something, but when the silence dragged on she offered him a half-hearted smile. 'Well, I think I should rejoin my aunt—'

'Lady Nicola, is it true that you…that is, that Lord Blackwood has…I mean, is your betrothal to Lord Blackwood really at an end?' O'Donnell cried.

Nicola blinked and quickly glanced away.

'Forgive me, I didn't mean to discomfort you,' he said, 'but I did want to know—to hear from your own lips— that it was over between the two of you.'

Swallowing the despair that rose in her throat, Nicola forced herself to say, 'Yes, it is…over. I came to the conclusion that…we should not suit.'

Then why was she still having so much trouble admitting it?

'Perhaps it was not so much a case of Lord Blackwood not suiting you, as your not suiting him,' said the smug voice of Arabella Braithwaite.

Nicola flushed as she turned to see Arabella regarding her with an expression of thinly veiled triumph. She brought the blades of her fan together with a snap. 'I would prefer not to discuss the subject, Mrs Braithwaite,' she said frostily.

'But why not? Surely you are not embarrassed about it?'

'Not in the least. I simply do not believe it to be an appropriate topic for conversation.'

'Oh, now, that is good,' Arabella said, smiling up at Mr O'Donnell. 'Lady Nicola Wyndham telling *me* what is and is not appropriate behaviour. Do you not think that a little feeble coming from a woman who picks up mice in her bare hands, and carries hunting falcons around on her arm?'

O'Donnell went quite pale. 'I'm sure I don't know—'

'To say nothing of her risking life, limb, and reputation, to rescue a fox,' Arabella sneered. 'Come now, Lady Nicola, you must realize how…inappropriate the objection sounds, coming from someone like yourself. Had you acted a little more circumspectly when you were engaged to Lord Blackwood, there might still be some hope of

your becoming the next marchioness. Though, if you recall, I did offer to help you in that regard.'

Nicola swallowed hard, trying not to reveal how angry
she truly was. 'And as I recall, Mrs Braithwaite, I told
you that I did not need or want your help.'

'Yes, I do recall. Which is no doubt why you and Lord
Blackwood are no longer betrothed,' she retorted sca-
thingly. 'From where I stand, Lady Nicola, it seems to me
that my help might have done you some good.' And, without another word, Arabella turned and walked away.

Beside her, Mr O'Donnell noisily cleared his throat.
'M-may I secure a glass of ratafia for you, Lady Nicola?'

Nicola nodded, thankful to be given a reason for spending a few precious moments alone. She closed her eyes
as he moved off in search of the promised refreshment,
and wondered if she had ever liked anyone less than Arabella Braithwaite.

'I see your gallant Mr O'Donnell is not letting the grass
grow under his feet,' David remarked mockingly.

Nicola stiffened, aware that the evening was going from
bad to worse. She hadn't noticed David walk across to
the room to join her—and was heartily displeased that he
had witnessed her brief conversation with Mr O'Donnell.

'He is not *my* Mr O'Donnell,' Nicola informed him
coldly. 'And he has merely gone to procure a glass of
ratafia for me, as any gentleman might offer to do for a
lady.'

David clamped down on his opinion of Mr O'Donnell's
gentlemanly graces, and offered her a tight smile. 'Of
course. Forgive me for supposing an interest where there
is none.'

Nicola glared at him. 'At least Mr O'Donnell is not
afraid to admit that he holds me in some regard, Lord
Blackwood,' she retorted. 'You hide behind your shield

of duty and devotion, and say that you *hope* such feelings might arise. Well, I can assure you, they are far more likely to occur where there is willingness of heart than prejudice of mind!'

A muscle jumped in David's cheek. He hadn't come here to argue with Nicola. He had come to show anyone in the room who doubted it that he was neither intimidated nor angered by her presence, and that he could converse with her in a totally civilized fashion.

Which was becoming harder and harder to do the longer he stood here!

Unfortunately, before he had a chance to retaliate, O'Donnell returned, carrying the promised glass of ratafia for Nicola and a glass of champagne for himself. David saw him hesitate for a moment, as if uncertain of his reception, but then, obviously deciding that *he* could not be the unwelcome one in the party, he continued to walk towards them with a swagger that set David's teeth on edge.

'Evening, Blackwood,' O'Donnell greeted him. 'Didn't expect to see you here this evening.'

'I can't think why,' David drawled. 'I received an invitation the same as everyone else.'

'Yes, but I thought you weren't socializing much these days. And I understood functions of this nature weren't to your liking. Your ratafia, Lady Nicola.'

Nicola accepted the glass, wishing that the floor would suddenly open up and swallow her.

'Thank you.'

'I am socializing as much as I ever did,' came David's bland reply.

'Yes, I suppose you would have to, now that Lady Nicola has rejected your suit.'

Nicola's cheeks flamed. 'Mr O'Donnell!'

'Do not trouble yourself with the gaping hole in Mr O'Donnell's education, Lady Nicola,' David said, his opinion of the young man's character confirmed. 'For I can assure you it is of no concern to me. However, you will understand if I choose not to linger in the present company. Good evening.'

David walked away, cursing fluently and vehemently under his breath. Idiot! What anyone could see in a thatch-gallows like O'Donnell—least of all an intelligent woman like Nicola—he would never understand. Perhaps she had been correct in her conviction that they were ill suited to each other. If Nicola *could* be content in the company of a man such as that, truly they had nothing in common!

Nicola watched David's stiffly retreating figure and bit back the angry words that had been trembling on her lips ever since Mr O'Donnell had uttered that audacious comment a few moments ago, and wondered when this dismal evening would come to an end.

Was O'Donnell mad? No gentleman would speak of a broken engagement in such a manner—and certainly not in front of both parties. What in the world must David think of her for spending time in the company of such a coxcomb?

Unfortunately, it appeared that Mr O'Donnell was of the impression that he had done her a considerable favour. 'Well, I doubt he will be troubling you again, Lady Nicola,' the young man said in a tone of supreme satisfaction. 'And I for one am glad.'

'Mr O'Donnell, for your information, Lord Blackwood was not troubling me. We were having a perfectly civil conversation before you returned,' said Nicola, forgetting for a moment that she had, in fact, been reprimanding

Lord Blackwood at the time, 'and I did not appreciate your ill-mannered comment.'

'But Lady Nicola, I only thought—'

'Yes, I know what you thought, Mr O'Donnell. You thought that because *I* admitted to being the one to break off the engagement I had also cast Lord Blackwood in the role of the villain. Well, that is not the case, and I would thank you not to trouble me again. Good evening, sir.'

Nicola marched back across the floor towards the music room, fuming at the pomposity of the entire male species. How irritating was their way of simply…assuming things. First David, high-handedly telling her how to behave, and then Mr O'Donnell, intimating that she needed his help. How arrogant they were! The only help she needed was in choosing the right man—something with which she had definitely *not* had any success to date!

'Well, thank goodness that's over!' Nicola exclaimed some hours later as the lights of the Ramsland mansion finally began to fade into the distance. 'I thought we would never be able to leave.'

'Yes, it was an exceedingly boring affair,' Lady Dorchester agreed. 'The tenor was dreadful, and Miss Howlett's skills on the harpsichord left a great deal to be desired. However, the evening did serve its purpose. You conducted yourself splendidly, my dear, and I am very proud of you.'

Nicola stared moodily out of the window. 'I managed to get through the evening, though I have my doubts as to how well I carried it off.'

'Nonsense, you did fine,' said Lady Dorchester. 'It was noted by everyone in attendance that you and Lord Blackwood enjoyed a few minutes of polite conversation before that odious Mr O'Donnell returned to monopolize you.'

'The conversation was hardly polite, nor was it enjoyable,' Nicola said, fiddling with the strings of her reticule. 'Indeed, I fell out with two gentlemen this evening, not just one.'

'Oh?'

'I ended up having words with Mr O'Donnell too.'

'Well, I hardly consider that a loss,' Lady Dorchester observed dryly. 'In my opinion, Mr O'Donnell was never a suitable companion for you.'

'Yes, but the only reason I had words with him was as a result of his shocking treatment of Lord Blackwood,' Nicola admitted wretchedly.

'Shocking?' Lady Dorchester glanced at her niece with renewed interest. 'Dear me, what ever did he say?'

'He said that…the only reason Lord Blackwood was in attendance at the musicale, was because he was once again looking for a wife now that *I* had refused him.'

'Gracious! Mr O'Donnell was ill mannered indeed to say such a thing.' Lady Dorchester turned away to hide her smile. 'You did well to put him in his place.'

'Yes, but now Lord Blackwood has some…misplaced notion that I was seeking Mr O'Donnell's company, and I had no opportunity for putting the matter straight.'

'But why should you care what Lord Blackwood thinks, my dear?' her aunt asked casually. 'Surely it is of no import to you any more?'

'It isn't. I do not care what Lord Blackwood thinks,' Nicola asserted defiantly. 'I just don't want him to believe—that is, I wouldn't like him thinking— Oh, botheration,' she said, returning her attention to the window in frustration. 'You are quite right, Aunt. What does it matter what anyone thinks any more? Lord Blackwood despises me, our engagement is over, and I sincerely wish that I had never come to this wretched gathering in the first place!'

Chapter Eleven

The next few days were not easy for Nicola. Once her feelings of anger had subsided, she was left with the bitter emptiness of despair. She tried to put on a brave face for her father and her aunt, but the strain of pretending to be happy took its toll. Especially when she awoke late one morning to the sound of the excited yapping of the hounds. She had completely forgotten about the hunt!

'Quickly, Maire, help me get ready,' Nicola said as she threw back the covers and jumped out of bed. While her maid attended to her clothes, Nicola cautiously moved towards the window and glanced down. There looked to be about twenty riders assembled in the courtyard below, and though she told herself she wasn't looking for anyone in particular Nicola knew differently. She was looking for David; and the realization that she was in love with him as much as ever brought the tears to her eyes once more.

In his cage on the window ledge, Arthur danced up on his back legs in an obvious attempt to catch her attention. Nicola glanced down at the little mouse with a sorrowful smile. 'Are you trying to distract me, Arthur? Because I fear it will take more than you to do that today, pet.'

A short while later, Nicola descended the main staircase, dressed in the rather plain, dove-grey habit that she had worn in the latter days of her mourning. It was a comfortable outfit, and one that Nicola liked to wear on these cooler mornings. Given the fact that she was late, however, and that everyone was already gathering in the courtyard, Nicola decided to wait until the field set off before calling for her own mount. She had no desire to walk out into the midst of the hunters, recalling all too painfully the humiliation of her last exposure to them. Instead, she sought the peaceful seclusion of the breakfast parlour, intending to partake of a light breakfast before heading for the stables.

Or so she thought. Upon opening the door, Nicola stopped dead at the sight of David sitting quietly at the table, his gaze focused on the window in front of him. 'Oh, I…beg your pardon.'

'*Nicola!*' The cup clattered to the saucer as David leapt to his feet. 'That is…forgive me, Lady Nicola, I was not expecting to see you this morning. Your father told me that you had…already ridden out.'

Tormented by a stream of confusing emotions, Nicola hesitated in the doorway, not sure whether to turn and flee, or to go forward and pretend indifference. Certainly the former would have been the easier, but she was not a coward by nature. Besides, there was nothing to be gained by it. Given their positions in Society, it was unrealistic to believe that their paths would not cross again.

'I…I slept late this morning,' Nicola stammered, 'and consequently thought I would…wait until everyone left before heading down to the stables.'

David's shadowed eyes skimmed over her face, noting the pallor in her cheeks and the shadows beneath her eyes, and he wished with all his heart that he could take her in his arms and beg her for another chance. But he could not. For he was too proud. And she too unforgiving.

'Have you breakfasted?' David asked at length. 'I could ring for fresh coffee.'

'No, that is…quite all right. I had a tray in my room,' Nicola lied.

The silence between them lengthened. From somewhere in the depths of the house, Nicola heard the sound of a door slam, and then her father's voice bellowing orders. Moments later, the door opened again and he walked into the parlour. 'Come along, Blackwood, the field's about ready to— Oh!'

Lord Wyndham broke off as he suddenly caught sight of his daughter standing off to one side. 'Nicola, my dear, what are you doing here? I thought you had already left.'

'I fear I am a little behind this morning, Papa,' she admitted. 'I came down thinking to wait until the field had gone before venturing out. I was not expecting to find Lord Blackwood already here.'

'A few minutes longer, and you would not have,' David said briefly. He turned to address Lord Wyndham. 'Are we ready, my lord?'

The brief flicker of hope which had appeared in Lord Wyndham's eyes at finding both his daughter and Lord Blackwood in the same room abruptly died as he realized that theirs was strictly an accidental meeting. 'Er, yes, that's why I came to get you.'

'Good. Then I shall be away.' David swallowed the rest of his coffee in one gulp, then sketched Nicola a brief bow before taking his leave.

After he had gone, Lord Wyndham sighed heavily. 'What a pity. For a moment there, I thought perhaps the two of you were talking over your differences.'

Nicola managed a weak smile. 'There is nothing to talk

over, Papa, since our differences are unlikely to be resolved.'

'Is it not worth the effort to try?'

Nicola studiously avoided her father's eyes. 'I do not
see that there is anything to be gained by it. I cannot be
the type of wife Lord Blackwood needs. He is looking for
a woman who will put duty to her title above all. Someone
who will not bring scandal to the name, whereas I have
already disgraced Lord Blackwood *three times* in public,
and am likely to do so again, given the differences in our
fundamental beliefs. What more is there to talk about?'

Lord Wyndham's brows drew together in a frown.
'There is more to marriage than…fundamental beliefs, Nicola. What about emotions? Are you telling me that you
haven't any feelings for the man?'

Thankfully, Trethewy chose that moment to intervene.
'Excuse me, my lord, but I believe they are waiting for
you.'

Lord Wyndham muttered something unintelligible, and
then reluctantly nodded. 'Very well. Tell them I shall be
there directly.'

When the door closed again, Lord Wyndham crossed
the room to stand in front of his daughter, and gazed down
at her with eyes that saw a great deal more than he let
on. 'Nicki, my dear, you are all I have left in the world,
you know that, don't you?'

'Yes, Papa.'

'Good, because I don't want you to misunderstand what
I'm about to say, but I think it important that you hear it.
I do not hold Lord Blackwood guilty for his treatment of
you that day in the woods.'

'Papa!'

'No, let me finish. I know that he spoke sharply to you,
but I believe it was solely as a result of his deep concern

for your safety. Lord Blackwood is a good and honourable man, and if the two of you are able to smooth things over and find happiness together I shall be very happy. However, if you truly believe that there is nothing left between you, and that you are happier this way, then that is fine with me too. Your happiness means more to me than anything else in the world, my dear, and I would not wish to see you compromise that happiness for anything.'

Nicola slipped into his arms, her heart aching as she pressed her face into his shoulder. 'Thank you, Papa.'

'These things are never easy, my dear, but they do pass.' He held her close a moment longer, before gently putting her away. 'Now, I'd best be off before they start raising a hue and cry!'

'Papa, if by chance you happened to see…Alistair on one of your hunts, you would not…?'

Lord Wyndham sighed. 'No, Nicki. As unpopular as it would surely make me, I would not allow the hunt to continue. In fact, short of climbing a tree myself, I would do everything I could to spare him.'

A reluctant smile tipped the corners of her mouth. 'Thank you, Papa. It is all I can ask.'

'Now, go and enjoy your ride. And this time do not venture out without suitable accompaniment. I have no desire to witness a repeat of that unfortunate episode with Mr O'Donnell.'

Nicola laughed. 'Rest assured, Papa, I have learned my lesson. I will not ride out unescorted again.'

As soon as the field set off, Nicola made her way down to the stables, surprised to find that Roberts had already saddled Nightingale, and that Jenkins was waiting to accompany her. Obviously Lord Wyndham was taking no chances.

Roberts also told her that, according to Widgin, the hunt would be sticking close to the river valley today, which left Nicola free to roam the upper pastures. This she did for nearly an hour, letting the mare have her head to gallop unchecked over the fields. But her hopes that the exercise might help to clear her troubled mind were destined to be disappointed, and she finally slowed the mare to a walk. It seemed that nothing had the power to do that. Try as she might, thoughts of David kept intruding, as well as questions about everything that had happened between them.

Was he happy with the way things stood now? Nicola wondered sadly. It was hard to tell. He hadn't seemed overly despondent when she had bumped into him in the breakfast parlour this morning. Startled, yes, but that probably had more to do with her timing than it did with any feelings of regret he might have suffered upon seeing her.

No, more than likely, David had resented her intrusion into what would otherwise have been a quiet period of rest before the hunt.

A tiny rabbit, startled by the sound of the approaching horse and rider, dashed across the field and disappeared into a small clump of bushes off to her left. Nicola smiled, suddenly envying the rabbit the simplicity of his life. He suffered no emotional upheaval because he wasn't loved. His happiness was not compromised because he didn't observe the rules and restrictions imposed upon him by Society. All he cared about was eating, sleeping and staying alive.

Somehow, it seemed a much simpler philosophy all round.

Immersed in the depths of her thoughts, Nicola did not at first notice the horse and rider standing in the field below. They were very close to the fence and were all but hidden by the lower branches of a thick tree. But when Nicola heard the sharp crack of a whip, followed by the terrified whinnying of an animal in pain, all other thoughts disappeared. She gathered the reins in her hands and quickly urged her mare in their direction, signalling Jenkins to follow behind.

It didn't take long for Nicola to see what was happening. The rider was beating what was obviously a very expensive horse. But what was even more horrifying to Nicola was the realization that the person cruelly raining lashes upon the poor animal was a woman.

'Hold there,' Nicola shouted as soon as she came within range. 'Stop that at once! Do you hear me?'

The woman raised her arm and struck the animal again, totally oblivious to the warning. The mare, which was securely tethered to the fence, shied and bucked violently, pulling hard at the reins in an attempt to free herself. But it was to no avail. The whip was rising again.

'I said stop!' Nicola shouted, shock turning to fury as she saw the angry welts rising on the horse's rump and withers. 'You're hurting her.'

'I'll do a damn sight more than hurt her if she doesn't start minding what I say!'

Had she been less angry, Nicola might have recognized the woman's voice, but, as it was, she was more concerned with getting the whip out of her hand than she was at discovering her identity. She slid out of the saddle as Nightingale came to a prancing halt and ran up behind the woman, wrestling with her for the whip. 'I said…no more!'

'How dare you?' the woman shouted in outrage. 'This is none of your…concern!'

Nicola wasn't sure what happened next. She might have been pushed, or she might simply have trodden on the hem of her gown. Either way, she stumbled—giving her adversary the time she needed. The woman turned around, and, with no sign of remorse at all, brought the whip down with vicious force across the back of Nicola's gloved hand. 'There. That will teach you to meddle in other people's business, my girl!'

Nicola screamed, recoiling in pain and horror. She had never been struck by anyone in her life, and certainly not by a woman. As the tears sprang to her eyes, she glanced up at her assailant—who was already turning back towards her horse—and blanched.

The woman was none other than Arabella Braithwaite!

In seconds, Jenkins was at his mistress's side. 'Lady Nicola, are you all right?'

'Lady Nicola!' Arabella spun around, shock draining the blood from her cheeks as she realized that the meddlesome creature she had struck was not a girl from the village at all, but the very woman who had taken David from her. She had been momentarily fooled by the plain grey habit. 'My God, am I never to be rid of you?' she spat contemptuously.

The throbbing in her hand was making Nicola feel light-headed, but she gulped a few deep breaths of air and willed herself not to pass out. 'Why were you…flogging your mare?'

'Because she required discipline.'

The words were uttered so callously that Nicola felt as though she had been struck again. 'Drawing blood is hardly disciplining, Mrs Braithwaite. I would call it beating.'

'Yes, well, unlike you, I believe that animals have their place,' Arabella told her haughtily. 'This one has a vicious temper and she needs to be taught. She will not refuse a jump again.'

Nicola glanced at the skittish mare. Her sides were lathered and there was foam on her bit, but her eyes weren't rolling, nor were her ears laid back flat against her head. 'Your mare has no more temper than my own,' Nicola informed the woman frigidly. 'Perhaps it is your lack of skill in the saddle which has caused her to rebel.'

Two bright spots of colour stood out on Arabella's white cheeks as she angrily stamped her foot. 'I am a superb rider, and I would thank you to mind your own business. She has been fidgety all morning, and has kept me behind the rest of the hunt.'

Nicola slowly walked towards the tethered mare.

'What do you think you're doing?' Arabella demanded. 'Get away from my horse.'

Nicola ignored her, but hesitated when the mare suddenly pulled away and laid her ears back flat against her head.

'There, you see!' Arabella said triumphantly. 'I told you she was vicious!'

Nicola watched the horse for a moment longer, and then sadly shook her head. 'Those aren't the actions of a vicious horse. This animal is terrified and I would advise you to step away from her.'

'I beg your—'

'I said, step away!'

There was no mistaking the anger in Nicola's voice, and, for the first time, Arabella faltered. 'You've no right to talk to me that way. I shall tell David.'

'I don't care a fig what you do, Mrs Braithwaite,' Nicola replied in an angry whisper. 'The only thing I care about is your mare. And if you do not step away from her I shall have my groom pick you up and physically remove you!'

'You would not dare!'

Nicola glanced at the waiting groom and nodded. 'Jenkins, would you kindly remove Mrs Braithwaite?'

'With pleasure, my lady.'

'All right, all right!' Arabella cried, hastily stepping back as the groom took a step forward. 'But I am warning you, Lady Nicola, that horse in none of your concern!'

Clearly untroubled by the woman's threats, Nicola turned back towards the mare, who was now standing quietly, albeit guardedly, beside the fence, watching her. 'All right, girl, easy there,' Nicola said softly. 'I'm not going to hurt you. I just want to have a look.'

Moving slowly and patiently, Nicola approached the frightened horse, all the while keeping a watchful eye on the animal's powerful hindquarters. She'd seen a strong man knocked unconscious by a kick from legs like that and she knew how fast it could happen. 'That's it, easy now. Easy, that's my girl.'

Not surprisingly, the mare responded well to the sound of Nicola's voice, and her ears pricked forward, confirming Nicola's opinion that the horse was not vicious at all. When she was close enough to touch her, Nicola ran her good hand gently along the mare's sides. She could feel the heat rising from her body, and a sudden, uncontrollable trembling as her hand moved closer to the saddle.

Nicola suddenly wished that she could take a whip to the arrogant Mrs Braithwaite herself! Perhaps that would make her think twice before lashing a harmless animal.

'I don't know what you're trying to prove,' Arabella taunted. 'A bad-tempered horse can't be cured.'

Nicola ignored her. Her hand was close to the saddle now and the mare was pulling away more vigorously. Was the saddle itself the source of the irritation? Or something which lay beneath it?

Carefully, Nicola reached under the horse's belly and

loosened the girth. It was an awkward thing to do with only one good hand, and in the end she had to ask Jenkins for his help. But within a matter of moments she had her answer.

'This is what has been causing your mare to fidget, Mrs Braithwaite,' Nicola said, holding out a large clump of prickly burrs which had been embedded in the blanket under the saddle. 'She is neither bad-tempered nor difficult, and had you spared a little more time and attention to her you would have found that out.'

Arabella glanced at the handful of burrs and laughed. 'Well, well, so the Lady Nicola comes to the rescue again. It seems your time would have been better spent cultivating the affections of a veterinarian, my dear. Certainly, he would be in a better position to appreciate your unique talents.'

Nicola flushed at the mocking tone, but offered no reply. There wasn't even a pretence of affability in Arabella's manner now. It was clear, since Nicola was no longer betrothed to the Marquis of Blackwood, that she obviously deserved no special recognition from the marquis's cousin.

Nicola glanced down at angry welts on the chestnut's withers and felt anger rise anew. 'You should have your groom see to those gashes as soon as possible, Mrs Braithwaite. Left unchecked they will fester and you will find yourself with a much bigger problem than burrs under the saddle.'

Deciding that it would not be prudent to ask Nicola's groom for assistance, Arabella led the now docile mare to a nearby tree stump, and mounted. 'Thank you for the advice. I shall be sure to tell him that the Witch of Wyndham Hall told me to do so.'

Nicola's cheeks flamed, but once again she let the insult

go. Nothing would be gained by retaliating in kind. She understood now exactly what kind of person Arabella was.

'She is a fine animal, Mrs Braithwaite,' was all Nicola would say. 'It would be a shame to see her scarred.'

Arabella's smile flashed like the sharp edge of a dagger. 'Spare me your lectures, Lady Nicola. A horse is like any other commodity. If it fails to serve, it can easily be replaced. In fact, I am sure David would buy me a new one tomorrow, if I so desired. He has been most considerate in his attentions to me of late,' she gloated. 'But then, unlike you, I know *exactly* how to behave around him, and how to get what I want.'

Nicola heard the note of triumph in Arabella's voice, and suddenly all she wanted to do was to go home. Her hand was throbbing, and she felt sick to death over the entire affair.

She slowly walked back to where Jenkins stood holding Nightingale, and with his assistance, and mindful of her injury, carefully climbed into the saddle. 'Yes, I am sure that you do, Mrs Braithwaite. However, I am not concerned with your relationship with Lord Blackwood, or with the welfare of your *next* horse. I am concerned with the welfare of this one. And if I ever see you whipping it again, or any other creature for that matter, I shall see to it that you never hunt in this county again.'

'You don't frighten me,' Arabella retaliated spitefully. 'I know why you and David broke up, and I'm glad, because you don't deserve him. You and those stupid animals. And if you're harbouring any thoughts of a reconciliation between the two of you I would advise you to put it out of your mind. David was very explicit when he told me what he thought of your conduct. And I can assure you, Lady Nicola, none of it was flattering.'

And then, pressing her heel sharply into the mare's side, Arabella rode away.

Breathing a heavy sigh, Nicola set off for home too, so disgusted with the woman's conduct that she could scarcely see straight. But it was her comments with regard to David that hurt Nicola the most. It was obvious now that her behaviour with Mr O'Donnell at the musicale had served to destroy whatever remaining affection David might have felt for her.

It seemed that their relationship was well and truly over.

Nicola decided not to tell anyone how she had come by her injury. For one thing, she did not care to admit to the world at large that she and Arabella Braithwaite had come to blows. It seemed so…sordid. And, given that Nicola already had a reputation for eccentricity when it came to animals, she had no doubt that if the story leaked out Arabella would twist it around so as to make her part in the proceedings sound even more bizarre. For that reason, Nicola decided that she would just have to keep the injury out of sight as much as possible.

Unfortunately, she reckoned without the sharp little eyes of her maid.

'Oh, my lady, your poor hand!' Maire exclaimed. 'How ever did you come to give yourself such a nasty injury?'

It did look severe, Nicola was forced to admit. She had eased the buttery soft leather glove down from her wrist to expose an ugly red wound, the skin all around it having already turned a dark blackish blue. There were even flecks of dried blood where the whip had cut into the skin. Nicola hated to think how bad it would have been had she not been wearing a glove.

'I'm afraid I was rather…careless this morning, Maire,'

she said, hoping that the lie sounded better to the maid's ears than it did to her own. 'I wasn't watching where I was going and hit it against a gate post as I passed through.'

'Well, we had better see to it straight away,' her abigail said promptly. 'We wouldn't want it leaving a mark on your lovely fair skin.'

Feeling of a like mind, Nicola allowed her maid to minister to her hand, wincing as she dabbed away the dried blood with a wet cloth. She knew that the girl was being as gentle as she could, but, even so, it took very little to set the hand to throbbing.

'This is one of my mum's remedies,' Maire told her as she applied a salve. 'She used it on all eight of us when we were growing up. Swears it's the only reason I don't have scars on my knees and my elbows now.'

Nicola smiled, then smothered a cry of pain as Maire began to wrap a length of clean gauze around the injury. 'Will it prevent my hand from…swelling any further?' she gasped.

'It should,' Maire said, carefully fastening the gauze. 'But it's going to be tender for a while. I doubt you'll be able to wear your gloves to Lord and Lady Bently's ball tomorrow night, my lady.'

That was the least of her worries, Nicola thought narrowly. She was far more concerned about how she was going to explain the injury to her father and Aunt Glynnis than to a room full of strangers.

Unfortunately, Maire's words turned out to be all too true. By the following morning, Nicola's hand had stopped swelling, but she could scarce credit the number of times it pained her, even when attempting to do the most simple of things. And needlework became a positive chore. 'Oh, bother!' Nicola said at last, all but flinging the tambour aside. 'This hand is the most dreadful nuisance. I am sick to death of it.'

'Now, dear, you must give it time to heal,' Lady Dorchester cautioned. 'Maire's salve can only do so much.'

'I suppose.' Nicola sighed. 'I had no idea how much I took my hands for granted.'

'Of course not, because I doubt you have ever had such a nasty cut on them before,' Lady Dorchester scolded. 'Indeed, how you came to deal yourself such a dreadful injury, I shall never know. Gently reared young ladies do not ride pell-mell through the countryside, throwing aside caution and care, and flinging themselves against gate posts.'

'It was not the manner in which I was riding that caused the accident, Aunt Glynn,' Nicola murmured, detesting the fact that she had to lie to her aunt about the cause of the injury. 'It was because I was not paying sufficient attention to where I was going.'

'Mmm. And might *that* not have had something to do with the fact that you came upon Lord Blackwood in the breakfast parlour yesterday morning?' her aunt enquired innocently.

Nicola flushed. 'I assure you, it had nothing to do with Lord Blackwood whatsoever. It is of no concern to me whether I see him or not.'

'No, of course not.' Lady Dorchester put down her own tambour and studied her niece's hand. 'Well, I suppose that is of secondary importance at the moment. Right now, we must concern ourselves with your injury. We cannot have you walking around Lord and Lady Bently's this evening with a bandage on your hand. People are bound to ask what happened, and those who don't may put their own interpretation on it. And with the memory of your last injury still fresh in their minds I don't like to think what those interpretations might be.'

'No doubt they will be wondering which of my pets had a go at me this time.' Nicola gazed down at her hand and her smile faded. 'I had hoped that the swelling might have gone down enough for me to wear my gloves, but when I tried one on this morning I could not even pull it up over my fingers.'

'Then you shall have to wear one of mine,' Lady Dorchester offered. 'I am one glove size larger than you, and though the fit may still be a touch uncomfortable at least it will not restrict movement. And it will keep the sight of that bandage away from prying eyes.'

'Thank you, Aunt Glynn, that will be perfect. Then all I shall have to worry about is the occasional gentleman wishing to press my hand.'

'Simply offer them the other one. I am sure they will not mind which hand they kiss, so long as it is one of them.'

'*If* there are any gentlemen wishing to kiss them at all,' Nicola pointed out ruefully. 'After the debacle with Arthur in the drawing room and Alistair in the woods, I seriously doubt any gentleman of breeding is going to risk an association with me.'

'Tosh, you are a beautiful woman. And, more than that, you have a warm and loving nature. Any gentleman of breeding who cannot see that is blind and does not deserve you to begin with.'

'There is always Mr O'Donnell.'

Her aunt sniffed disdainfully. 'I do not consider Mr O'Donnell a gentleman of breeding. He cannot hold a candle to—'

'Thank you, Aunt,' Nicola interrupted quickly, 'but I would rather not hear that name mentioned again. It is enough that I have to live with the memory of what passed between us, let alone hear him held up as the model by which I should compare all others. The gentleman and I simply did not suit. It is…better this way.'

Chapter Twelve

Unfortunately, upon their arrival at Lord and Lady Bently's ballroom that evening, Nicola was hard-pressed not to seek David out before anyone else. Her eyes, seemingly of their own accord, sought his handsome face from amongst all the others. Which was silly, given that he likely wasn't even in attendance. Since the night of Lady Ramsland's musicale, Blackwood had been conspicuous; not by his presence at Society functions, but by his absence from them.

'Heavens, what a crush,' Lady Dorchester gasped as they inched their way through the crowded assembly rooms. 'I vow Henrietta has invited everyone she knows along with a few hundred she doesn't.'

Nicola was inclined to agree. She had already been bumped and jostled so much that her head *and* her hand were beginning to pound painfully. 'Never mind. We can stay as long as is polite and then take our leave. I am quite sure Lady Bently will not miss—'

And then she saw him, standing alone at the far edge of the room.

For a moment, it was as though Nicola's entire being was filled with a curious sense of…waiting. David's dark hair glistened like jet in the moonlight, and as he raised a glass to his lips and gazed around the room she felt her heart begin to beat uncomfortably fast.

He is nothing to me, Nicola reminded herself, desperately needing to believe it. *He shuns that which I hold dear. Our interests are completely different. Not to mention the fact that I have already disgraced him horribly.*

It was that thought more than the others which brought the blood rushing to Nicola's cheeks, and she quickly opened her fan. Unfortunately, it was also the movement which caused Blackwood to turn his head and look at her. And for those few, brief moments it was as though all the noise and the heat faded into the background, and they were two alone in a room full of people.

David had not been aware of Nicola's advent into the room. Since his own arrival at the sprawling country house, he had been in something of a brown study, his thoughts following their own unhappy path. Indeed, since the morning at Wyndham Hall when Nicola had unexpectedly burst in upon him in the parlour, David hadn't been able to think of anyone or anything else. Nicola's face had haunted him; her eyes followed him, and everywhere he went she was there.

Now, upon seeing her in person again, the haze dropped away and he stared at her outright. His gaze travelled over the softly rounded cheeks, the delicate contours of her nose, and the smoothness of her chin. It searched the depths of her eyes, probing for the answers he hoped to find there. And in that one piercing glance he saw everything: the heightened colour of her skin, the brief flash of defiance mingled with lingering regret in those beautiful green eyes—and the look of uncertainty, as their eyes met and held across the wide expanse of floor.

God in heaven, how had he ever let her go?

'Ah, David, there you are,' Sir Giles said affably. 'Hard-pressed to get across the room in such a crush. Don't know why I keep coming to these dashed things.'

The moment passed. In the blink of an eye, the contact was broken and Nicola was once again allowed to escape into the privacy of her thoughts. But not before David had seen the tell-tale softening in her face. There *was* still something between them, he knew that now. And he vowed that, next time, he would not let her go so easily. He would have his answers.

For now, however, the only one awaiting an answer was his uncle. 'I venture to say that you keep coming to these things,' David drawled, 'because you hate the thought of missing anything of import which might take place in your absence.'

'Humph! Doesn't seem to bother you much,' Sir Giles quipped.

'No. But then, the idiosyncrasies of Society never have.'

Their light-hearted banter was interrupted by the arrival of the outspoken Lady Grantley and her only daughter, Lucinda, a rather timid girl who was clearly in awe of the two illustrious gentlemen before whom she found herself standing.

'Evening, Sir Giles, Lord Blackwood,' Lady Grantley said in a voice that was more suited to the hunting fields than it was to the ballroom. 'Glad to see you out and about again. Began to wonder whether you'd gone abroad or just into retirement.'

Amusement flickered in the depths of David's eyes. 'As you can see, I have done neither, Lady Grantley. Good evening, Miss Grantley, are you enjoying the festivities?'

Unfortunately, the softer tone Blackwood used to address the daughter did little to ease her discomfort. The poor girl blushed a most unbecoming shade of red and stammered an all but incoherent reply.

'Mustn't mind my Lucinda,' Lady Grantley said brusquely. 'A touch reserved, that's all. A suitable quality in a wife, don't you think, Sir Giles?'

Sir Giles blinked. 'Er, yes, I suppose.'

Lady Grantley nodded. 'So I always told Lord Grantley. Better than being too brazen, wouldn't you agree, Lord Blackwood?'

'I am sure no one would ever think Miss Grantley brazen.'

David was rewarded for his trouble by a grateful glance from the pale blue eyes, and on impulse said, 'Perhaps I might request the honour of a dance, Miss Grantley? If your card is not already full, that is,' he added with a smile.

'Full? Of course it's not full,' Lady Grantley assured him with a snort. 'Hand over your card, Lucinda.'

David duly wrote his name beside a country dance and handed it back to the girl, feeling decidedly sorry for her. The kindest thing that could happen to her would be for some amiable gentleman, or even a clergyman, to offer for her and take her far away from her mother's domination. 'I look forward to it.'

Well satisfied, a beaming Lady Grantley retired back to the chairs along the side wall, dragging Lucinda with her.

'I say, there goes a dragon in disguise,' Sir Giles whispered when the two were safely out of earshot. 'Damned if I don't feel sorry for the poor girl.'

'You and me both, Uncle,' David agreed. 'Can you imagine what it would be like having Lady Grantley as a mother-in-law?'

'It would be enough to make one consider moving to the Americas.' Sir Giles let his gaze travel over the as-

sembled crowd, his eyes brightening as they lighted on
the two ladies across the room. 'Ah, now there is a much
more pleasant sight for these old eyes. The fair Lady
Dorchester and her niece. Pray do not tell me you had not
noticed their arrival.'

David shrugged in a matter-of-fact way. 'I did chance
to spot Lady Nicola moments before you arrived.'

'Yes, I'm sure you did.' Sir Giles wisely kept his smile
to himself. 'I must say, she's looking quite the thing tonight, albeit perhaps a touch pale. Doesn't seem to be
pining away, though.'

'No reason why she should be,' David replied. 'It was
her decision to end the betrothal, not mine.'

'Yes, but given the circumstances—'

'The circumstances have nothing to do with it,' David
snapped, uncommonly out of curl. 'I was perfectly willing
to talk to her and try to work things out between us. It
was Nicola who shut me out.'

'Perhaps she felt it was the only honourable thing she
could do after embarrassing you to such a degree. After
all, you did make your feelings perfectly clear to her when
you proposed, dear boy,' Sir Giles said softly. 'And Nicola knew precisely what type of woman you were looking for when she accepted. I venture to say that, for that
very reason, she knew better than anyone how badly she
had let you down.'

David glanced across the room, and realized that his
uncle was right. He remembered every word Nicola had
said to him, just as he remembered the tone of her voice
when she had spoken them—the undeniable note of regret
that she could not live up to his expectations. And the
unmistakable sadness that he could not live up to hers.

'She thought we were…too different to make it work,'
David said softly, his eyes fixed on the slender form of

the woman at the other side of the room. 'And sometimes I thought she was right. At times, Nicola can be as gentle as a lamb, and at others as wild and unpredictable as any of her creatures.'

'I believe she calls them pets,' Sir Giles reminded his nephew with a grin.

'Pets, creatures, they're all wild animals, whatever she chooses to call them. Have you ever known a lady to keep a mouse in her bedroom, Uncle Giles? Or a mischievous fox for a pet?'

'Pray do not forget the falcon.'

'Lord, yes, how could I forget Guinevere?' David murmured dryly. 'God only knows what other wild and woolly creatures she is tending.'

'Well, I'll say one thing for the girl,' Sir Giles commented, removing one of his prized antique snuff boxes from his coat pocket and flicking back the jewelled lid. 'Lady Nicola may be a trifle out of the ordinary, but life with her would never be dull. And, knowing you as I do, I would venture to say that she is far more suited to being your wife than any meek and mild miss who would smile and agree with everything you said. I wager you'd be bored out of your brain-box within a year. And I know you're not the type to trifle with lightskirts and actresses once you're wed.'

No, he wasn't, David acknowledged silently. The vows of marriage might be no more than words on a page to some men, but, to him, they were sacrosanct. The woman he married would not only be the right choice for his marchioness; she would be the right choice for him. She would be a woman whom he could love and respect, and admire for her beliefs. A woman who had values and who stood by them.

A woman—like Nicola.

* * *

Across the room, Nicola stood alone in the shadow of a huge decorated pillar, and tried to look as though she was having a wonderful time. Her aunt had gone to have a word with her good friend, Lady Alderly, and had promised to return directly. In her absence, Nicola smiled serenely at acquaintances who stopped to say hello, and offered her card to the few gentlemen who asked for the pleasure of a dance. She kept up a light and witty stream of conversation when she was with her partners and looked, to all outward appearances, to be having the time of her life.

Inwardly, however, she was shattered. Because the look David had given her earlier in the evening had left her reeling.

Had she mistaken the smouldering passion she'd seen in his eyes? Indeed, she must have, for, by all accounts, Blackwood had no interest in her any more. Arabella had made that perfectly clear. And yet Nicola couldn't deny that *something* had passed between them. Something wonderful—

'Good evening, Lady Nicola.'

Nicola jumped. 'Lord Blackwood!' Her throat suddenly tightened, making it difficult for her to speak. 'Pray, forgive my lack of attention, my thoughts were…elsewhere.'

David bowed formally from the waist, but when he straightened his gaze bore into her, silent and searching. 'Somewhere pleasant, I hope?'

'But of course.' Nicola swallowed hard, and then affected a light-hearted laugh. 'Do daydreams not usually take one away to a place more pleasant?'

'To a place more pleasant—or to people more so?'

Nicola quickly opened her fan and plied it briskly to her cheeks. 'I am sure that one can always find places and people who are more to one's liking than those with whom we are forced to associate on a daily basis.'

David shrugged. 'That is easy enough. Simply do not attend functions at which such people might be encountered.'

'Is that why you have been absent from Society this last week?'

He smiled enigmatically. 'I am flattered that you would even notice. I wouldn't have thought my whereabouts would have given you a moment's pause.'

The caustic tone brought a flush to her skin, but Nicola matched his look with one just as direct. 'They did not. I merely thought you would have been anxious to resume your search for a suitable marchioness.'

She was gratified to see David look somewhat taken aback. 'You do not mince words, Lady Nicola.'

'No, but then I do not believe you would wish me to. You have always been most…painfully honest with me, Lord Blackwood. Surely it would be uncharitable of me to be anything less in return.'

In spite of himself, David felt a smile work its way to his lips. 'At times, I wish you could see your way clear to being a little less honest and charitable with me, Nicola.'

The sound of her name was sweet on his lips, but Nicola knew that she could not allow him to use it. 'It is not seemly for you to address me in such a manner. We are no longer betrothed.'

'No, and how I wish it were otherwise,' he whispered softly.

Nicola's eyes flew up to his, confusion and dismay clouding the emerald depths. 'My lord, I really do not think—'

'Are you engaged for this dance, Lady Nicola?'

If possible, his question threw her into even greater confusion. 'No, but I do not think it…appropriate that we dance.'

'Then perhaps you would care to join me for a stroll on the balcony?' he suggested, holding out his arm. 'The room has grown uncommon warm and your colour is a touch high. I promise, I will keep you no more than a few minutes.'

Nicola's first impulse was to refuse. She was having trouble enough maintaining an air of detachment, in view of the startling things he had just said to her. But she also knew that a breath of fresh air would be very welcome.

'Surely you are not so afraid of me, Nicola, that you would begrudge me a few moments of your time?'

'I am not afraid of you at all,' Nicola asserted, the challenge helping her to make up her mind. 'And, yes, a stroll in the evening air would be most welcome, my lord. But a brief one, as you say.'

'To quote my uncle,' David said roguishly, 'a moment spent with you would be as fine as an hour spent with anyone else. Shall we?'

He offered his arm, and, after a moment's hesitation, Nicola placed her gloved hand upon it, and in silence they made their way onto the balcony.

The night sky was breathtakingly clear, the stretch of midnight-blue dotted with the twinkling light of a thousand stars. It did indeed make for a welcome change from the oppressive heat of the room, and once they were clear of the French doors Nicola tipped back her head and breathed deeply of the cool evening air. 'Mmm, what a beautiful night.'

'I thought you would find it so. It was worth bringing you out here if only to bring the colour down in your cheeks,' David teased her.

In spite of herself, Nicola smiled. 'It is an unfortunate failing of the female members of my family.'

His mouth quirked with humour. 'Of course.'

They walked on in silence, Nicola content to savour the blessed peacefulness of the cool night air and not to have to worry about conversation. David was content just to have Nicola by his side. 'Your father is well?' he asked finally.

'Yes, thank you.'

'And Lady Dorchester?'

'They are both in excellent health. Aunt Glynnis is here with me this evening.'

'Yes, I know. My uncle keeps me informed of her whereabouts at all times.'

'I noticed that he was still most…attentive towards her.' Nicola glanced off to the left where the ornamental pond—its waters turned silver by the moonlight—formed the centre of a large formal garden, and said, 'Sir Giles seems such a pleasant man. How is it that he has never married?'

'I believe it stems from a desire to find the right woman, rather than from any less noble reasons. He is one of the few men I know who has not enjoyed a succession of romantic liaisons, if you understand.'

'I understand perfectly,' Nicola said hastily. 'And I appreciate your candour. Is he…that is, would his income provide a comfortable living for two?'

'Lady Nicola, why do I get the impression that you are more interested in my uncle than you are in me?'

His lazy smile set Nicola's pulses racing, but her voice was steady as she said, 'Perhaps because I find older men so much more interesting than younger ones.'

'Do you, indeed? I am relieved to hear it, given my own somewhat advanced age,' David observed in a dry tone. 'However, I do not think that is the truth of the matter.'

'Oh? And, pray, what is?'

'I believe that you have set yourself up as Lady Dorchester's guardian, and mean to find out whether my uncle's intentions are honourable or not.'

'Now you are laughing at me,' Nicola accused.

'Not at all. I merely find it amusing to hear you asking the type of questions that are usually the domain of an anxious father quizzing a prospective son-in-law.'

'I hardly think they are the same at all,' Nicola replied as she sank gracefully onto one of the stone benches set out along the balcony. 'If your uncle's intentions do run in that direction, I should simply like to know what kind of man he is. My aunt was very happily married the first time, and is naturally cautious about marrying again. I would not wish to see her hurt.'

David set one foot on the bench next to her and braced his elbow on his knee. 'Nor would I. And, for what it's worth, Sir Giles is one of the finest gentlemen I have ever met, quite apart from the fact that he is my uncle. We grew very close after my father died.'

For all the coolness of the air, the proximity of David's body generated its own kind of heat, and Nicola quickly rose. 'Well, now that we have settled the matter of Sir Giles's suitability to court my aunt, perhaps we should return—'

'No, not yet,' David said briskly. 'We have not spoken about our own situation.'

Nicola hastily averted her eyes. 'I was not aware that we had…a situation.'

'On the contrary, Nicola—'

'Lord Blackwood, I would remind you that you no longer have permission to address me by my first name.'

'Not so long ago, you were willing to allow me to address you with a deal more intimacy than that.'

'Be that as it may, the situation now is very different,' Nicola said, turning to go.

'Damn it, Nicola, wait!' And, without thinking, David grabbed for her hand.

Nicola's reaction was swift and totally beyond her control. She cried out in pain, her face turning deathly white as she jerked back her hand. Stars danced in front of her eyes, and she staggered back towards the bench, fighting as hard as she could not to pass out.

David stared at her in horror. 'Dear God, Nicola, what's wrong?'

Nicola shut her eyes against the throbbing in her hand, and fought back the tears which bubbled in her eyes. 'Nothing, I'm…fine.'

'The hell you're fine! What did I do? Obviously I hurt you in some way.'

'Yes—I mean, no. That is…it wasn't…your fault.'

'What wasn't my fault?' David glanced down at her hand, and then swore softly under his breath. 'My God, look at your hand. Even under your glove, I can see how swollen it is.'

'It's nothing. Truly. I suffered a slight accident.'

'What kind of an accident?'

'A…riding accident. I…hit it against a gate post,' she lied, blinking back tears.

David's eyes darkened as he carefully took her by the forearm. 'Nicola, kindly take off your glove.'

'My lord, if you will just take me back inside—'

'I want to see what you have done to your hand.'

'I would prefer that you do not, my lord.'

'Nicola, if you do not remove your glove this instant, I shall sit you down on my lap and take it off myself!'

Aware that he was very likely to make good on his threat, and realizing that making a bigger fuss would only give him more cause to be suspicious, Nicola defiantly raised her chin. 'Very well. Though I fail to see why such a simple injury should warrant such attention.' She rolled down her glove and carefully drew it off, biting her lip as she did so. 'There, you see. It is nothing.'

Unfortunately, even in the semi-darkness, Nicola could see that it looked a great deal more than nothing. The gash itself was healing, but the skin all around it was still swollen and badly bruised.

'This isn't the result of any riding accident,' David said tersely.

'I assure you—'

'Is that why were you so reluctant to remove your glove? Because you didn't want me to see what really happened?'

'My lord, I told you, I was careless and brushed it against a post—'

'No, you told me what you wanted me to hear, Nicola. If you had hit your hand against a post, the skin all around here would be scraped, whereas this has the appearance of an entirely different kind of injury,' David interrupted. 'Besides, I've ridden with you before and I know what a competent rider you are. For you to have come this close to a gate post would have meant risking injury to your horse, and that is something you would not do.'

'My thoughts were…momentarily distracted,' Nicola said desperately.

'Damn it, Nicola, stop lying to me! I know how you came by this, and it has nothing to do with some cock-and-bull story about a gate post. I know the type of damage they can do, and now you're trying to pass it off as a riding accident.'

Nicola glanced at him in bewilderment. 'The damage *who* can do?'

'You know perfectly well who. Those damned…pets of yours.'

Nicola went pale. *'My…pets?'*

'Yes. Which one of them got out of hand this time? That wretched bird? It looks like something a sharp claw could have done. Or perhaps you have some other kind of wild and wonderful creature lurking in your bedroom that I've not had occasion to meet. Is that it?'

David was furious, but it was pale in comparison to the rage that Nicola suddenly felt. 'You really believe that one of *my* animals did this to me?'

'Of course. Why else would you be so reluctant to tell me the truth? You knew how I would feel about the matter, and so you thought to lay the blame for it on a riding accident.'

Nicola was all but trembling. 'How *dare* you? The poor creatures under my care are not so savage as you think, my lord. Indeed, I find the human species a great deal more vicious.'

'Nicola, be reasonable!'

'I am being reasonable! It is you who are not!' Nicola cried. 'This injury did come about as a result of a riding accident, though not, I admit, by hitting it against a post.'

'Then what did happen?'

'That is no concern of yours.' Nicola quickly and carefully donned her glove, before sweeping up the train of her gown and turning back towards the French doors. 'Since you do not choose to believe the answer I gave you, or to see beyond your prejudices, we have nothing further to say. And thank you for reinforcing my decision, Lord Blackwood. I see now that I was right to end our betrothal. We should never have suited.'

'Nicola!'

'Goodnight, Lord Blackwood. Pray do not trouble yourself to see me in.'

With that, Nicola hurried back inside, anxious to put as
much distance as she could between David and herself.
Once again he had jumped to conclusions, willing to believe that such a grievous injury had been inflicted by an
innocent animal. What would he have said, Nicola wondered, if she had told him the truth? That his dear cousin
Arabella had lashed out at her in a fit of anger? Would
he be as quick to forgive her as he was to condemn others?

Inside, Nicola found her aunt in comfortable conversation with Sir Giles. It was a sight which, at any other
time, would have brought a smile of pleasure to her lips,
but at the moment it only exacerbated her frustration.
'Aunt Glynnis, I wonder if we might…take our leave?'

Lady Dorchester turned, but her smile quickly gave
way to a look of concern when she saw the expression on
her niece's face. 'Nicola, are you all right?'

Nicola nodded, too upset to offer any kind of explanation. 'I am…fine.' She saw Sir Giles cast a fleeting
glance in the direction of the French doors, and forced
herself to add, 'Really. It's just a touch of the megrim.'

'No doubt due to the heat,' Sir Giles said thoughtfully,
his attention still on the door.

'Just so,' Nicola replied.

'Well, then, yes, of course we shall leave. My poor
dear, now I can see that you are, indeed, very pale,' Lady
Dorchester said kindly. 'Sir Giles, will you excuse us? I
think it best that I take Nicola home.'

'Of course, dear lady. May I…call upon you tomorrow,
as we discussed?'

Lady Dorchester blushed, looking a little like a flustered debutante. But she quickly nodded her agreement, saying, 'Yes, I should like that.'

'Good. And now please allow me to call for your carriage. I shall escort the two of you outside.'

Sir Giles was as good as his word. As he handed Nicola up into the carriage after her aunt, he said quietly, and for her hearing alone, 'I regret that the evening came to such an abrupt ending, Lady Nicola. I would like to think that it was not as a result of anything my nephew may have said, but somehow, under the circumstances, I think that highly unlikely.'

Nicola turned and offered him a stiff smile. 'Sometimes discovering the truth is worth the sacrifice of an evening, Sir Giles, and I must say that tonight was very illuminating. My only regret is that I have taken my aunt away from what was obviously a very pleasant situation for both of you. Pray, accept my apologies. Goodnight, Sir Giles.'

'Goodnight, Lady Nicola,' he replied, smiling back at her a touch sadly. His eyes brightened momentarily, however, as he looked into the carriage and met those of Lady Dorchester. 'Until tomorrow, my lady.'

Sir Giles stepped back as the carriage set off, watching until it rounded the corner of the drive and disappeared into the darkness. Seconds later, he realized that he was not the only one watching its departure.

'Did she say anything about me?' the voice said quietly from behind him.

Sir Giles did not turn around. 'No, but it is obvious that she is in high dudgeon over something.'

'Yes. It would seem that I have committed *le grand faux pas.*'

'Oh? And what have you done this time?'

David sighed. 'Nicola has a terrible gash on her hand,

and I laid the blame for it squarely on the head of one of her much beloved pets.'

'And were any of them at fault?'

'She would have me believe that they were not.'

Sir Giles spun around. 'Oh, dear. That could indeed cause a problem, given Lady Nicola's loyalty to them. And the fact that you were not in her good books to begin with.'

'Her good books!' David's expression was rueful in the extreme. 'Rest assured, Uncle, I am now so far beyond contempt as to make Mr O'Donnell look like a saint!'

Chapter Thirteen

The next day, Nicola stayed in her room with the curtains drawn and the door tightly closed. The events of the previous evening had brought about a megrim in earnest, and it was as much as she could do just to draw breath without wincing. Lady Dorchester, after having assured herself that her niece was resting as comfortably as could be expected, headed back to her own room to prepare for the arrival of Sir Giles Chapman, who was coming to take her driving.

It had been a very long time since Glynnis had felt the stirring of excitement that she did now, and she realized with some surprise that she was actually looking forward to the outing. Sir Giles had turned out to be a witty and entertaining companion, who was softly spoken and rather endearingly unsure of himself—qualities that Glynnis found charming in a gentleman, having grown used to the swaggering confidence displayed by so many of the young bucks about Town.

Yes, all in all, she was very pleased at being escorted by Sir Giles Chapman this afternoon, and with the comfortable rapport that was developing between them. Now, if only she could bring herself to feel happier about the situation between Nicola and her marquis, everything would be quite wonderful.

'Does the new style please you, my lady?' Maire asked as she put the finishing touches to Lady Dorchester's coiffure.

'Hmm? Oh, yes, Maire, truly, you work wonders with my hair.' Rousing herself from her thoughts, Glynnis peered into the looking-glass atop her dressing table, and smiled her pleasure at the young girl's efforts. 'I dare say Sir Giles will be pleased.'

'Thank you, my lady.'

As Maire turned to go, Glynnis said, 'Would you look in on Lady Nicola a few times this afternoon, Maire? Though she claims that it is her head which keeps her to bed, I am concerned that her hand is causing her far more pain than she is letting on. Mayhap more of your wondrous salve would help.'

'Yes, of course, my lady. I went to see my mother yesterday morning and brought a quantity back with me, fearing that Lady Nicola might be needing it,' Maire assured Lady Dorchester, before adding, ''Tis a sad thing, though, her taking such a dreadful blow. What ever could have possessed the woman to strike Lady Nicola in such a cruel manner, I'll never understand.'

Carefully arranging her new bonnet over the freshly styled curls, Glynnis asked, 'Which woman, Maire?'

'Why, Mrs Braithwaite.'

'Arabella Braithwaite?' Glynnis frowned. 'But...what has she to do with this?'

'Well...everything, my lady,' the maid replied in some surprise. 'It were her that struck Lady Nicola across the hand. Did she not tell you?'

Lady Dorchester gasped in dismay, and spun around on

the stool. 'No, indeed she did not! This is the first I have heard of it!'

Maire's face turned pale. 'Oh, dear. There, and I hope I've not said anything out of turn. Perhaps she didn't want you to know.'

'It doesn't matter whether she *wanted* me to know,' Glynnis professed in considerable agitation. 'The fact is that she has not uttered a word about it to me. Mercy, how on earth could such a thing happen? Was it an accident?'

'I don't believe so, my lady. It seems that Lady Nicola came upon Mrs Braithwaite that morning she went out riding, and that Mrs Braithwaite was beating her poor horse something fierce. But when Lady Nicola shouted at her to stop Mrs Braithwaite told her to mind her own business and whipped her across the hand for her trouble!'

'Never!'

'I'd not tell you a lie, my lady.'

'But Nicola told me that she had struck her hand against a gate post. Why would she lie?' Confused, Glynnis nibbled thoughtfully at her lower lip. Could it be that Nicola was trying to…protect Arabella for some reason? 'Did you hear this story from my niece, Maire?'

'No, my lady. Jenkins told me.'

'Jenkins?'

'One of the grooms. He was there when it happened. Jenkins said that Mrs Braithwaite's horse was jumping around, a bit wild, like, and that Mrs Braithwaite was having trouble controlling it. Lady Nicola told her to get out of the way and then took to feeling under the mare's saddle. That's when she found a clump of burrs stuck in the blanket. She showed them to Mrs Braithwaite, but the lady didn't seem to care. She only laughed and called

Lady Nicola the Witch of Wyndham Hall, and galloped off. That's what really happened, my lady.'

The story was so…incredible that Lady Dorchester was forced to close her eyes and draw a long, deep breath. That wretched woman! How dared she strike her niece? How *dared* she?

Fighting to control the rising edge of her temper, Glynnis quickly turned back to her reflection in the looking-glass and fastened her bonnet beneath her chin. She knew it would be dreadfully bad form to let forth the spate of angry words that even now were trembling on her tongue, but, indeed, it was all she could do not to. It was only her many years of training that allowed her to hold the vitriolic spate in check.

She took a few more deep breaths and said, 'Thank you, Maire. I am very glad I have found out the truth of the matter at last.'

Maire wrung her hands in dismay. 'I hope Lady Nicola won't be angry with me for telling you, my lady. I sure and didn't mean to tell tales out of school—'

'You haven't told tales, Maire. For whatever reason, Nicola has chosen to protect Mrs Braithwaite by not telling the truth about her injury. Probably because she is too kind-hearted to let people know what kind of a beast the woman really is. Fortunately, I suffer no such pangs of conscience. Something must be done about the contemptible Mrs Arabella Braithwaite!' Glynnis said as she stood up. 'And I intend to do just that this very afternoon!'

David was just settling down with a book and a glass of brandy in his study after dinner that evening, when his uncle appeared at the door. 'Evening, David,' the baronet said. 'Mind if I join you?'

David chuckled and put down his book. 'This is getting to be quite a habit of yours, Uncle Giles.'

'Not an unpleasant one, I hope.'

'Not in the least. I simply never know when I'm going to look up and find you propping up the door. Brandy all right?'

'Yes, fine. But I should tell you, the purpose of my visit is not entirely social.'

'Oh?' Something in the tone of his uncle's voice prompted David to pause in the act of pouring out the brandy. 'Something wrong?'

'Yes, and I thought I should make haste to tell you something which I only learned myself late this afternoon. Something you must know.'

David thought for a moment as he put the crystal decanter back down on the table. He knew that his uncle had taken Lady Dorchester driving that afternoon. Was it possible that the lady had imparted some vital piece of information which might ultimately help him in his quest to be reunited with Nicola?

'I take it this is about Nicola.'

'It is. And, more specifically, about her injury.'

'Her injury?' David hadn't been expecting that. He frowned as he carefully replaced the stopper in the decanter. 'What did Lady Dorchester tell you?'

'That you did, indeed, malign the wrong creature,' Sir Giles said, accepting the glass his nephew held out to him.

'Are you telling me that the gash to her hand was not inflicted by one of her pets?'

'Most assuredly not,' Sir Giles confirmed. 'In fact, I would go so far as to say that you could not have been more wrong, and that you will not be at all pleased when I tell you how it actually did come to pass.'

'And that is?'

'That your cousin Arabella purposely struck Lady Nicola across the back of her hand with her riding whip.'

David stared at his uncle in utter disbelief. 'She did *what*?'

'Yes, I thought you'd be shocked,' Sir Giles acknowledged dryly. 'I was myself.' He quickly went on to relate the rest of the story to David, exactly as it had been passed on to him by Lady Dorchester. As he did, he watched his nephew's expression go from one of startled disbelief to one of white-hot fury.

'And you are absolutely sure of the facts?'

'I have no reason to doubt Lady Dorchester's word,' Sir Giles said. 'In fact, she was as horrified as I when she learned the truth of it.'

'Did Nicola tell her what happened?'

'No. Lady Dorchester said that Nicola hasn't offered a word about it, other than to maintain that she hit her hand against a post when she was out riding. But I understand that Lady Nicola's groom was present when it happened, and that he was witness to the entire affair. He then passed it along to one of the housemaids, who in turn passed it along to Lady Dorchester. In fact, Lady Dorchester admitted to me that she questioned the groom herself before joining me this afternoon.'

David stood up, his mouth drawn into a tight, angry line. 'I saw the marks on Arabella's horse when she came in after the hunt that day, but I had no reason to believe that she had inflicted the injuries herself. By God, she told me the mare had jumped badly and brushed hard against a post, and I believed her.'

'Coincidental her using exactly the same excuse as Nicola did,' Sir Giles drawled.

'A coincidence indeed,' David muttered. He stared into the empty fireplace, his thoughts as dark as the coal-blackened bricks. 'But it doesn't make sense, Uncle. Why would Arabella be so cruel? Nicola has done nothing to her.'

'Other than steal your heart,' Sir Giles pointed out kindly. 'And I regret to say that a woman's jealousy can be a frightening thing. Hell hath no fury, and all that.'

David tossed back his brandy and promptly refilled his glass. 'And they call them the fairer sex.'

'Yes, and the black widow spider eats her mate after lovemaking, too,' Sir Giles pointed out wryly. 'Hardly the behaviour of a gentler species, to my way of thinking.'

David grimaced. It seemed that both his uncle *and* the Duchess of Basilworth had been right in their assessment of Arabella's character. They had both warned him about her, and he had laughed at them. It had taken one horrible incident to show him how right they really were.

But that was not the most important issue here, David realized with a sinking heart. That was his lack of belief in Nicola. He thought back to the occasion of his last meeting with her, remembering all too clearly the disappointment in her face, and how very cold her eyes had grown as he'd hurled accusation after accusation at her. He had all but called her a liar, refusing to believe that one of her animals hadn't turned on her.

Had he but stopped to think for a moment, he would have realized that *none* of Nicola's animals had ever harmed her. Not the little fox at the height of his terror, nor the mouse when she had picked him up in the drawing room, nor the falcon when she had been trying to put her safely back into the cage. None of them had so much as *tried* to harm her. Why, then, had he just arbitrarily assumed that it must have been one of her creatures which had inflicted such a grievous injury?

What a fool he had been! David cursed himself. He had

forfeited Nicola's love as a result of his own stupid prejudices. He had cut her as deeply as though he had wielded the whip himself. And now he must bear the burden of knowing that a member of his own family had inflicted such a vicious injury, simply because Nicola had had the misfortune to love him. It was, indeed, an onerous charge.

'This isn't your fault, David,' Sir Giles said gently, as though sensing the inner turmoil that was tearing his nephew apart. 'Whatever you said to Nicola, you said in ignorance of the facts.'

'That is no excuse, Uncle Giles. My behaviour was unpardonable, and all I can do is try to make amends. It may be too late, but I can at least try. First, however, I intend to deal with Arabella.' David's eyes turned as black as stone. 'I swear she will not have occasion to hurt anything or anyone again.'

David's meeting with his cousin was not a pleasant one. Because, not surprisingly, Arabella vehemently denied any and all accusations.

'I cannot believe that you would entertain such an outrageous account,' Arabella cried, looking grievously wounded as she stood before him, one hand pressed to her heart. 'That you would listen to her—'

'Nicola did not tell me what happened, Arabella,' David said, his voice filled with icy contempt. 'The events were passed along to a third party by her groom.'

'Her groom!' Arabella's eyes flashed. 'You would take the word of a servant over mine? That is even worse!'

David shrugged. 'He had no reason to lie. And I myself saw the marks on your mare's flanks. Marks which you told me had been caused as the result of a hard brush against a gate.'

'And so they were!' Arabella maintained stubbornly. 'Why would I lie?'

'I don't know. That is what I am trying to ascertain.'

'Oh, David, David, you must know that I would never do anything to hurt Nicola. She was to have been your wife—'

'Which is precisely why you might have done it, according to some people,' David said quietly. 'It has been suggested that you were jealous of her.'

'Jealous? But that is absurd! Why in the world would I be jealous of the woman my cousin was going to marry?'

'Perhaps because you had hoped to become the Marchioness of Blackwood yourself?'

For a split second, Arabella's composure faltered, and she glanced away. She could not risk him looking into her eyes; not now, when he had come so close to the truth. Which meant there was only one thing she could do. One way she could extricate herself from the situation.

Walking slowly and gracefully towards the window, Arabella stood with her back to him, and said, in a soft, almost wounded tone, 'I am truly surprised that you would believe that of me, David, and very, very hurt. You and I have always enjoyed…a warm relationship, but surely you knew that I was not looking for anything deeper. Did I ever give you reason to believe that my feelings went beyond those of mere friendship?'

'No, you did not.'

'And did I not express to you some time ago my interest in Lord Wickstead?'

'You did.'

'Then, why would you accuse me of…harbouring secret hopes of becoming your wife now?' Arabella finally turned to face him, her features admirably composed—

and suitably injured—as she gazed across the room at him. 'You are my cousin, and, as such, I love you dearly, but I have never, ever looked upon you with anything but the most friendly of intentions.'

David watched her for a moment and marvelled at her ability to lie so convincingly. 'Then you deny any and all involvement in Nicola's injury?'

'I most certainly do.'

'And if I were to ask Nicola how she came by her injury, and ask her to swear it on her mother's grave, she would tell me that you had nothing to do with it, and that you were not, in fact, anywhere near her at the time?'

Arabella swallowed hard, and lifted her chin. She had gone too far to turn back now. 'I have no idea what Lady Nicola would say. If she wished to discredit me, this would provide her with a perfect opportunity to do so.'

'But why would she wish to discredit you?' David pressed. 'If you have been as agreeable to her as you would have me believe, surely there is no reason for her to be anything but gracious in her dealings with you.'

Arabella struggled to smile, fighting to maintain her poise in the face of his unrelenting attack. 'Yes, of course. She would have…no reason to behave…otherwise.'

David studied his cousin's coldly beautiful face, and wondered how he had misjudged her all these years. What a fool he had been.

'Nicola doesn't have a malicious bone in her body, Arabella, that much I do know,' David said quietly. 'I only wish that I could say the same for you.' He turned and walked towards the door, and, picking up his hat, said in a voice that he might have used to a stranger, 'I would prefer to have no further contact with you, Cousin Arabella. Do not seek me out, or present yourself at my home. If we should meet upon the street, do not address me, nor attempt to engage my attention. To all intents and purposes, you are no longer a member of my family.'

Arabella blanched, staggered by the magnitude of what he had just done. 'David, dear God! You cannot be serious?'

'I assure you, I am. And, in truth, I am sorry. But you have brought this on yourself. I will not have those I love slandered by your lies, nor made to suffer because of your petty jealousies. You have enough money to assure you of a comfortable living, and perhaps friends in the country who will, if they do not hear the gossip, stand by you as friends. But I doubt that you will be received in London. Perhaps this will teach you to behave differently in the future. Goodbye, Cousin Arabella.'

'David! Wait! Please, David, don't go!'

But her pleas fell on deaf ears. David went out and closed the door softly behind him, and moments later Arabella heard the sound of the front door closing. And she knew—because she knew her cousin well—that he would never set foot in any establishment of hers again.

By morning, Nicola's megrim had eased enough for her to get up and resume her normal daily activities—a fact for which she was extremely grateful. She had never been one to lie about in bed and the inactivity forced on her by keeping to her room had bothered her almost as much as the megrim had. Consequently, she donned a royal blue habit, trimmed at the shoulders and down the front of the bodice with black frogging, and, after partaking of a light breakfast, prepared to leave for the stables.

'Ah, there you are, Nicola.' Lord Wyndham greeted her at the door. 'Glad to see you up and about again, my dear. Feeling better?'

'Much better, thank you, Papa. I thought I would ride.'

'Splendid idea. It's a beautiful morning, though a little on the cool side.'

'I shall be warm enough,' Nicola assured him. 'And I shall be home in time for luncheon.'

'Nicola…'

She turned, and saw the concern in his eyes. 'Yes?'

'Are you really…all right?' he asked hesitantly. 'I mean, other than the megrim?'

Nicola did not pretend to misunderstand. She walked back to where he stood and, reaching up, pressed a kiss to his ruddy cheek. 'No, but I am trying to get over it. And I will, given time.'

Lord Wyndham glanced down into the eyes that were so much like his dear late wife's, and sighed. 'Do not let pride stand in the way of love, my dear. It is one of the biggest mistakes anyone can make. Pride is self-serving, and blinds us to the things which are most important in life. And I would hate to see you, of all people, lose something so very precious over something so foolish.'

Nicola's eyes clouded, though she managed a weak smile. 'I understand what you are saying, Papa, but it is not only pride which brings about the downfall of a relationship.' Her brow furrowed as she called to mind an image her father could not. 'A man must trust the woman he professes to love. And if he cannot there is no basis for love. I have not lied to Lord Blackwood about anything, Papa.'

'You did not exactly tell him the truth either,' her father pointed out gently.

'No, but omission cannot and should not be construed as lying. When David chose to believe that one of my animals had caused the injury to my hand, without asking me if such was the case, that evidenced a complete lack of trust in me.'

Lord Wyndham glanced down at his daughter's hand, noticing that it was still encased in a bandage, and said, 'You have not yet told *me* how you really came by the injury.'

'No, but then you did not jump to the conclusion that it had been inflicted by a mouse, or a fox, or a falcon. Lord Blackwood did, and in a most arrogant and high-handed manner.'

'I take it you are not going to tell me the true cause of the injury, then?'

Nicola hesitated. What would be gained by telling her father of Arabella Braithwaite's animosity now? There was nothing he or anyone else could do to change things. 'It really does not signify, Papa,' Nicola said finally. 'My hand is well on its way to healing and I think the less said about the matter the better.'

'I see. Well, I shan't press you for an answer,' Lord Wyndham said wisely. 'If you are content to let the matter drop, then so shall I be. Enjoy your ride, my dear.'

'Thank you, Papa, I shall.'

And fifteen minutes later, with Jenkins dutifully at her side, Nicola set off.

No more than ten minutes after that, Blackwood arrived at Wyndham Hall to see her.

He tossed the reins of his stallion to the waiting lad and then hurried inside, taking the front steps two at a time. He had to talk to her; to apologize for his behaviour, and to beg her to forgive him. He couldn't lose her now.

He was shown into the library, where a startled Lord Wyndham rose to greet him. 'Lord Blackwood, this is a surprise.'

'Lord Wyndham, pray forgive my calling at such an early hour, but I should like very much to speak with Lady Nicola.'

'I'm afraid that isn't possible.'

David felt a sharp stab of anxiety. 'Is she refusing to see me?'

Lord Wyndham carefully hid his smile. 'Not at all. She just left to go riding and is not expected back for a few hours.'

David's relief was palpable. At least she had not left orders that he be turned away.

'My lord, your daughter and I had…a terrible misunderstanding recently, one which I should like to see remedied at the first opportunity.'

'I see.' Wyndham studied the man in front of him. He hadn't missed the look of concern on the younger man's face and he was pleased by it. 'If I may be so bold, why are you suddenly so anxious to set these wrongs to right? I had been led to believe that a good deal of the fault lay with you.'

'The fault was mine entirely,' David admitted. 'I… erroneously accused one of Nicola's pets of having inflicted a grievous wound to her hand. You may have noticed it.'

'Yes, I did.'

'Did she tell you how she came by it?'

'Only that it was the result of a brush with a gate post.'

David nodded. How like Nicola to spare Arabella the censure she so rightly deserved.

'You said you *erroneously* accused the animal, Lord Blackwood,' Lord Wyndham said. 'What have you learned to make you believe otherwise?'

'That it was not an animal which caused the injury at all, but my…cousin Arabella.'

'Mrs Braithwaite? Good Lord!' Wyndham said, obviously finding it hard to get to grips with this new and highly disturbing piece of information. 'But why on earth would the woman do such a thing? Was it an accident?'

David shook his head. 'I believe it to have been an intentional act of malice, and one for which there can be no excuse.'

The earl's face darkened as anger moved in to replace his earlier feelings of shock and surprise. 'Have you spoken to your cousin about this?'

'I have. And I have told her that she is…no longer welcome in my home.'

Wyndham glanced at the man sharply. To cut a member of his own family—especially a woman like Arabella Braithwaite—was more punishment than he would have expected. When word of Blackwood's treatment leaked out, Arabella would be shunned by the society in which she moved. She would be forced to retire to the country and live out the remainder of her days as a social outcast. It was retribution indeed.

'Well, I must say I am shocked by her actions,' Lord Wyndham said at length. 'And saddened by them. Socially, she is ruined.'

David's eyes were wintry. 'That is not my concern. Arabella should have thought of that before she struck Nicola. Right now, my only concern is to apologize to your daughter and to see if there is any way we can resolve our differences.'

'And do you think there is?'

'I have no idea after the wretched way I've treated her,' David admitted. 'I doubted her, I questioned her motives, and I even tried to make her into someone she was not. But I love Nicola with all my heart, and if she will still have me it is my dearest wish that we be married.'

Lord Wyndham was about to reply when the door

opened and the young stable lad, Jamie, rushed in. 'Beggin' your pardon, my lord,' he said breathlessly.

'Jamie, what's the meaning of this?' Lord Wyndham said, annoyed by the boy's temerity.

'I 'ad to see you, m'lord. It's about Alistair.'

Lord Wyndham frowned, momentarily at a loss. 'Alistair?'

''Er ladyship's fox. The one wot run off.'

'Ah, yes. That one.' Lord Wyndham gruffly cleared his throat and took care to avoid Blackwood's eye. 'Well, what about him?'

'I found 'im, m'lord,' Jamie announced triumphantly.

'You did?'

'Aye. In the far woods, down by the stream.'

'And you are sure it was the same fox?'

''Ad to be, my lord. There was a big patch of white on 'is foreleg, and I've never seen another fox with a mark like that.'

Clearly puzzled as to why the lad had thought it necessary to burst into the room and impart such a piece of information, the earl said brusquely, 'Well, it was good of you to tell me, Jamie, but as you can see I am busy at the moment.'

Jamie's eyes flicked briefly to David's impassive face. 'I know that, my lord, but I thought you might want to tell Lady Nicola—'

'Yes, of course. And I shall, just as soon as she returns from her ride,' Lord Wyndham said, walking the boy back towards the door. 'Now, away you go, there's a good lad.'

Looking decidedly crestfallen, Jamie took himself off. The earl chuckled as he turned to resume his conversation with David. 'Sorry about that, Blackwood. Don't usually have servants bursting into the room with messages for my daughter.'

'Quite all right, sir. Nicola does tend to inspire a loyal and impassioned following amongst all manner of creatures.'

'Yes, she does indeed.'

'Are you going to tell her about…Alistair?'

Lord Wyndham thought about it for a moment, and then shook his head. 'I think not. The lad has a good heart, but I doubt it was the same fox. That little fellow had quite a scare the other week, and I am sure that he is long gone by now. Reminding Nicola of him now will only upset her more. I'll have a word with Jamie later on, and tell him not to mention it when he sees her. Now, I believe you were saying something about patching things up with my daughter.'

'Yes, I should very much like to do so.'

'And how do you propose to go about doing that?'

'Therein lies my problem, sir. Nicola doesn't believe that I care about her animals at all. She thinks I am heartless and uncaring when it comes to such matters.'

'And are you?'

It was a direct question, but one to which Blackwood took no offence. 'Perhaps I was in the past,' he admitted slowly, 'though I would venture to say no more so than any other gentleman of our class. I have always considered foxes and falcons to be sporting creatures, not pets to be taken in and loved. As for mice, well, I'm sure you would agree that the servants spend far more time trying to rid the house of them than in encouraging them to take up residence. However, since meeting Nicola, I find that my opinions have…changed somewhat.'

'Huh! Mine certainly did,' Lord Wyndham confessed with a wry smile. 'Given my wife's extraordinary talents, it would have been impossible for them not to. And there's no denying that Nicola has inherited many of her mother's gifts. I used to tell her that it would cause problems for her in the future and I fear my prophecy is coming true. But you have to admit, Blackwood, there is something almost…magical about the way Nicola is able to communicate with her creatures. It's as if they feel no fear in her presence.'

David nodded grimly. 'How I wish I had given more thought to that before speaking out against them, my lord. But that is precisely what I wish to set to rights now.'

'Well, Nicola did say that she would be back by lunch. You are more than welcome to stay. Or, if you would prefer, you could come back and speak with her later this afternoon. I do not recall her saying that she was intending to pay calls.'

Encouraged by Lord Wyndham's sentiments, David nodded. 'Perhaps I shall do that, sir. If I still have your blessing as regards marrying Nicola, that is?'

A twinkle appeared in Lord Wyndham's eyes. 'I have always believed that you and my daughter were right for each other, Blackwood. I just wondered how long it would take the two of you to work it out.'

Chapter Fourteen

David did not, however, depart from Wyndham Hall as he had planned. When he took his leave of the earl, it suddenly occurred to him that it might be well worth the trouble to ride out after Nicola. He had spent most of the night awake, planning what he would say to her, and, frankly, he was reluctant to wait until the afternoon to begin the discussion. If he could find her and somehow convince her of how much he loved her, perhaps she would be willing to forgive him, and they could begin planning their future together that much sooner. And if they were both on horseback it might help Nicola to feel more at ease. Certainly, it was worth a try.

'Is anyone likely to know where Lady Nicola might have ridden this morning?' David asked the young lad who was patiently holding his stallion's reins.

'Roberts would, my lord,' the boy volunteered. 'He always sees to the saddling of her ladyship's mare. He'll know where she went.'

David flicked the grateful lad a shilling, and then rode off in the direction of the stables. If he could find out which route Nicola had taken, perhaps he might come upon her in the fields. It was a slim chance, but one definitely worth taking.

David soon located the wiry groom and asked for Nicola's whereabouts.

'I think she was planning to ride over by Upper Broughton, my lord,' Roberts advised him. 'There's a church in the village that Lady Nicola likes to visit. But, if you'll pardon my saying so, it might not be a good idea for you to ride after her this particular morning.'

'Oh?' David frowned. 'Why's that?'

'Well, I don't think her ladyship was expecting to see anyone this morning, and in spite of my urging she's gone out without a groom again. So if you did find her—'

'Thank you, Roberts, I see the predicament,' David said, not needing to have it spelled out for him. He wasn't surprised to discover that Nicola had flaunted convention yet again, but he was impressed that the head groom cared enough for her reputation to point it out to him. 'You may rest assured that if I do come upon the lady our only destination will be straight back here, and I doubt even she can come to harm in that short a distance.'

'I don't know about that, my lord,' Roberts muttered. 'That was what her ladyship said the day she encountered Mr O'Donnell on the road too.'

David wisely decided to ignore that one. 'Which way do you suggest I go?'

Moments later, armed with the information he required, David turned the stallion around and set off in the direction indicated. He knew the old church the groom had referred to. It was a pretty little place, and he could well understand Nicola's attraction to it. Nestled on the edge of the forest, it was set amongst large shady trees and neatly tended headstones. It was also a place where deer,

rabbits and other small creatures were known to gather—
a fact which could only add to its appeal for Nicola.

For that reason, he was somewhat surprised when, a
short while later, he discovered that it was *not* the church
that Nicola had been intending to visit that morning at all.
When he was still some distance away, he spotted Nicola's mare. She was tethered to the lowest branch of a
linden—and her mistress was nowhere in sight!

Frowning, David quickly urged his mount forward.
Where could Nicola have gone? There was a stone farm-
house off in the distance, but she would hardly have left
her horse all the way back here if she had planned on
paying the tenants a call. Had she simply decided to stop
and go for a walk on foot?

'Nicola?'

Nightingale pricked her ears forward and nickered
softly, but there was no response from Nicola.

David swung down from the saddle and tied the stallion's reins to a tree a short distance from the mare.
Glancing down at the soft ground, he spied what was un-
mistakably the impression of a lady's boot! So, she *had*
gone for a walk. And, by the looks of things, straight into
the dense growth of forest nearby.

Cursing whatever impulse had compelled Nicola to ride
out alone this morning, David began to walk towards the
trees. A raw wind was blowing and the skies overhead
had turned grey and ominous-looking. He only hoped that
she had thought to dress warmly, especially when he
passed through the first line of trees and into the forest
proper. It was damper in here, and considerably colder. A
lightweight jacket would offer little protection in this kind
of weather.

The path of footprints veered to the left and right, and
in places it disappeared altogether, forcing David to re-

trace his steps any number of times. What the devil had Nicola been doing? It was almost as though she had been…looking for something. But what?

'Nicola!' David's voice echoed in the heavy stillness of the forest, the huge trees seeming to absorb the sound. 'Nicola, can you hear me?'

When there was still no answer, David pressed on. It was tough going, given the way the lower branches of the trees had grown into each other, but he refused to give up. His feelings of concern were rapidly giving way to alarm as the forest continued to close in all around him. He didn't like thinking about Nicola, alone and unprotected, in the midst of all this.

'Nicola?' he shouted. 'Nicola, are you there?'

He was just about to turn to the right when he heard it—a faint sound coming from the small clearing just up ahead. 'Nicola?'

'David…'

David froze, trying to pinpoint her location. Her voice had sounded strangely hollow, as though it were echoing off walls, but there was no doubt that it was her. Unfortunately, he had absolutely no idea where it was coming from. 'Nicola, keep calling,' David shouted as he hurried towards the clearing. 'It will help me locate you.'

'I'm here,' the voice said weakly. 'The well.'

Abruptly, David halted. A well?

Then, seconds later, he saw it—barely visible through the dense undergrowth just at the front of the clearing— the crumbling top of an old dry well. And, caught on a twig next to it, a lacy bit of fabric from a lady's petticoat. *Nicola!*

Heedless of the sharp thorns that tore at his buckskins, David ran the last few yards. 'Nicola! Are you all right?'

'David, we're…down here…in the well.'

We? David pushed his way to the edge of the well—marvelling that Nicola had been able to get through the dense foliage at all—and then saw that the vines and undergrowth covering the top had indeed been disturbed. Dropping to his knees, he peered down into the wide opening—and saw Nicola standing in a deep pile of leaves at the bottom. She looked to be about nine feet down—and she was clutching a tiny ginger kitten in her arms.

'Nicola! How in the name of God did you fall in?'

Fear sharpened his voice and reverberated off the masonry walls, causing Nicola to flinch. 'There is no need to shout, my lord; I can hear you perfectly well.'

Wondering if she could hear his curses as clearly, David carefully lowered his voice. 'Are you all right? Are you hurt?'

'No. At least, not very much. I think I may have… twisted my ankle when I landed, but it's not too bad at the moment. And I did hit my hand on the way down, but at least I was able to save Merlin,' Nicola said, gleefully holding up the kitten for him to see.

Merlin, David reflected grimly. He might have known.

'Are you telling me that you fell into the well because you were trying to rescue a cat?'

'He is only a kitten, and there was no other way of getting him out,' Nicola explained. 'He couldn't climb out because the walls are too steep and his claws aren't very big at all.'

And he obviously shares none of the more useful traits of the wizard for whom he's named, David thought darkly. All he said, however, was, 'Did you give any thought as to how *you* were going to get out, once you had accomplished your rescue?'

Nicola bit her lip. 'Actually, no.'

'No, I thought not,' David muttered, trying to keep his

temper in check. The little fool! She might have broken her neck—and all because of some wretched cat!

Well, he couldn't say that he was terribly surprised. It was typical behaviour for the woman he loved. He was just going to have to get used to it.

'All right, darling, don't worry; I'll have you out in a trice.'

'Oh, David, I'm so glad you came,' Nicola whispered weakly, his tender use of the endearment causing her carefully erected defences to fall.

The softening in her voice was all he needed to hear. Quickly making his way back to where he had left Knight, David untied the reins and led the stallion into the woods. He would have walked across hot coals if she had asked him to.

The matter of how to get her out of the well, however, gave David a moment's pause. But for the injury to her hand he could have used the stirrup leathers to pull her up, but with the wound still being as painful as it was there was no question of her being able to hold on as tightly as would have been necessary. Which meant that he had no choice but to try to lift Nicola out of the well himself.

'All right, Nicola,' David said when he finally reached the edge of the well again—which was no small task with the stallion in tow. 'You showed me how well you could climb a tree. Now you're going to have to show me how well you can climb a wall.'

'*What?*'

'I am going to lean into the well and pull you out.'

'David, you *mustn't*! You'll fall!'

'Not if I can help it,' David said, bringing Knight as close to the edge of the well as he dared. Moving around to the saddle, he let down the stirrup leather as far as it would go, then checked the girth to make sure that it was tight. If the saddle slipped in the middle of this, they might *both* find themselves at the bottom of the well!

'I'm going to lower myself down until I can reach you. That's when I need you to tuck up your skirts like you did before, and put your feet against the wall. When I start to lift, you start to climb. Otherwise you'll be dragged up against the stone.'

Nicola felt a tiny flicker of apprehension. 'But...if you're leaning into the well, how will you be able to pull us both out?'

'Don't worry, Knight will take care of that.' David stripped off his jacket, knowing he would have more freedom without it, and said, 'Are you ready?'

Nicola nodded gamely. 'Yes, I suppose, but...I'd like you to take Merlin up first.'

'Merlin be—' Just in time, David caught the remark which would definitely not have earned him a kindly reception, and grudgingly nodded. He kneeled down, bracing his knees against the wall of the well, and reached in as far as he could. 'All right, pass him up.'

'Be good, Merlin,' Nicola whispered. She pressed a kiss to the kitten's furry brow, and then, standing on her very tiptoes, stretched her arms up as high as she could.

David easily grasped the kitten in one hand and brought him up to the surface. He was a funny-looking mite, with eyes that looked too big for his head and his fur all matted. But for all that he was an endearing little fellow, and David was surprised to feel a smile work its way to his lips.

'There you are, old chap, safe and sound.' He put the kitten on a patch of soft grass a short distance away and watched for a moment to make sure that he didn't run away. The last thing David wanted was for Nicola to come through all this, only to find the kitten gone. He also didn't want the little ball of fluff heading back towards the well, where the stallion might inadvertently step on him. That, too, would make for a sad conclusion to the day's activities!

Fortunately, whether the kitten was surprised at finding himself in the open air again, or merely exhausted as a result of his adventure, he seemed quite content to stay where he was, which thankfully allowed David to get on with his preparations for rescuing Nicola.

Resting his hands on the edge of the well again, he reached back with his left leg and placed his booted foot through the stirrup cup, wedging it firmly against the metal. Then he hooked the toe of his right foot over the edge of the well, and slowly and carefully began to lower himself down.

'All right, Nicola, it's your turn,' David said, trying to ignore the tempting sight of her smooth white legs which were bare now from knee to ankle. 'Reach up your arms towards me.'

It was a daring manoeuvre and Nicola doubted that a man less muscular than David would even have attempted it. She raised her arms as he instructed, and felt his hands close firmly around her wrists. But when he began to lift the pressure caused her injured hand to start throbbing, and she gasped, tears springing sharply to her eyes.

'Are you all right?' David whispered, immediately letting her go.

Nicola bit down hard on her lip, and nodded. David was risking a great deal to get her out of here, and she wasn't about to show him weakness in return. After all, she had only herself to blame for the predicament she was in.

'Forgive me, my lord, I shall…be fine. I was simply…unprepared for you to lift me.'

David drew a deep breath, knowing that it was the pain she was unprepared for, and wished there were some way of sparing her. 'I'm sorry to hurt you, Nicola, but I can't think of any other way of getting you out. Other than riding back to Wyndham and putting together a rescue party.'

'No! Please, I'd…rather not be left alone down here for that length of time,' Nicola admitted. 'I'm sure we can make this work. Perhaps if you were to grasp my arms a little higher up it might make it easier on my hand.'

David nodded his agreement and changed his hold. 'All right, let's give it another try.'

The next few minutes would stay in Nicola's memory for a long time. As David again began to lift, she valiantly ignored the pain in her hand and concentrated instead on walking her feet up the wall. The leverage to pull them out of the well came from the magnificent stallion who, at a soft whistle from his master, began slowly to back away, pulling his master with him. With David executing a series of jerks and twists as his body was dragged upwards, and Nicola using her feet to keep her body away from the wall, the short trip to the top was soon accomplished.

When she was close enough to do so, Nicola gripped the edge of the well with her good hand and pulled herself the rest of the way out. Seconds later, she collapsed on the grass, exhausted by her efforts.

'My lord, your face is…uncommon red,' she said, when at last she was able to catch her breath.

David carefully extricated his foot from the stirrup, and then, after sweeping back the dark curls that had fallen forward onto his face, dropped to his knees in the grass

beside her. 'You try hanging upside down for that length
of time and we shall see what colour *your* face is.' He
reached out to brush back a wispy tendril of copper-kissed
hair from Nicola's forehead, and asked, 'How is your
hand?'

'It's…fine,' she fibbed. In truth, it was throbbing like
the devil, but it seemed ungracious to say so after everything David had just done to save her. Instead, Nicola
closed her eyes and lay back, enjoying the gentle caress
of David's fingers against her temple. For a moment, it
didn't matter that they were all alone in the middle of a
cold, damp forest, or that she was lying in the grass, with
her gown torn and her hair in disarray. All that mattered
was that they *were* alone, and that David's touch was as
gentle and as comforting as any she had ever felt.

Quite unconsciously, she turned and pressed her face
into his hand.

David caught his breath. 'Nicola!'

Slowly opening her eyes, Nicola looked up and saw the
tenderness in his face—and knew that he was going to
kiss her. And, suddenly, it was all that she really wanted.
It was as though everything that had gone before had been
leading up to this moment; as if it was inevitable. Her
lashes fluttered closed, she tipped back her head, offering
her lips up to his—

And then shot bolt upright as something sharp and furry
landed on her bare calf!

'Merlin!'

True enough, the mischievous kitten had struggled
across the narrow strip of grass and was now using his
needle-sharp claws to pull himself up her bare leg. And
if that wasn't bad enough, Nicola suddenly realized that
her skirts *were* still up around her knees and that she had
a huge tear in the fabric. Her entire body felt as though

it had been severely pummelled, David was staring at her in dismay—and suddenly, and quite helplessly, she began to laugh.

'Well, I'm glad you find it so amusing,' David muttered, aware that the feisty ball of orange fluff had just robbed him of a much desired kiss. He reached over and carefully plucked the kitten from Nicola's leg, then set him in the long grass beside her. 'Good Lord, what a voice,' he observed when the kitten promptly set up a series of howls. 'He certainly doesn't seem to have suffered for his adventure in the woods. Or to realize that it was his clumsiness that started this whole thing in the first place.'

'Oh, David, it's really not his fault,' Nicola said, wiping tears of laughter from her eyes as the plaintive chorus of meows continued. 'Cats are curious by nature. But I do believe this little one may have just used up the first of his nine lives.'

'Yes, you're probably right.' Then, taking pity on him, David reached over and lifted the kitten out of the grass, and set him in Nicola's lap. 'Let's just hope you're around for his next eight.'

Nicola picked up the sorry-looking sight and held it to her cheek. 'Oh, bless his heart, he's purring for all he's worth. Listen.'

She held the kitten to David's ear and watched as the expression on his face changed. 'Good Lord, what a strange sound. And you say that's what he does when he's happy?'

'Yes.'

'Then what does he do when he's annoyed?'

Nicola's mouth curved in a rueful smile. 'Something quite different, I can assure you. But that is hardly important at the moment, my lord. What matters is that Merlin and I are safe because of you.'

David glanced at the sight of Nicola cuddling the kitten to her breast—aware that he would have given his entire fortune to have changed places with it—and slowly got to his feet. His buckskins were ruined and his boots were scuffed beyond repair, but that was of little consequence at the moment.

The lady was safe. Everything else was secondary.

The ride back to Wyndham Hall was a painful one for Nicola. The throbbing which had started in her foot when she had awkwardly fallen into the well was now painful in the extreme, and it was all she could do not to cry out every time it brushed against the side of her mare. Her hand was throbbing too, and, consequently, she and David were obliged to walk their horses nearly the entire way back. This resulted in a problem of another kind, since Merlin was clearly not used to being held for any length of time. In the end, David was forced to stuff the kitten into one of his saddle-bags, where his muffled cries of outrage could be heard for most of the trip. When eventually they did stop, David peeked into the bag to make sure that everything was all right, and was relieved to see that Merlin had finally fallen asleep. The rest of the trip was completed in relative silence.

As for his own intentions of trying to persuade Nicola to change her mind about him, David decided that this was definitely not the time to open the discussion. She was clearly exhausted by the morning's activities. Her face was white, and it was obvious that she was in considerable distress.

David had removed her boot prior to their setting off, fearing that when the foot began to swell the boot would be painfully constricting. In the end, however, it had done little to lessen her discomfort. And her hand was still throbbing as a result of his lifting her out of the well.

No, the only thing that mattered now was getting Nicola home, where the combination of a hot bath and her aunt's loving ministrations would surely help to ease her suffering. The time for them to talk could wait. What he had to say was far too important to be said in a rush.

Because David knew that if he said the wrong thing, or in the wrong way, he ran the risk of losing *everything*.

'Well, my dear, that was quite a little adventure you had this morning,' Lady Dorchester said as she tucked the covers up around Nicola's chin later that night. 'And you are a very lucky young lady to have come through it relatively unscathed.'

'Yes, I suppose I am,' Nicola agreed ruefully. 'I dare say I should still be at the bottom of that well had it not been for Lord Blackwood.'

To Nicola's relief, her aunt had not reprimanded her too harshly for her careless behaviour in the forest. Once she had learned that the welfare of an animal had been involved—and, in particular, that of a rather lovable little kitten—her annoyance had all but vanished. After all, what would have been the point?

'Yes, how very fortunate you were that he happened upon your horse and came looking for you,' Lady Dorchester said. 'I hope you were suitably appreciative.'

Nicola smiled. What would her aunt have said, she wondered, if she knew just how close she had come to allowing David to kiss her as a sign of her…appreciation? 'Is Papa still annoyed with me?' she asked instead.

Lady Dorchester chuckled. 'Yes, but he'll get over it. He knows as well as I do that when it comes to an animal in distress you act first and think later. And Merlin is a dear little fellow. I can see why you felt the need to try to rescue him. But, for what it's worth, Nicola, you really must be more careful in the future. Lord Blackwood was right—you could have done yourself a very serious injury climbing into that well. Or falling into it, as the case may be.'

Nicola sighed, and shifted her foot to the left, trying to find a more comfortable position in which to lay it. 'Yes, thankfully it is only my ankle which suffered in the fall. In truth, I did not expect the pile of leaves at the bottom of the well to be so deep.'

Lady Dorchester tutted audibly. 'Well, never mind that now, my dear. Try to get some sleep. I shall bring you a tray in the morning and then we shall see how you are feeling. But I think it goes without saying that you will have to stay close to home for the next little while. Goodnight, my dear.'

'Goodnight, Aunt Glynn,' Nicola said, before leaning over to blow out the candle. Yes, she would have to stay at home. And given the rampant state of her emotions, and everything that had happened today, she could not say that she was overly sorry.

Chapter Fifteen

Four days later, a very different David set out for Wyndham Hall.

Different because, over the course of those four days, David had had time to come to terms with the intensity of his feelings for Nicola. He had spent many long hours thinking about her, and about everything that had happened to him since he had met her. And, for the first time in his life, he began to understand exactly what it was to love someone—a discovery that had both startled and overwhelmed him. He began to comprehend the incredible power that love commanded. How it could change people, and enable them to see truths which they had never seen before—both about themselves, and about others.

For the first time since his father's death, David began to fully understand just how deeply his father had suffered when the two women he had loved most in the world had died.

That had probably been the most enlightening discovery of all. He was finally able to understand why, after Stephanie de Charbier had died, his father had lost the will to go on living. Because David knew now that to live without love was far more painful than dying. It left a man empty, and without direction. It allowed him to exist, but not to thrive.

That was what David learned over the course of the four days he spent away from Nicola. And it was the reason he knew that he had to get her back—at any cost!

He found Nicola reclining on the chaise longue in the yellow salon at Wyndham Hall. Her foot was covered with a warm blanket, and she was working on a piece of embroidery. David could tell from the look on her face that she was surprised to see him, but hoped that the telltale colouring of her cheeks indicated that she was not displeased.

'Good afternoon, Lady Nicola. I trust I find you in better health than I did upon the occasion of our last meeting four days ago?'

Nicola glanced up at her handsome visitor and felt her heart begin to race within her breast. Was it really only four days since she had last seen David? It seemed like an eternity. He was dressed for riding, in a well-tailored frock coat and top boots, and his hair was casually dishevelled by the wind, as though he had been riding hard. Nicola thought him quite the most devastatingly attractive man she had ever seen.

'Very much, thank you, Lord Blackwood. The… swelling in my foot has gone down a little, though not enough to allow me to wear shoes. And the injury to my hand is healing nicely, given frequent applications of a most wondrous salve.'

'I am relieved to hear it,' David said, in a voice that warmed her right through. He glanced down at the carpet, where the mischievous ginger kitten—who had obviously been given a bath and was now looking much more handsome for it—was playing with a thick ball of yarn, and smiled. 'Merlin seems to have suffered no ill effects. In fact, he's looking quite at home here.'

'No doubt due to the fact that Cook gives him milk when she thinks no one is looking, and that my aunt plays with him for hours on end,' Nicola remarked wryly. 'Everyone seems to be quite taken with him.'

David chuckled softly. 'I'm not surprised. There is a certain appeal to that furry little face.' He glanced around the room. 'I am surprised that Lady Dorchester is not with you.'

Nicola blushed softly. She was not about to tell him that her aunt had left the moment she'd learned that David had called. 'She was here a moment ago, but left to have a word with Cook. I am sure that she will return... shortly.'

David carefully kept his smile to himself. Yes, no doubt she would—shortly *after* he had left. He walked towards the armchair closest to the chaise longue where Nicola rested, and sat down. 'My uncle wished me to pass along his regards to her.'

'I shall make sure that she receives them, Lord Blackwood. I am pleased to hear that she is still in his thoughts.'

'Of that there is no doubt,' David reassured her.

There was a momentary silence, before Nicola said, 'My lord, I do not know if I...thanked you properly for everything you did for me the other day. Had you not found us, Merlin and I should certainly have been stuck at the bottom of that well for a good deal longer than we were.'

'Your thanks are not necessary, Lady Nicola. The only thing I ask is for your assurance that you will not ride out unescorted again,' David replied. 'Your penchant for doing the unusual puts you at greater risk than most young ladies, and I know that I—and indeed all those who care about you—would be relieved to know that you were not venturing out alone.'

'I give you my word that I will not flaunt the conventions again. In fact,' Nicola added, looking somewhat embarrassed, 'I do not think Roberts will even allow me to ride out unless I am accompanied. He told me that he was considerably shaken by our appearance upon arriving back at Wyndham.'

'Yes, I'm sure he was, given the wretched state of our clothing.' David suddenly started to laugh. 'Between the grass stains on my buckskins, and the wet patches on your dress, I dare say he wondered precisely what manner of *accident* had befallen you.'

Aware that the circumstances had looked rather condemnatory, Nicola felt her cheeks burn as brightly as they had that day in the woods. 'I fear you may be correct. I…didn't think about it at the time, but I am sure my aunt harboured similar…concerns when she saw me. Until I explained what really did happen. And then she was extremely grateful for your assistance. As was my father.' Nicola hesitated again, trying to find the right words. 'Roberts told me that…you asked him where I might be found.'

'Yes, I did.'

'So your…coming upon me in the woods that morning was not…entirely coincidental, as I thought.'

Feeling there was no point in denying it, David bent his head. 'The only coincidence was that I managed to find you at all. Roberts told me the direction in which you had set out and I likewise set out upon that route. But the fact that I traced your footprints into the forest and ultimately found you at the bottom of a well was, I think, good luck rather than good planning.'

'I confess, I was…astonished to learn that you had

come looking for me at all. Papa told me that you wished to speak with me on a matter of some importance, but I thought we had said…all that needed to be.'

It was hardly an auspicious beginning, but David refused to be discouraged by it. He would not leave this house until she had heard everything that he had come to say. 'Lady Nicola, I will come straight to the point. I came to Wyndham on Thursday morning for two reasons. The first was to apologise for my abominable behaviour at Lord and Lady Bently's ball. I had no right to say the things to you that I did. They were hurtful and cruel, and I regret them deeply. Especially having since learned that they were as far removed from the truth as can be imagined.'

A flicker of alarm cast a shadow across her face. 'And what truth is that?'

'That the injury to your hand was not inflicted by one of your pets as I so firmly believed, but rather by my cousin, Arabella Braithwaite.'

Shock drained the colour from Nicola's cheeks and rendered her momentarily speechless. Arabella! But…how in the world had he found out? Surely the woman hadn't confessed to the deed? No, of course she hadn't. Arabella would hardly jeopardize her position with her beloved cousin by admitting to such an act of aggression against the woman he had once planned to marry. But how else could he have found out?

Needing time to gather her thoughts, Nicola fiddled with the blanket covering her foot. 'Why would you believe such an unlikely thing to be true, my lord?'

'As you once said to me, it doesn't matter how I know, only that I do. And I apologize from the bottom of my heart for ever having doubted you.'

Nicola wasn't overly surprised that David would not

divulge the source of his information. He was not the type
to cast blame, any more than she was. However, it was
of little consequence now. 'I accept your apology, my
lord,' she said simply.

'You do?'

'Yes.'

David glanced at her with renewed hope. 'I am delighted to hear—'

'You said there were two matters upon which you
wanted to see me,' Nicola interrupted, not wishing him to
read more into her words than she intended. 'What is the
second?'

'Ah. Well, the second is in regard to…you and I, and
to our relationship.'

Somehow, Nicola managed to ignore the sudden flurry
of butterflies in her stomach, and said, 'We no longer have
a relationship, Lord Blackwood. I thought that was clearly
understood.'

David sighed. 'Yes, it was. But I was hoping that we
might remedy that situation. Because I am not ashamed
to admit that, for me, these past few weeks have been
pure hell.'

The words were spoken with a quiet conviction that
carried far more weight than had he raised his voice and
shouted the roof down. Nicola was surprised to find an
uncomfortable tightness in her throat, and wondered how
much she should say. 'They have…not been easy for me
either,' she admitted finally. 'I find that you are…not an
easy man to forget.'

'Then do not try to,' David said, in a voice as gentle
as she had ever heard him use. 'I love you, Nicola, with
all my heart. More than I ever would have believed possible. You are everything that is good and beautiful, and
it is my dearest wish,' he said, as he reached across and

took her hand in his, 'that we forget what has passed between us, and once again plan to be married.'

It was an impassioned speech, and, just for a moment, Nicola was sorely tempted to forget everything that had happened, and to go along with him as he asked. But even as the temptation loomed the cold hard light of reality returned, and, with it, all of Nicola's fears. 'I am…truly sorry, my lord, but I fear it…would not work.'

'But why? Do you doubt that I love you? Because if you do I am well able to understand why,' David confessed. 'I have not exactly been forthcoming about my feelings for you at any time during our engagement, Nicola. But until these last few days I really had no idea of how deeply I felt.'

Nicola knew that the words were intended to make her feel loved and to communicate fully the depth of his feelings. But hearing the heartfelt sentiments now from the man she loved more than any other only made her feel worse. She gazed into the clear blue eyes that were so filled with hope, and sadly shook her head. 'I do not doubt that you love me, or that you wish to marry me. But we cannot change what has passed between us, nor can we forget it.'

'If you are referring to the way in which I have behaved towards your animals, I understand fully. But I want you to know that you are welcome—indeed, I urge you—to bring any and all of your pets with you when you come to your new home at Ridley Hall.'

'Oh, David, I wish it were that simple,' Nicola said sadly. It was an indication of her state of mind that she allowed herself to address him by his Christian name. 'But the fact of the matter is that you do not like animals, nor do you trust them.'

'Do you not believe that a man can change?'

'In some things, yes, but not, I think, in this. I find it difficult to believe that, were I to show you a gash on my arm or leg at some time in the future, you would not automatically assume that it had been inflicted by whatever kind of animal I happened to be keeping at the time,' Nicola told him. 'And, while you might be able to understand the animal's reasons for injuring me, you would always resent it for doing so. Like my father, you believe that wild animals belong in the wild.'

'Your father was willing to concede a great deal for the woman he loved,' David pointed out gently. 'Are you saying that I cannot?'

Nicola's expression was pragmatic. 'My father was not aware of the nature of my mother's abilities before he married her, my lord, whereas you are. And, more importantly, so is Society. They have been witness to it on several occasions. Do you really believe that the gentlemen who saw the incident with Alistair in the forest will ever forget it? Or that the aristocratic ladies who come to call will not furtively be casting their eyes into every corner of the room, looking for a mouse? I fear that people will always regard me as an oddity, and that they will secretly be saying, "I wonder if the Marchioness of Blackwood really *is* a witch?"'

'I don't give a damn what people say,' David said fiercely.

'Ah, but you did. Was it not you who told me that you were looking for…a woman of breeding? A woman who knew how to conduct herself in Society, and who was not prone towards…unacceptable behaviour. Pray tell me, David, during the last few weeks, what have I evidenced *except* unacceptable behaviour?' Nicola said, her voice catching slightly. 'This latest episode with Merlin is nothing if not proof of what I just said.'

'Nicola—'

'No, please, do not make this any harder than it already is. You are a sportsman like your father, and like his father before him. Your attitudes cannot change, nor have I any right to expect them to. And since I cannot undo the damage I have already brought to your name the only way I can exonerate myself is by avoiding any further association with it.'

David dropped to his knees in front of her. 'I love you, Nicola. I want to spend the rest of my life proving that to you. Can you honestly tell me that you have no similar feelings? That you care nothing for me in return?'

Nicola gazed down at him and was surprised that he could not read what she felt for him in her face. 'I love you so much that it hurts,' she said, in a voice that was barely above a whisper. 'I have for a long time. But I will not marry a man who does not believe me, or trust me. I can't spend my entire life trying to make my husband feel as I do about the matters which are closest to my heart. It would be too…emotionally draining. Especially when those are the very matters which would serve to bring scandal and disgrace to his name.'

'It did not stop your mother and father from being happy together,' David said, desperately wishing that he could make her understand. 'You cannot tell me that your father did not adore your mother, or that she loved him any the less for knowing that he hunted the very animals she cared for so deeply.'

Nicola sighed, knowing that it was true. 'No, but you and I are not our parents, and we both know how things stand going into this marriage. And, knowing that, I cannot see how I would not continue to be hurt, and you would not be angered and frustrated in the future. It is the existence of feelings such as these which lead to further resentment and to the eventual breakdown of a marriage altogether.'

David studied the woman in front of him and sadly shook his head. He couldn't deny that her arguments made sense. They were logical, rational, and well thought out. And at the moment he could have happily tossed each and every one of them out of the window. 'Is there nothing I can say which will make you change your mind?'

Nicola turned her face away, aware of an emptiness that was so deep, it went far beyond tears. 'No, my lord. I fear that in this instance there is not.'

As he stood up and gazed down at her, David felt the bitterness of despair slash open his heart. She loved him, and yet she would not have him. A rejection which effectively condemned them both to a life of misery and solitude.

David said nothing as he turned to leave. He feared that, if he did, it might be something he would have cause to regret later. He merely closed the door with a soft click, and left. He did not encounter Lord Wyndham or Lady Dorchester as he walked down the long quiet hallway, and for that he was grateful, since he had absolutely no idea what he would have said to them. Other than that...it was over.

In the yard, he swung up into the saddle, his eyes staring blankly ahead as he gathered up the reins, and started down the long gravelled drive.

He had lost her. That much was now painfully clear. There was nothing he could do. Nothing more that he could say to convince Nicola that he loved her and everything else that she held dear. Including a kitten named Merlin, a mouse named Arthur, and even a fox named...

Alistair.

David's head shot up. *Alistair.* But of course! Why hadn't he thought of it before?

Whirling the stallion's head around, David galloped back up the drive towards the young lad who had just brought up his horse, and shouted, 'I say, you there!'

Fearfully, the boy turned. 'Y-yes, m'lord?'

'Where can I find a young lad named Jamie?'

'Jamie?' Obviously relieved that he was not the cause of the marquis's displeasure, the lad said, 'He'll be down by the stables, m'lord.'

With a crisp nod, David set off in that direction. Yes, it was true that there was probably nothing he could *say* to Nicola that would convince her of how deeply he loved her. But if he could *show* her that he was serious, and that the things that mattered most to her mattered equally to him, perhaps he would have a better chance. He had to try. Because, right now, even the slimmest of chances was worth pursuing.

'On your feet, Jamie, me lad,' Roberts said briskly. 'His lordship would like a word.'

Jamie glanced up into the face of the head groom, and then at the Marquis of Blackwood standing behind him, and nervously scrambled to his feet. 'Wiv me?'

'Aye. Take off your cap.'

Jamie quickly dragged the offending article from his head and stood with it in his hands, wondering what he could have done to warrant the attention of the mighty Marquis of Blackwood. 'Yes, m'lord?'

'Jamie, in the library the other day, you told Lord Wyndham that you had found Alistair. Is that true?'

Jamie regarded the peer with a hint of suspicion in his eyes. He hadn't forgotten that this was the man who had spoken to his beloved Lady Nicola so harshly, and he

wasn't quite sure whether to forgive him or not. 'Aye, my
lord. I saw a fox that looked just like 'im out in the far
woods, so I tracked 'im down.'

'And?'

'It was Alistair, all right.'

'You're sure?'

'I'm sure. 'E 'ad the same white patch of fur on 'is
foreleg.'

'Do you think you could find him again?'

Jamie blinked his surprise. 'I suppose I could.'

'Good. Because I have a very large favour to ask of
you, Jamie,' David said, refusing to acknowledge how
desperately he needed the answer to be yes. 'Would you
be willing to take me to him?'

The young lad was clearly shocked at the idea of taking
a marquis into the woods to look for a fox, and it showed
in his face. 'Why? You wouldn't want to be 'unting 'im,
would yer?'

'Good God, no, that's the last thing I want. All I want
to do is to make perfectly sure that it *is* Alistair before
we raise Lady Nicola's hopes. You know how much she
loved that little fox, and it would break her heart if it
turned out to be another.'

Jamie bristled. 'It *was* Alistair, my lord, I know it was.
'E 'ad the mark, and I ain't never seen another one like
it.'

'Nevertheless, we have to be sure. And that's why I
want to go and see him for myself. Then we can surprise
Lady Nicola by taking her to see him so that she can see
that he really is safe. Will you help me?'

The lad hesitated for a moment, but then, deciding that
the marquis wasn't such a rum cove after all, nodded his
agreement. 'Aye, m'lord. When do you want to go?'

David glanced briefly at the head groom, and then

smiled back down at Jamie. 'Saddle a mount for the lad, Roberts. We have a very important mission to undertake.'

The following afternoon, David returned to Wyndham Hall once more. But this time he did so in the company of Sir Giles Chapman.

When his uncle had asked him whether he might accompany David the next time he ventured to Wyndham, David had agreed willingly enough. However, it was clear from the onset that the older man was in a considerable state of nerves.

'Is it my imagination, Uncle, or are you in more of a pucker this afternoon than usual?'

Clearly preoccupied with his thoughts, Sir Giles jumped, and then gruffly cleared his throat. 'Can't think what you mean, David. I'm as calm as the breeze on a summer's day.'

'Then why have you been fiddling with the buckle on your rein all the way over here?'

Abruptly letting go of the offending article, Sir Giles said, 'I am not fiddling. I'm just...thinking.'

'About anything in particular?'

'No.'

David nodded, pretending to watch the flight of a small bird above them. They rode in silence for a few more minutes before he said, 'By the by, I did mention that Lady Dorchester asked about you the last time I saw her, didn't I?'

It seemed to David that his uncle suddenly grew even more tense. 'A number of times.'

'Ah, good. I just wanted to be sure that you knew,' David said, tactfully hiding a smile.

Sir Giles slanted his nephew a perceptive glance. 'You

seem to be in rare spirits today. Dare I ask if there has been a change in the lady's feelings?'

'There has not,' David confessed, his own confidence ebbing just a little. He knew that he was taking perhaps the biggest gamble of his life today, but he had to try. The alternative was untenable. 'However, I am hoping that, with a little luck, I may yet win the day. One never knows with the fairer sex.' He glanced at his uncle again, noting that the colour had deepened in the older man's cheeks. 'I say, Uncle, are you sure you're all right?'

'Yes, of course. Never better,' Sir Giles said quickly.

But a little too quickly, David thought in amusement. He said nothing, however, as they drew the horses to a halt in front of Wyndham Hall and tossed the reins to the waiting groom. After all, David reflected, every man had a right to his privacy.

Nicola and her aunt were both in the yellow salon when David and Sir Giles were announced. Nicola was reclining on the chaise longue once again, her head bent over her embroidery, while Lady Dorchester sat in a chair by the window, reading. She looked very fetching in a gown of jonquil silk, and as she rose to greet them David thought he detected a definite sparkle in her lovely eyes.

'Lord Blackwood, Sir Giles, what a pleasant surprise. Just what we needed to brighten a dreary afternoon. Wouldn't you agree, Nicola?'

David knew that his presence in the room would be painful for Nicola, but, like the lady she was, she put aside whatever she was feeling, and offered them both a warm smile. 'Indeed. The weather has certainly closed in on us.' She glanced at David once, smiled, and then abruptly looked away. 'You are…looking well, Sir Giles.'

'I am? Oh, thank you, Lady Nicola,' Sir Giles said a

touch self-consciously. 'And may I say that you…that is, that both of you are looking all the crack?'

'Sir Giles, you are as charming as ever,' Lady Dorchester observed as she crossed to the bell pull. 'Please, won't you both be seated? I shall ring for tea.'

The gentlemen advanced into the room. Sir Giles glanced longingly at the vacant chair next to Lady Dorchester, but decided on the settee opposite. David took the vacant chair, which placed him directly opposite Nicola. He was relieved to see that her foot was on the mend, since she had both shoes on this afternoon. She was wearing a becoming gown in a soft shade of pink that was extremely flattering to her complexion, and, to David, she was all that was beautiful.

For a moment, an awkward silence filled the room. Then, abruptly, everyone started talking at once.

'Well, it would seem that we are all of a like mind this afternoon,' Lady Dorchester commented, her words accompanied by a silvery ripple of laughter. She noticed Nicola's studiously averted face, and glanced rather pointedly at Sir Giles.

'Ah, yes,' that gentleman said, taking his cue. 'Well, Lady Nicola, how fares your injured falcon?'

Nicola blanched. It was the last thing she had been expecting to hear. Even Lady Dorchester seemed taken aback, and glanced nervously at Blackwood, obviously expecting him to be just as confounded. To her surprise, however, he showed absolutely no signs of discomfort at all.

'Yes, indeed, Lady Nicola, I was of a mind to ask after the bird's welfare myself,' David remarked casually. 'Is the wing improving?'

Nicola glanced from one gentleman to the other, clearly suspecting them of having sport with her, and said, 'I hardly think the topic is appropriate for the conversation, or that either of you are truly interested.'

'On the contrary, I am very interested,' David assured her. 'In fact, I was wondering if you had ever thought of training the bird, now that it has apparently become accustomed to the wrist?'

Not convinced of David's sincerity for a moment, but knowing that it would be impolite not to answer at all, Nicola lifted her shoulders in a delicate shrug. 'To tell the truth, I have never given any thought to the possibility of training Guinevere. My only concern was in getting her well again. However, as I doubt that the wing will ever be strong enough to allow her to return to a life in the wild, it is reasonable to believe that she might be useful as a sporting bird.'

'My sentiments exactly. In fact, I would be interested in handling her myself,' David offered. '*If* you feel she is trainable.'

Nicola stared at him for a moment, searching for any sign—even a hint—that he was mocking her, but could find nothing. He looked to be in total earnest—and genuinely interested.

'I believe she…could be good at it,' Nicola said cautiously, 'though I am not aware of what is involved in the training of falcons.'

'Uncle Giles, did you not mention that a friend of yours does just that?'

'Indeed, I did, my boy. Bit of a queer fish, old Lord Sharpe, but a talented one nonetheless. I'm sure he wouldn't mind passing along a few tips if I asked him.'

'Splendid. Perhaps you could speak to him in the near future about the possibility of handling Guinevere himself?' David suggested.

'Consider it done.'

'Thank you.'

Silence descended again. This time it was broken by the arrival of the tea tray.

'Ah, tea. Capital,' Sir Giles said, obviously in some relief.

David glanced sharply at the older man, again wondering what was afoot. There was definitely something on the baronet's mind; David had never seen him this agitated before.

'Thank you, Trethewy, you may set it down next to Lady Nicola,' Lady Dorchester said. 'Perhaps you would be so good as to pour, my dear?'

Nicola regarded her aunt in surprise, but graciously complied. 'Yes, of course, Aunt Glynnis.' She wasn't sure why her aunt had chosen to deviate from the norm, but she nevertheless reached for a cup and saucer and, lifting the silver teapot, began to pour. Her hand had come along well in the last few days, and she was pleased to see how steadily she was able to hold the cup and saucer as she added sugar, and then passed it to her aunt.

'Sir Giles?' Nicola asked, reaching for the second cup.

'Just a little milk, my dear.'

Nicola duly poured in a drop of milk and then added the hot tea. Funny how loud the ticking of the clock on the mantel suddenly seemed to have become in the room. She passed the cup to Sir Giles, and then raised her eyes to David's. 'Tea, my lord?'

'Thank you.'

Not needing to ask, Nicola prepared his tea the way she knew he liked it. No milk, no sugar.

'Was that a new mount I saw you riding today, Lord Blackwood?' Lady Dorchester asked conversationally as the tray of warm, buttery scones was passed around.

'It was indeed, Lady Dorchester. I picked him up at Tatt's just this week.'

'Aye, and a prime bit of blood he is too,' Sir Giles piped up. 'But then, most of David's cattle are.'

'Perhaps you would care to take a look at him later on, Lady Nicola,' David offered. 'I would value your opinion.'

Nicola flushed, clearly not having expected such an invitation. 'I am flattered that you would ask, my lord, but my knowledge of good horseflesh is hardly superior to yours. If he is a sound galloper in your opinion, mine is scarcely worth the trouble of obtaining.'

This time, however, it was Lady Dorchester who inadvertently came to David's aid. 'Now, Nicola, you know that isn't true. You have always been a most shrewd judge of an animal's character, especially when it comes to horses. I vow you truly do have your mother's gift in that regard.'

Instinctively, Nicola cringed, hearing again the type of remark that was guaranteed to make David squirm. But once again he surprised her.

'Which is precisely why I asked, Lady Dorchester,' David concurred. 'I would venture to say that Lady Nicola's perception allows her a far greater insight into the matter than anyone else has. And, as I have not had the animal long, and am not acquainted with all of his tempers, I was hoping that perhaps she could lend me some assistance in that regard.'

Nicola inclined her head, albeit cautiously. 'I would be...pleased to have a look at him, my lord.'

'Thank you, Lady Nicola.'

Silence descended for a third time. This time, it was broken by Sir Giles, who abruptly set the china cup on the table next to him and hastily got to his feet. 'Lady

Dorchester, I wonder if you would…do me the honour of walking with me in the garden?'

Nicola looked immediately at David, wondering if he knew what had prompted the sudden invitation. But judging by the look on his face he was as puzzled as she. Lady Dorchester, however, did not seem to find the request in the least surprising. In fact, she set her own cup and saucer down and rose with a composure that Nicola found quite remarkable.

'Thank you, Sir Giles, I would like that very much,' she replied, then glanced at her niece with a smile that Nicola had not seen in a long, long time. 'Nicola, you do not mind if we leave you and Lord Blackwood for a moment?'

'N-no, Aunt Glynnis, of course not,' Nicola said, stumbling.

'Actually, with your permission, Lady Dorchester,' David said, also rising, 'I should like to ask Lady Nicola to accompany me on a ride. It appears that the sun is trying to break through the clouds and it seems a pity to miss such a pleasant opportunity.' His eyes turned to regard the woman he loved. 'Naturally, Lady Nicola will be accompanied by her groom.'

'You certainly have my permission, Lord Blackwood,' Lady Dorchester replied amiably. 'But I think that, in this case, it is Nicola who must give you her answer.'

Three pairs of eyes turned towards Nicola, all of them displaying varying degrees of hope. Nicola hesitated as she weighed up the merits of both staying and going. If she refused David's offer to ride, she would be obliged to remain alone here in the salon with him until such time as her aunt and Sir Giles returned. But if they rode together she could, if necessary, escape at a gallop. And, as

David had pointed out, they would be accompanied by her groom.

'Very well, Lord Blackwood, I shall accompany you,' Nicola said, quickly deciding that riding was the lesser of two evils. 'If you will allow me a moment to change, I shall meet you outside.'

Heartily relieved that she had not refused him outright, David bowed. 'I shall see to the horses and await your return. Shall we say, half an hour?'

'That would be fine.'

Meanwhile, Sir Giles walked slowly to Lady Dorchester's side, and proffered his arm, his smile tremulous. 'Shall we?'

And so the four of them quit the salon—Nicola to attend to a change in outfit, Lady Dorchester and Sir Giles to enjoy a pleasant stroll through the gardens, and Lord Blackwood to arrange for the horses to be saddled and brought round. Certainly innocent activities all.

And yet, as Nicola stood before the cheval-glass while Maire attended to the fastening of her habit, she truly began to wonder. She had seen the way Sir Giles had looked at her aunt just now. The adoring, puppy-dog look had suggested the behaviour of a man in love. And, given the tenderness with which her aunt had greeted that glance, Nicola felt sure that her aunt reciprocated the feelings. Was there, then, a more meaningful purpose to a simple stroll through the gardens that the baronet had in mind?

And why was David being so…amenable to everything she said today? Nicola wondered. He had not made one derogatory comment about…anything. Indeed, listening to him, one might be sorely tempted to believe that his interest in her animals was as genuine as her own. Was this the same David who had berated her for bringing home an injured falcon, and for giving a poor, tatty-eared mouse a home in her bedroom? To say nothing of how he had reacted to Alistair!

Well, only time would tell. And as Nicola set the jaunty crimson cap on her dark red curls and pulled the fine black net over her eyes she wondered whether they weren't all due for a surprise this afternoon!

Chapter Sixteen

David stood by the front steps of the house and waited for Nicola to appear. The groom had brought around his new hunter, a flashy piece of work that David had wanted from the moment he'd laid eyes on him, as well as Nicola's pretty dapple-grey mare, who had the manners of a queen.

David couldn't help but smile. She and her mistress were a fine pair.

Moments later the door opened and Nicola appeared. David turned—and for a moment found himself quite at a loss for words. He hadn't seen this outfit before, but there was no question that it was spectacular. The well-cut habit flattered the perfection of Nicola's figure, while the rich crimson fabric brought out the roses in her cheeks. Or perhaps it was his own forthright appraisal that was doing that, David mused. Either way, he was convinced that he had never seen her looking lovelier.

'I hope I did not keep you waiting too long, my lord,' Nicola said, rendered suddenly shy by the intensity of his gaze.

David shook his head, knowing that he would have

waited a lifetime for her, had she but asked. 'I am in no hurry, Lady Nicola. The afternoon is young. Shall we go?'

Holding the mare's head while the groom helped Nicola to mount, David then swung up into his own saddle and gathered the reins. For the first few minutes, he concentrated on controlling the animal beneath him, rather than in admiring the beautiful lady at his side. The tightly leashed power of the young horse was considerable, and David smiled in anticipation of a memorable ride.

'He is indeed magnificent, Lord Blackwood,' Nicola complimented. 'And surprisingly well behaved for one possessed of such fire and spirit. You have made an excellent choice.'

David's blue eyes swung round to meet hers. 'I am more pleased than I can say, Lady Nicola. Your approval of him means a great deal to me.'

Nicola purposely avoided his gaze as she pressed her heels gently into the mare's flanks. She was quite at sixes and sevens with this new David. His behaviour was not at all in keeping with the man with whom she had argued, fought, and eventually broken off their engagement.

Not in a hurry to disclose the true nature of the ride, David set off in a direction at right angles to the one he would eventually take and put the hunter to a trot. Nicola followed half a length behind on his left, while the groom held back at a discreet distance.

'Are you game for a race to the high pasture?' David threw back over his shoulder.

'A race!' Nicola's eyes sparkled at the prospect. 'But of course. I dare say it will give your mount a chance to prove his mettle.'

'The hunter's ability isn't at question here,' David replied, his lips curving in a devilish smile. 'Your mare's is. But are you sure you are sufficiently recovered from

your injuries to participate? I would not wish to hear that
the cause of your losing was a pain in your hand, or a
twitch in your foot.'

The sparkle in Nicola's eyes ignited to a flame. 'I am
well enough recovered to hold my own against you, my
lord. And do not be deceived by Nightingale's meek appearance; she has a heart as big as all England. However,
given the fact that she is somewhat smaller than your
hunter, I would suggest a modest head start to make things
more equitable.'

The look of amusement in David's eyes changed to one
of warm approval. By God, she was beautiful. The wind
had whipped the colour into her face, and the eyes smiling
back at him through the wispy veil of net were an incredible, breathtaking green. He suddenly wished he could
have a portrait painted of her, just as she looked now.

'Very well.' David glanced into the distance and then
pointed to a small cluster of trees at the base of the slope.
'I shall give you to the point where the hedge meets the
trees. Jenkins will go and mark the spot. Will that do?'

'Admirably,' Nicola said happily as the groom rode
ahead to take his place. She had been expecting a lead
half that distance. Truly, Blackwood did not know what
her trusty little mare was capable of. She gathered her
reins in her hands and took her position beside the hunter.
'Ready?'

David's smile was as intimate as a kiss. 'Fly away,
Lady Nicola,' he whispered. 'For know that I will soon
be in hot and heavy pursuit.'

The blood began to pound in Nicola's ears, but it had
nothing to do with the race. Only a fool could have misinterpreted the deeper meaning behind David's words,
and, knowing that only a fool would attempt a response,

Nicola didn't even try. Using the lightest of touches from her whip, she let the mare go.

Behind her, the thoroughbred whinnied, clearly confused as to why the mare was being allowed to run while he wasn't, and danced a jig on the spot. Nicola paid him no mind, however, as she concentrated on her mare. The ground beneath them flew as the distance between her and David widened.

All too soon, however, Nicola reached the cluster of trees and knew that her brief head start was over. Behind her the hunter whinnied again, this time high and excited as it recognized the start of the chase.

The race had begun in earnest.

'Come on, sweetness,' Nicola whispered into the mare's ears. 'Let's show them what we're made of.'

The mare pricked her dainty ears forward and back, as if listening to every word, and then Nicola felt the long limbs stretch even further as they headed onto the slope. The wind whistled past her ears as hedgerows flew by. But it wasn't long before Nicola caught the thunderous sound of the thoroughbred. She could hear the hunter's breath as the powerful hooves dug into the soft turf, narrowing the distance. She finally risked a quick glance back over her shoulder, and gasped.

David was riding hard, his hands steady on the reins, his head down low over the stallion's. Nicola could see the predatory gleam in his eyes as he closed the gap between them, almost as though *she* had become the fox, and he the hunter. And, suddenly, she feared that the outcome would be the same.

One would succeed; one would succumb.

The thought came out of nowhere, but it made Nicola feel weak at the knees. Within seconds, however, reality returned and she thrust the foolish thought aside. This was a race, nothing more. And one, she realized with a sinking heart, that she was now in definite fear of losing!

Three-quarters of the way up the hill the two riders were neck and neck. Nightingale was starting to tire and Nicola was about to ease her back when the hunter flew past them in a startling burst of speed, easily cresting the hill first. By the time Nicola drew even, a few minutes later, David had already turned the hunter around to watch Nicola cover the last few yards.

'Well done, Lady Nicola. A valiant effort indeed!' David complimented her, white teeth flashing in the sunlight. 'At one point, I wasn't even sure that victory would be mine.'

Good-naturedly accepting the jibe, Nicola pulled the sweating mare to a halt and gave her a well-deserved pat. 'It wouldn't have been, had we been racing on flat ground,' she said, laughing. 'But on an incline, I admit, your hunter has the advantage. Well run, my lord. He's a splendid animal.'

David acknowledged the tribute by flourishing his high-brimmed beaver towards her. 'My lady is too kind. And now I have a different kind of treat in store for you. At least, I hope I have,' David said, aware that it was still possible for his surprise to fail.

Nicola sent him a quizzical smile. 'You hope? Am I to believe that you are not in total control of everything, my lord?'

His eyes, as he looked at her, were carefully shuttered. 'In most things, I would say, yes. But when it comes to…certain other matters I find that I have precious little control at all. However, all that aside, there is something that I would very much like to show you, Lady Nicola, if you would allow me to.'

Nicola studied him for a moment, wondering what he

could possibly show her on her own land that she had not seen before.

Still, she was curious. And, more importantly, she was reluctant to see their time together come to an end. After today, it might be some time before she saw David again. She was quite sure he had come today because of his uncle, but in the future there would be no such excuses.

She had told him once that it was over. David was not a man who needed to hear it twice.

'Very well, Lord Blackwood,' she said huskily. 'Lead on.'

David chose a different route back from the one by which they had come. It crossed over the top of the hill and then wound sharply down until it eventually led into the wooded area which bordered the property.

'My lord, are you sure you know where you are going?' Nicola asked as they walked their horses into the dense forest. 'The path here is extremely overgrown.'

'Do not worry, Lady Nicola,' David said softly. 'I'm not about to get us lost. But what I wanted to show you is down this way.'

'It must be something very special indeed to go to all this…trouble,' Nicola said, ducking quickly as a low-hanging branch nearly knocked her hat off.

'I assure you, it is well worth the effort.'

'Am I not to be given a hint?'

'No. Other than to say that, hopefully, you will not be disappointed.'

Puzzled, Nicola resumed her silence as the horses continued to pick their way slowly through the thick brush. The path wasn't wide enough here for them to ride side by side, and Nicola was forced to drop behind, while Jenkins brought up the rear. In truth, she didn't mind. Her position allowed her to admire David's broad back and shoulders, without having to worry that he might see her interest.

They rode for another ten minutes or so before the path suddenly disappeared altogether, and David drew to a halt. The trees had closed in all around them, so that even the light was dim. 'I'm afraid we have to go on foot from here, my lady,' David told her.

'On foot?' Nicola glanced up ahead. 'My lord, there does not appear to be anything but brush ahead. Are you sure you know where you are going?'

'Trust me, Nicola,' David said softly. 'I would not lead you on a wild-goose chase. That which I hope to show you will be well worth the effort, I promise you.'

His eyes did not lie, and Nicola felt her reservations dwindle. Whatever lay at the end of this path was terribly important to him—or, at least, it was terribly important to him that she see it.

Sliding out of the saddle, David walked back to hold the mare's head while Nicola dismounted. 'Are you sure your foot is up to a short walk?'

'It is, though even if it were not I vow I should force myself to go on, if only to assuage my curiosity.'

Indicating with a nod that the groom should stay and watch their horses, David took Nicola's hand and began to lead her deeper into the forest. His steps were slow and measured; almost, Nicola thought, as though he was stalking something.

'David, I wish you would tell me—'

'Shh,' he whispered over his shoulder. 'We haven't much further to go now.'

Intrigued, Nicola kept her silence and followed him through the thickening undergrowth, grateful for the protection of her leather riding boots. When she was sure they could penetrate no further, however, David finally stopped. He peered up ahead for a moment, and then, with a smile lighting up his face, drew her to his side and pointed. 'Look there, in the clearing just below the rocks,' he whispered. 'What do you see?'

Nicola followed the direction of his arm. It seemed to point to a small patch of ground that was littered with rocks, small shrubs and tangled undergrowth. At first Nicola saw nothing. Then there was a flash of colour against the green undergrowth, and Nicola's eyes widened in delight. 'A fox. Oh, how wonderful. And a female most likely.'

'And what else do you see?'

Nicola focused her eyes on the clearing again. For a moment, she saw only the one fox, and the rocks and trees close by. Then, seconds later, she saw him.

'Alistair!' Nicola gasped, hardly able to believe her eyes. 'Oh, dear heavens, it's Alistair! It truly is!'

Nicola was embarrassed to feel the wetness of tears in her eyes, but there could be no mistake. The fox that was making its way across the clearing to join its mate was most definitely Alistair. His reddish-gold fur and his white front leg stood out like a brilliant flag against the muted colours of the forest. She would have known her little pet anywhere!

'Oh, David, I can't believe that I am really seeing this,' Nicola whispered breathlessly as she watched Alistair make his way towards the trees. 'He's all right. Alistair truly is all right.'

'He's better than just all right,' David murmured against her ear. 'He has a mate now, and in the spring there will be cubs for him to care for. Neither of which he was likely to have if he'd stayed at Wyndham Hall.'

Fascinated, Nicola watched her former pet trot towards the female, aware that he looked quite cheeky—and per-

fectly at home. And when his mate disappeared, only to
return a little while later and drop a plump brown hare at
Alistair's feet, Nicola knew that he was exactly where he
belonged.

'Seen enough?' David murmured.

Too moved for words, Nicola nodded. In silence, and
as quietly as she could, she turned and followed David
back along the path and towards the horses.

Nicola was very quiet on the ride back to the house.
Wisely, David did not push for conversation. He knew
that Nicola was happy, and that what she had just seen
had made a profound and lasting impact on her. And he
was content in the knowledge that he had been the one
able to provide it for her.

Finally, when they were at last within sight of Wyndham Hall, Nicola reined in her mare and turned to look
at him. 'You went to a great deal of trouble to take me
out there this afternoon, Lord Blackwood. Why?'

'Because I knew how very important it was for you to
be sure that Alistair was safe,' David told her quietly. 'I
wanted you to see that he had returned to a way of life
that was natural to him. I also knew that I had to convince
you, beyond a shadow of a doubt, that what was important
to you was equally important to me. And I thought that
by finding Alistair—which I freely admit I could not have
done without Jamie's help—and by showing you that he
was well, it would mean more to you than anything I
might have been able to say.'

Nicola stared at his cravat, not sure what would happen
if she looked up into his eyes at that moment. She had
never expected him to go to such lengths to prove a point.
'I wanted to hate you that day in the forest,' she admitted
unsteadily. 'I wanted to scream at you for being so heart-

less. I so desperately needed you to understand what I was feeling, and how I felt about Alistair, but all I could see was your anger. And that blinded me to everything else.' She glanced up at him then. 'I didn't realise until later on that…it wasn't really anger at all.'

David shuddered slightly. 'You will never know how I felt that day, Nicola. My heart was in my mouth when I saw you so high up in that tree. All I could picture was you…falling, and my not being able to catch you. And then, later, when I turned around and saw you hanging from a branch—and not even holding on with your arms—I swear I aged ten years on the spot.'

Nicola uttered a shaky laugh. 'I thought you were furious at me for embarrassing you in front of all those people.'

'I didn't give a damn about the people,' David growled. 'I was terrified that you were going to fall. The only thing I was *angry* about,' he conceded, 'was that you were out riding with O'Donnell. I thought perhaps that I had misunderstood your feelings, and that you had…'

When he hesitated, Nicola reached out and laid her hand upon his arm. 'Say it, David, please. If we are making a clean breast of things here, you must be as honest with me as I have been with you.'

'Yes, I suppose I must. But it is not easy for me to say, even now.' He took a deep breath, and said, 'I was so afraid that…you had changed your mind, and that you no longer wished to marry me, that I could barely speak. I thought perhaps you had decided to choose O'Donnell over me. And my insecurity about that, combined with my overwhelming fear for your safety, turned me into someone even I didn't like very much. And for that, Nicola, I am so very, very sorry.'

Turning to signal to the groom to stay behind, David

rode on with Nicola at his side, until they finally rounded a bend in the path and he knew they were alone. There, David stopped.

Nicola pulled up too, and watched as David slid out of his saddle and walked back towards her. To her surprise, he said nothing. He only held out his arms—and waited.

Nicola knew that the time for her to choose had come. If she went into his arms now, there would be no turning back. David had been honest with her. He had told her exactly how he felt, and, by his actions today, he had more than demonstrated the depth of his feelings. Now it was up to her to tell him where she stood. And she did.

Kicking free the stirrup, Nicola slid out of the saddle and went willingly into his arms.

There was no need for words. As David's arms closed tight around her, Nicola shut her eyes and knew that she was right where she belonged. She felt David's heart beating against hers, and marvelled that she had ever thought to question his love, or the rightness of their being together.

And when he tipped back her head and kissed her Nicola gave herself up fully to his caress, welcoming the warmth of his mouth on hers and kissing him back with all the passion and love she possessed.

'Nicola, darling,' David whispered at length, 'I owe you...such an apology. For all the things I said, and for all the things I did, and for all the things I should have said, but didn't. I've learned...so much over the last few days,' David told her fervently. 'I was so wrapped up in my damned notion of duty and obligation that I almost lost the most precious thing in the world. But I don't care what anyone thinks any more. I only care about you. I love you with all my heart, and I want you to be my wife. But—'

'David—'

'No, please let me finish, because it may be the only chance I get to say it.' David took a deep breath, and put her away from him, knowing that what he had to say must be said now. 'If your heart is still hardened towards me, or if you feel that there will never be any hope of a reconciliation between us, then…tell me now, and let that be an end to it. You have my word that I will not ask you again, nor will I try to persuade you. Only know that I will never, ever stop loving you, my beautiful, bewitching lady.'

Nicola gazed up into the face that she loved so well, and blinked back tears of joy. 'Oh, David, there will never be an end to this. Because I love you too, with all my heart. And I want so very much to be your wife. But— are you *sure* about this?' she asked him for the very last time, needing him to know how terribly important his honesty was. 'Whatever…abilities I have will likely be with me for the rest of my life, and you will never know what you may come home to find.'

'As long as whatever I come home to find doesn't take up my side of the bed, I think I can live with it,' David replied lightly. 'Because to love you, my darling, is to love everything about you. Especially the things that matter most in your life.'

'And it won't bother you to know that those abilities may be passed along to our children?'

David threw back his head and laughed. 'Lord help us, I'll end up being a gamekeeper in my old age, but no, Nicola, the only thing I care about is that we *do* have children. Lots of them, laughing and playing with as many pets as we've room for.' He reached up and stroked the side of her face with his fingers, loving the softness of her skin, the softness of her. 'And if we have daughters their husbands will have to learn to accept the wonderful gifts that they bring, as your father did with your mother, and as I have done with you. But, in truth, I don't think it will be such a difficult task. For if they are anywhere near as lovely and as enchanting as you no man could possibly help but fall in love with them.'

Nicola caught his fingers in her hand and squeezed them tightly. 'Oh, David. I may not end up being the typical wife and marchioness, but I will do everything I can to make you proud. And you shall be happy every day of your life. That much I can promise you.'

It was promise enough for David. As he bent his head to kiss the woman he loved, he said, 'What more could I ask for, lady mine, than to be made a happy man for the rest of my life?'

Epilogue

B<small>Y</small> the time they returned to Wyndham Hall, Lady Dorchester and Sir Giles were anxiously waiting for them.

'Nicki, my dear, I am so glad that you're back,' Lady Dorchester said earnestly. 'We were truly beginning to worry about you.'

'David took me to see Alistair, Aunt Glynn,' Nicola breathed happily. 'We saw him and his mate out in the deep woods. He's all right, Aunt Glynn, and he's happy.'

Lady Dorchester saw the joy and love shining from her niece's eyes—as well as the happiness in Lord Blackwood's—and knew that Nicola had found a great deal more than her lost fox in the woods this afternoon.

'Thank you, Lord Blackwood. That was a very special thing you did for my niece today,' Lady Dorchester said quietly. 'You have no idea how much it meant to her.'

'I could do no less for the woman I love,' David replied in all sincerity. 'After all, since Nicola is going to be my wife, I may as well get used to the fact that I am probably in for all manner of surprises.'

Sir Giles was positively beaming. 'Then all's well between the two of you?'

Nicola smiled and slipped her hand into her fiancé's.

'Everything is just perfect, Sir Giles. David and I are going to be married, as we had planned.'

'Well, I am very glad to hear it. And here is one more piece of news to add to your day,' Sir Giles said as he slid one arm around Lady Dorchester's waist in a gesture that was as natural as it was loving. 'Dear Glynnis has just agreed to become my wife.'

'You are to be married!' Nicola gasped. 'Oh, but this is simply too splendid. I am so very happy for you both! David, is this not the most wonderful news?' Nicola cried, rushing forward to embrace her aunt.

'It is indeed. Well done, Uncle Giles.' David grinned broadly as he shook his uncle's hand. 'No wonder you were in such a state all the way here.'

'Well, I couldn't very well tell you what I had in mind,' Sir Giles said gruffly. 'Felt Glynnis should be the first one to know.'

'Have you told Lord Wyndham yet?'

'No, we thought we would wait until you returned,' Lady Dorchester told him. She glanced warmly at Sir Giles, and then back at Nicola. 'We wanted to see how the two of you fared before sharing our own news. But now that we have I think we should find him at once and tell him all the good news. I know that he is going to be *very* happy for you.'

Unfortunately, just as they were about to make their way to the library, Nicola turned to see Trethewy hesitating uncomfortably in the doorway. 'Yes, Trethewy?'

'Pardon me, my lady, but—'

Suddenly, the irrepressible Jamie ducked under his arm and took up a position in front of him, his little face unusually woebegone. 'Beggin' your pardon, my lady, but I desperately need your 'elp.'

Trethewy blanched. 'My lady, I am so very sorry—'

'That's quite all right, Trethewy,' Nicola said with a smile as she quickly drew the boy forward. 'Jamie and I know each other very well, don't we, Jamie?'

'Aye, miss, we do.'

'Good. Now, tell me what's wrong.'

'Well, there's a deer out in the forest, m'lady, and, well, she's got a real bad leg. She's not very big, but she looks to be in a bad way. I was wondering if you could…well, that is, would you mind…?'

'Of course I'll come and see her,' Nicola said, automatically moving towards the door. Then, suddenly aware that the room had gone very quiet behind her, Nicola stopped and turned towards her fiancé, her green eyes softly questioning. 'David?'

She needn't have worried, however. David had already signalled to the butler to have the horses brought round, and, after taking Nicola's hand firmly in his, he kissed her on the cheek and then winked at the young boy.

'Lead on, Jamie; the three of us have work to do. Because I doubt you're strong enough yet to bring an injured deer home all on your own!'

* * * * *

MILLS & BOON®

Makes any time special

Enjoy a romantic novel from Mills & Boon®

Presents™ *Enchanted*™ *Temptation*®

Historical Romance™ *Medical Romance*™

Perfect Summer

The perfect way to relax this summer!

Four stories from best selling
Mills & Boon® authors

JoAnn Ross

Vicki Lewis Thompson

Janice Kaiser

Stephanie Bond

*Enjoy the fun, the drama
and the excitement!*

Published 21 May 1999

*Available at most branches of WH Smith, Tesco, Asda,
Martins, Borders, Easons, Volume One/James Thin
and most good paperback bookshops*

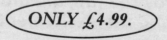